FLASH DRIVE

Dick Thornby Thriller #3

Donald J. Bingle

Cover Design by Juan Villar Padron

This book is published by 54°40' Orphyte, Inc.
St. Charles, Illinois

ISBN 13: 978-17323434-5-0

March 2021

Dedication

To Christine Redford, who has always encouraged my storytelling.

Prologue
May 28, 1993

Thwack! Yet another grasshopper slammed into the glass, splattering yellow-green ichor. The windscreen wiper shoved the smashed insect's shell and one still twitching hind leg into a curving wall of accumulated goo and viscera at the edge of the wiper's reach. Archie stared ahead, peering through the messy windscreen into the black void of the Outback at night. He reckoned the multitude of twinkling stars were outnumbered by the flashes from his headlights glinting off insects fluttering in his path. Still, he held his semi to a constant hundred kilometers per hour on the lonely road seven hours east and north of Perth.

Archie didn't really care if he could see well. The road was reasonably straight and he knew better than to swerve if a 'roo wandered into the big rig's path. But he did need to stay awake. If his ride wandered off the road into open ground, there was no telling what might happen. He could hit a rock, slide into a dry wash, or get caught up by bushy vegetation or soft soil, with no one around to help get his tractor-trailer back on the straight and narrow.

He turned up the heavy metal on the cab's tinny radio and cracked his side window enough for a stream of air, but not so wide as to suck in a torrent of hoppers. For the thousandth time, he wished he'd left the coast earlier so he'd be driving this small stretch from Menzies to Leonora in the arvo, when it was still light out. Sure, it would be warmer and the scenery was pretty damn boring when it could be seen, but at least he would be able to see something besides the flashes of insects in the black through a filter of insect guts. He squinted his eyes and peered into the empty.

A moving slash of intense yellow-white light assaulted his eyes, forcing them fast shut. At the same instant, the radio music dissolved into a mass of crackling static. Archie instinctively hit the air brakes, while simultaneously downshifting as fast as his bulky transmission allowed, even though he had seen—could still see in the scene momentarily imprinted on the back of his retinas—there was nothing in the road ahead. Nor was there anything unusual in the flat salt expanses and mounds of near-constantly dry Lake Ballard to the left—an area which should have been enveloped in blackness this time of night. He opened his eyes, catching a moon-sized streak of yellow-orange light in the sky ahead to his right. At the same time, a long, deep, thunderous, pulsing roar assaulted his ears and rattled the fenders of his slowing rig, like a rolling earthquake triggered by a mining explosion a hundred times stronger than he'd ever experienced.

Meteor strike?

No, the bright streak was still airborne, moving across the distant landscape too slowly for a shooting star by his reckoning, about the speed of a plane. Unlike what he knew about meteors, it also maintained a constant altitude as it progressed, rather than arcing down from the sky and slamming into the ground.

By the time Archie had come to a complete halt in the middle of the god-forsaken roadway and flipped on his hazards, the light had disappeared behind distant hills. But then a sudden horizon-to-horizon burst of blue-white light lasting several seconds emanated from behind the hills where the light had gone down. He sucked in a breath and waited. Moments later an overwhelming, low rumble thundered across the barren terrain, like a freight train and an earthquake and a gargantuan explosion all rolled into one. Where the blue-white light had flashed, a red, spherical—or, at least, hemispherical—dome pulsed above the horizon.

He flicked off the staticky hiss of the radio, but let the truck idle as he got out to take a clearer—less bug-smeared—look at the strange phenomenon. Now the engine's throaty chug was the only thing breaking the silence. Diesel was dear, but he let it run. He worried whatever this was might mess with the electrical system of his engine and he might not be able to start her up again.

Nuke?

He couldn't see a mushroom cloud, but the glowing red ball was much dimmer than the flash, or even the streak of light which preceded it, so he couldn't be sure. Besides, that didn't make a lick of sense. There was nothing out here in the never never worth nuking. Route 49 wandered northwesterly past Leonora; the red orb throbbed to his north but seemed too far east to be near the road. Lake Darlot? No, farther east. Maybe down Bandya way. Nothing between the two fly-specks 'cept maybe a few mines and even fewer sprawling sheep stations.

Maybe that was the point. Nothing there. A perfect place to test nuclear weapons—maybe even nuclear missile systems. But that meant a military presence: facilities, equipment, personnel. And that meant large scale, convoy type movement: Bushmasters, G-Wagons, personnel carriers, and trucks of all sorts. And he hadn't seen or heard of anything like that, not on the roads he traveled and not on the roads—or godforsaken excuses for roads—that the drivers he hung with at the diners and diesel pumps of local truck stops traveled. That meant black helicopters and all that crazy conspiracy shit which went with 'em. He hadn't gone troppo. He didn't subscribe to such nonsense on a regular basis, but God knows, there was nothin' regular 'bout what was goin' on in the lonely nowhere tonight.

A jet crash? Maybe. Not a likely route, though, even for Qantas.

There wasn't really anything to do ... anything he could check or investigate ... not with the source of the lights beyond the horizon, but he couldn't just drive on. Instead he waited, his rig's hazard lights flashing behind him as he stood on the side of the road, watching something unknown pulse in the distance. An apocalyptic hazard light?

Two hours later, the red orb suddenly winked off and he was alone in the dark with nothing but a strange story, a million stars, and a billion or three 'hoppers, flies, and midges.

He'd barely have enough diesel to make Leonora.

What the hell was that?

Chapter 1

"What the hell is that, Dad?"

Dick Thornby looked up from the wheel of the stopped, but bobbing, SeaRay 400 Express. Seth's arm was outstretched, his index finger pointing at a white concrete circular structure with red vertical stripes. It connected to another, lower, wider, less colorful concrete structure via an elevated footbridge over the choppy waters of Lake Michigan. There was really no reason for his son to point—more than two miles out from the shore, there really wasn't much else around to prompt his question.

Before Dick could respond, Seth continued: "It seems awful short to be a lighthouse."

Dick snorted, causing his wife Melanie to look up at him from the cabin tucked in the front of the speedy power boat, then responded. "That's because it's not a lighthouse. It's a water crib. Two actually. I think the painted one is still active, but the drab one isn't operational anymore."

Seth lowered his arm and gazed back at him. "Thanks, Dad. That explains ... absolutely nothing."

Dick smiled. He didn't mind his kid's heavy sarcasm; he was just glad Seth was finally recovered enough from his injuries from more than a year ago that he was able to laugh and tease and even be a wise-ass on occasion. "Well, you've got one of the world's largest cities on one of the world's largest lakes. Where did you think Chicago—and a bunch of its suburbs—get their drinking water from?"

Seth tilted his head to one side. "I dunno. The Chicago River? Seems a whole lot closer to everything."

Dick sighed. Although his job as a wastewater treatment consultant for Catalyst Crisis Consulting, LLC was only a cover for his real job as an agent for The Subsidiary, he would have hoped his kid would care enough about municipal water systems and treatment facilities to know at least the rudimentary principals of water supply. Instead, his kid had figured out Dick was a spy and gotten himself and Dick in a whole lot of trouble by trying to mimic his dad's missions and heroics. But enough of that, the family was on vacation. They were out to have a good time, not ponder regrets and recriminations, and certainly not to start an argument on a small boat—okay, a large, very fast boat—far from shore. Even with room for six, a boat could get pretty chilly if people weren't in a good mood. And Lake Michigan was chilly enough even in midsummer.

"I'll explain while we cruise over and take a look." Dick powered up the Cat 3400 horsepower inboard diesel engines and eased into a long, wide turn toward the structures. "The water cribs pull clean, fresh, lake water from an intake sixty to eighty feet below the surface and send it down a shaft that drops almost two hundred feet, sixty or more feet below the bottom of the lake. Then the water is pumped through tunnels under the lake to and past the shore, where it is treated and inserted into the city's distribution system or piped out to suburban water systems."

Seth made a face. "They tunneled under the lake? That doesn't sound very safe."

"Hmmmph. They tunneled under the lake in the nineteenth century, and again in the mid- thirties ... by hand. Not pleasant. And, no, not safe. I think the older crib was retired because the tunnel to it collapsed a long time ago."

"Like I said," replied Seth. "The Chicago River seems a lot closer and a lot easier."

"The Chicago River is filthy … or, at least, was filthy. The whole point of reversing the flow of the river ..."

"Say, what? The Chicago River flows backwards?"

"Of course. Don't they teach you anything in school?" Dick regretted that last bit even as he heard himself say it, but Seth didn't take umbrage. He hurried on. "It's why Chicago is a premier city instead of a small-scale port like, well, Toledo." Dick straightened out the boat and headed for the crib at a leisurely pace. "You see, Lake

Michigan is off to the side of the main water flow of the Great Lakes, starting up in Lake Superior and then through Lake Huron, then past Detroit into Lake Erie, which is pretty shallow, and quickly over Niagara Falls into Lake Ontario and out to the ocean via the St. Laurence Seaway. Lake Michigan is a big cul-de-sac to the side. It takes forever for all the water to circulate out."

Dick gestured at the distant skyline. "So, when Chicago started to develop, all the sewage and pollution flowing into it, including from the Chicago River, just stayed where it was. The south end of the lake was a virtual cesspool. The Army Corp of Engineers, it dredged out the Chicago River and connected it up to the Des Plaines River basin, so water could flow away from Chicago, then eventually down the Mississippi River to the Gulf of Mexico. That's why there's locks between the river and the lake in Chicago. The river and the lake are not at the same level. The lock pumps actually control the flow of water in the river, pumping the pollution from the end of the lake into the river and, eventually, down to the Gulf. These days the effort is supplemented by the Deep Tunnel, a huge system of gigantic pipes, including under the river, that ferries sewage and storm water away from the lake."

Seth feigned a yawn. "There's not going to be a quiz on this later, is there?"

Dick shot him a slit-eyed look. "The point is, smart aleck, that the Army is why Chicago has a beautiful lakefront and clean drinking water." Dick may not have been in the Corps of Engineers, but he had been an Army Ranger and was proud of it.

Seth got his point. "Yay!" he faux-hollered. "Go, Army!"

Melanie made her way on deck from the forward cabin. "That's what the Army was. Go here. Go there. Fight bad guys. Go, go, go." She wrinkled her nose. "Not that the Chicago Police Department ... or the Subsidiary—"

Dick shot her a stern look.

"—er ... Catalyst Crisis Consulting ... are any different." She fluttered a hand at Dick's serious countenance. "Not trying to start a fight. Just enjoying some time together for a change."

Dick throttled back and let the cigarette boat slip forward from momentum now that they were closer. "Looks like they repainted it a couple years back. Maybe did some maintenance." He adjusted the wheel to make a wide spiral around the concrete structures.

Seth pointed at two yellow signs. "Should we be doing this? It says: 'Restricted Area.' And the other one says 'Violators Will Be Prosecuted.'"

Dick smiled. "I wouldn't worry too much. There's nobody there to bother; it's all mechanized. And it's not like we're going to get sucked down by the flow. They just don't want people tying up or clambering about or ... God forbid ... diving into the water and trying to swim down to see the intake. That would be the kind of stupidity that doesn't require prosecution."

"No, duh," replied Seth. "Evolution in action."

Melanie's brow furrowed. "That's not a very polite phrase, Seth. I seem to recall some questionable decision-making in your past."

Dick butted in. "And some life-saving decision-making in the end—" As the SeaRay continued its lazy spiral, another boat came into view. Close in to the far side of the smaller, brighter, newer crib, it hadn't been visible from their initial angle of approach. "Besides, I don't think anybody's going to bitch about our distance compared to those guys."

A few unmanned, but fixed, fishing rods with lines out came into view as more of the low, flat boat was revealed. Seth jerked a thumb toward the craft. "Yeah, they don't seem so bright. With the strong flow underwater, it's bound to be one of the worst places to fish out here."

Dick tilted his head in acknowledgment, but never took his eyes off the mystery boat. "Wouldn't catch me in a rig like that this far out on a lake this big, either."

Melanie stepped over to Dick, steadying herself with one arm and shading her eyes with her other to peer at the boat. "What kind of boat is that? It seems somewhat familiar, but I'm not sure where I've seen something like it before."

The rolling waves showed the stern of the boat for a moment and Dick noted it was angled to form a ramp into the water. Then he looked up and saw the center of the flat craft was jammed with large holding tanks of some sort.

"Jet skis," he murmured.

Seth wheeled around, his head swiveling from side to side. "Where?"

Dick put up his hand palm out. "No, not in the water." He pointed. "That's a floating fueling station for power boats and jet skis and stuff. They had a smaller one something like it at the marina on Lake Geneva when we went up there for a long weekend years ago. This one is much, much bigger, but same principle. Tanks and pumps on what amounts to a floating pier."

Seth turned back to look at the boat. "Cool. Probably fueling up some equipment on the crib."

Dick nudged the throttle and turned the wheel to tighten their spiral in. "Nah. They're not moored to the crib." That's when he saw the hoses from the tanks draped over the side of the tanker boat facing the crib. "And they seem to be pumping their payload into the water."

Melanie's hand tightened on his arm. "I don't think this is any of our business ..."

Realization slammed home. "Get in the cabin, Melanie. Stay out of sight." He ignored her questioning eyes and called forward to his son. Dick snatched up the radio receiver, its long, curled cord bouncing from the sudden movement. "Seth, call the Coast Guard. Tell them someone is dumping something into the intake at the water crib two and a half miles east of North Avenue Beach." Seth rushed toward him. Dick tossed the handset to him and grabbed the throttle. "Tell them to hurry and to put a bird in the air. And take cover with your mother."

"I don't understand," Seth said. "Gas floats. They can't possibly get enough fuel in the intake sixty feet down to screw with the water." Seth might be arguing, but he was still doing what he was told. He dropped down into the cabin as Dick slammed the throttle to jolt forward.

"Who the hell knows what they're pumping and who the hell knows how long the hoses extend under the waterline. They're fucking terrorists and we're the only ones close enough to stop them." He jerked the wheel to make a beeline for the fuel boat. "Ebola, coronavirus, ... prions for mad cow disease if they're patient terrorists." He, of course, had once stopped a bad guy dumping neurotoxins in the Glasgow water supply, but that was never made public, so he couldn't mention it. But he also remembered a couple bulletins which had circulated publicly some months ago to water treatment professionals—he, of course, was on their mailing list for cover reasons. "Some asshole recently engineered cryptosporidium, already present in lake water, to be a lot more virulent. And then there's that brain eating amoeba that was in the water down by Houston."

Now that they were fast approaching the fuel boat, he saw three guys who had been lingering near the hoses look up and reach under their jackets.

"Fuck! Fuck, fuck, fuck!" He glanced down the stairway, where he could see Seth speaking on the handset. "Let your mother finish the call," he commanded as they rapidly closed the gap to the other boat. He was headed straight for it at speed. "They've got guns. You need to take the wheel and steer away from the crib, then make as much distance as possible, in three ... two ... ONE!"

Dick spun the wheel hard to the right, slamming the SeaRay into a sharp turn away from his target as he took two steps and flung himself off the left side of the craft, barely clearing the fuel boat's low railing and landing on the flat deck. He twisted and crouched as he hit, rolling to his left, toward the stern, as automatic weapons fire ricocheted off the spot he had been on just an instant before. He kept rolling until he put one of the tanks between him and the bad guys with guns, taking only a second to glance right, where, thankfully, he saw the straightening SeaRay accelerating away from the crib on a beeline for shore.

"Good work, kid," he muttered as he turned his attention to his adversaries. He yearned to reach for his gun, but there was no point. While he would think long and hard about going weaponless in the field, he wasn't on a mission. He was on a damn vacation with his wife and kid. And while whipping out a Walther PPK might get a Bond babe all hot and bothered, carrying on vacay wasn't a smart thing to do when you were trying to work things out with your estranged spouse who was pissed off you'd kept her in the dark about being a spy. If things reached the point of fumbling and grabbing in the dark, he didn't want her finding his nine-millimeter instead of finding out he was happy to see her.

He flicked a hand out from cover for an instant to draw fire. His opponents obliged. That told Dick two things. One, the tank he was hiding behind and the connected tanks undoubtedly below deck weren't carrying gasoline or anything else flammable. Henchmen aren't usually terminally stupid. Two, the sounds of their Mac 10s firing gave him a rough idea of their relative positions, which was crucial.

If you don't have a gun and you are facing three mooks who do, your first task is to take a gun from the nearest bad guy.

He quietly took off his slip-on boat shoes, then flung them both out in a high arc to the side of the tank where the closest guy was—the side toward the crib. The shoes drew bursts from all three shooters—a bit longer from the closest adversary. While the burst was short, he knew that, combined with the shots already fired, the Mac 10 was empty or nearly so.

The click of an expended magazine falling to the deck followed in quick order.

That's when Dick charged out from behind cover, roaring as he rushed forward, arms wide. As expected, the shooter had glanced down to snick in fresh ammo, so Dick caught him off-guard. Dick stayed low and tackled his opponent using every bit of the training he'd gotten when he played football for the Fighting Illini, wrapping his arms around his opponent's mid-section, then heaving upward so the guy fell back. Then he flung his arms wide again just before the thug man hit the deck with a shuddering whomp, grabbing the barrel of the Mac 10 with his left hand and thrusting it down and back so the stock struck the guy's chin. With his right hand, he wrested the weapon away, then leapt up, stomping on his adversary's chest. He fired a couple shots from the just-reloaded gun without aiming, but in the general direction of where he'd last heard the others, just to make them duck for cover. Then, rather than retreating back from where he'd come, he pushed forward to the next cover, listening for his remaining enemies, while eyeing the hoses snaking off the side of the boat and tracking them back to the pumps feeding them.

Once he located the two pumps, he quickly fired two rounds into each. Sure, he might wish he had four more rounds to deal with the bad guys stalking him, but stopping the pumps—stopping the befoulment of the region's water supply—was the top priority. Getting out alive was second place, as always.

After a burst of sparks and a staccato sound of wrenching gears and whining rubber belts, the pumps fell silent. The flat deck rolled with the waves, slick under his now bare feet. He couldn't hear his pursuers, but he knew they were moving toward him with slow, careful steps. Sure, he could play cat and mouse with these bozos, but they had more ammo, better footing, and the luxury of teamwork.

Instead, he'd approach this with the same subtlety he was infamous for at the Subsidiary. He glanced about for the best way to blow the fucking boat out of the water.

He peeked around the edge of his cover and shot a round toward the likely location of his pursuers. He knew he wouldn't hit anything; he just needed to slow them down while he worked the problem.

He couldn't just shoot at the idling motors for the craft. That might damage them—maybe even break them completely like the pumps, but they wouldn't blow up. This wasn't the movies. Liquid gas or, more likely, diesel, wasn't explosive even though it was flammable. But the fumes were. That meant he needed a lot of fuel on deck where it could start to evaporate. The outgassing liquid would aerosolize sufficiently to become explosive in less than thirty seconds.

He shouldered his gun with the strap the previous user had ignored, pulled out the small pocketknife he always carried, and opened the main blade. Crouching into a runner's starting stance, he burst out from behind cover, dashing toward the stern of the craft. After a few steps, he dove, as if sliding into third base, hooking on to the protruding engine access cover and letting his body slide down the jet ski ramp behind it for protection and concealment. Dick reached around and popped the access while his confused adversaries popped off a few rounds.

The cover slid down the ramp into the water with a *sploosh* as Dick groped exposed parts of the inboard motors like a teen boy getting some under the sweater action in the front seat. Finally, his fingers closed on the Holy Grail. No, not a nipple—a fuel hose. He pulled himself closer and brought his other arm up, wielding his tiny knife and sawing at the end of the hose nearest a coupling.

Cool, pungent liquid shot out onto his hands, but he kept sawing until he could wrest the hose free. Then he grabbed the hose and jerked up as hard as he could to seize whatever slack the line allowed and pointed the spouting end toward the flat deck of the boat. Liquid pulsed out, but not as far as he wanted, so he used a thumb, like on the end of a garden hose, to reduce the opening and increase the pressure, spraying the fuel farther away and speeding its vaporization. Of course, between fumbling with the hose and some of the fuel slipping down the angled jet ski ramp, he was also covering himself in the same incendiary liquid he intended to ignite in short order.

It would be easy to slide down the ramp after igniting the fuel, but there was no guarantee he wouldn't still catch on fire. Besides, he didn't fancy dropping into lake water that was being polluted by God knows what toxin.

No, he'd have to do this the macho bullshit way.

He wedged the still pumping hose so it continued to spurt fuel onto the deck of the rolling boat, then waited ten, maybe fifteen, seconds for the fuel to aerosolize and for the goons with guns to creep closer to the stern. He used the edge of the engine access as a grab point to rapidly pull himself up, letting go as he reached a crouch and shoving one bare foot against the same edge to push off into a dash onto the deck.

Shots immediately rang out from the outboard side of the craft, but he paid them no mind. Instead, he angled inboard as he sprinted across the deck and leapt out over the edge for the water crib. As he pushed off, he twisted in the air and unleashed a burst of fire from his recovered Mac 10 at the rear most tank on the fuel boat. A spark was all it took.

The fume-laden air lit, the bright flash expanding outward in every direction in explosive destruction just like he learned it would from casting fireballs when he played *Dungeons & Dragons*. He only hoped he would save for half-damage.

He might not have made the distance to the crib, except the shock wave from the blast of exploding fuel vapors boosted his leap. That was the good news. The better news was that the fireball from the explosion quickly engulfed the rear and midsection of the fuel station. The best news was that he heard two distinct sets of screams from the far side of the craft followed quickly by splashes.

The bad news? He was propelled forcibly back-first into the circular concrete wall of the water crib with a breathtaking jolt. The only thing that kept the back of his head from cracking like a ripe melon as it snapped back toward the concrete was the taut neck muscles he'd developed during his days playing football. As it was, he banged his head hard enough blackness fluttered at the edge of his vision, but he struggled to maintain consciousness as he slid down the slick, glossy white paint covering the concrete. Fortunately, his shoeless feet caught the narrow concrete ledge along the bottom of the crib, stopping him from dropping into the contaminated lake water between a burning boat and the concrete superstructure.

Still soaked with fuel, he took no chances, edging away from the nautical conflagration and making his way to a somewhat safer perch.

Chapter 2

Dick didn't worry about what would happen when the Coast Guard and the Chicago Fire Department arrived. He was a former Chicago Police Department detective and, for all the world knew, a current wastewater treatment consultant. He'd leave the prefix "waste" off when he explained what had happened to the local powers-that-be. He knew Catalyst Crisis Consulting would back his play. Given his background and his expertise, his conduct would not result in charges, especially if—no, when—the authorities found out whatever shit the evil sons-of-bitches were trying to slip in everybody's kitchen tap.

Dick was worried the explosive encounter would generate too much attention on him, though. Spies don't like their photos on the news. He'd make sure to say he wanted to remain incognito so his family wasn't put at risk from the terrorists who planned this caper. City personnel would understand and respect that rationale. He just prayed he was picked up off the crib before Eyewitness 7 News got a chopper out to the burning boat in the water next to one of the city's two functioning water cribs.

He also worried Melanie was going to be more than a little pissed. This wasn't exactly the vacation they'd planned.

Truth told, he wasn't even sure it really was a vacation. Oh, sure, he'd told Melanie the brass at Catalyst Crisis Consulting had told him to take a rest and treat his family to an extended vacation on company expense as a reward for his successful mission in the Canary Islands some months back. And both his boss, Glenn Swynton, and his bosses' boss, Dee Tammany, had said just that with straight faces the last time he was at headquarters in Philadelphia. But Dick didn't buy the hard sell. For one thing, Ace Zyreb, his partner on the Canary Islands caper, wasn't vacationing; he had it on good authority she'd been sent to Europe for a piece of wet work. Something smelled fishy to Dick, and it wasn't the cool breeze sweeping over Lake Michigan.

He didn't even think Melanie was buying the all-expenses company-paid vacation story. At this point she knew Catalyst Crisis Consulting was merely a cover organization for the Subsidiary, the post-9/11 international espionage agency run by a consortium of nations to ferret out and quash the kinds of threats to the well-being of the globe which individual nation-states were ill-equipped or, due to political reasons, unwilling to handle. She might not be privy to all of the details of his Canary Island mission, but knowing where he was and having followed his urgent pleas to drive inland to higher ground, she had some inkling of what was going on. Hell, if she'd asked Seth for a bit of help doing Google searches on the internet, the two of them probably had a much better idea of exactly what had happened—or not happened—than the ninety-nine and forty-four one-hundredth's percent of mankind who remained as pure as Ivory Soap in their clueless ignorance.

Most likely, Melanie thought Dick had already been fired and was softening the blow by wasting his severance package on a vacation while he scrambled to find a new job. Maybe a real job in the wastewater treatment industry or a private security gig like many ex-cops. She didn't understand that spies don't get fired, they get terminated. It would never occur to her this "time off" might just be a euphemism for letting an agent who did good work, but had flouted way too many rules, most especially those about keeping his real work secret from his family, get his affairs in order. Letting him spend some quality time with family before disappearing ... dying in a tragic accident ... or simply getting whacked by one of his fellow operatives. Jeez, he hoped Ace wasn't doing that kind of work. They wouldn't be cruel enough to have her whack him, would they?

He thought about it for a moment, his mind replaying the events not that long ago in Denver with Luke Calloway. Of course, they could be—would be—cruel enough to do that. It kept the circle of knowledge about his actions as small as possible to have someone he recently worked with, someone who he had helped train ... to replace him ... do him in.

Had Ace really gone to Europe?

Of course, he could just be paranoid. Looking over your shoulder as you imagine all of the most horrible possibilities is part of the package of being a spy. Worse yet when the head of your agency's Internal Audit function is former KGB/SVR. He thought back to the end of his conversation with Pyotr Nerevsky, when he'd been summoned to the basement of HQ six weeks into his extended time off. Once the sinister, bald asshole had made clear the Subsidiary was aware of Dick's secrecy transgressions, Dick had been pretty sure he was going to be capped in the windowless conference room with its easy to clean stainless steel furnishings. But he wasn't. Instead of killing, the ferret-eyed fuck had kept talking.

#

"You're insolent and violent. You seem to enjoy using explosives, even though it might sometimes be smarter to be more discreet. You don't obey the rules because you think your own judgment and your personal code provide better guidance for what needs to happen when bad things go down. You're ruthless and reckless in equal measure, but you always do the job that demands to be done."

Dick kept his mouth closed, but ran his tongue over his upper incisors.

"If you weren't so successful in completing your missions, you'd be the worst employee in the entire organization."

Dick leaned forward in his chair. "I didn't know we were doing my annual performance review today. Is this a three-hundred-sixty degrees process?" He leaned in more and tapped on the cold steel table with the pointing finger of his right hand for emphasis. "Should I have prepared my assessments of my bosses, my peers, my trainees? Do you want my thoughts about the strengths and weaknesses of the IT Department, the Quartermaster, Internal Audit? Do you want to know what I fucking think about you?"

Nerevsky sat back, a wry, evil smile flitting across his lips. "Not necessary."

"Because you don't give a fuck?"

The former KGB stalwart wagged his finger. "Because I already know." He straightened up in his chair. "You're a free thinker. You consider yourself an independent spirit, an amiable, but effective rogue. You don't want to be a smoothly functioning piece of a relentlessly efficient gray machine. You want to be the showy flash that gets noticed and gets results. That's why you're willing to break the rules when necessary and even when unnecessary."

"Jeez, Nerevsky, get on with it. This is the longest 'Dear John' letter since the telegraph was developed and people started having to pay by the word."

Nerevsky barked out what might pass for a laugh in a speech to a room full of henchmen. "So much attitude; so little understanding. You're not a John and this is not a good-bye. You're a dick. A well-intentioned, hard-working dick, but a dick all the same. Fortunately for you, I'm the kind of man who needs a—"

"I'm flattered, but I don't swing that—"

Nerevsky slammed his open hands on the table. "Shut up. Shut the fuck up and listen." He took a couple deep breaths. "You know my background. You know my function here in this organization. You know what I can do." His brow wrinkled and his beady black eyes bored into Dick. "Sometimes I have need of agents who are willing to do what needs to be done, whatever it is, and who know when and how to break the rules to get those things done."

Nerevsky's forehead relaxed. He even blinked. Dick couldn't say for sure he'd ever seen the guy blink before. "Officially, you'll be on furlough—inactive, but still being paid. Everyone will assume you've been burned, but the Subsidiary has some sympathy for your wife and sick kid. They won't expect to ever hear from you again. What they will expect is that three or eight months from now, there will be an accident and a short obituary in your hometown newspaper. And they will shake their heads and think 'That Thornby guy was okay, but he just didn't know how to play by the rules.' More importantly, they'll think 'I sure don't ever want to piss off Nerevsky in Internal Audit.'" Nerevsky paused. "I know everyone thinks they're indispensable, especially coming off a mission like your last one. But we have other agents. Life at the Subsidiary will continue without your presence much as it has always continued, except with fewer explosions."

Dick wished for a glass of water to wet his dry mouth. He asked the obvious question. "And, unofficially?"

Nerevsky smiled a wide, thin-lipped grin that revealed just a glimmer of his canines. "You have a pleasant, relaxing life with your family, but when I call, you jump. When I ask, you do. No questions. No excuses." He chuckled. "In the meantime, just keep in shape and keep a low profile."

#

So much for a low profile.

Dick would have used his special Subsidiary sunglasses and called in to warn his megalomaniacal leash-holder about his latest explosive encounter, but at Nerevsky's insistence he'd turned in all of his high-tech gadgets "for updating" when he'd taken leave from the office. Doing so no doubt furthered the belief among the rank and file he was being retired, if not terminated with extreme prejudice. But Dick also knew it was just another way Nerevsky could make sure all of Dick's communications with the Subsidiary came through Internal Audit rather than Communications or IT. He'd probably never interact with Dee or Glenn again.

Oh, well. He couldn't help it if he had tripped over a mission that needed doing. If that complicated things with Nerevsky, so be it. He worried more about how much it complicated things with his wife and kid.

Chapter 3

Jesus, there's a lot of paperwork in being a Good Samaritan.

Even after the on-site debriefing, the boat ride back to shore, the full debriefing at the CPD, dealing with the Water Commission, and the bevy of calls reconnecting with his family and talking Seth through getting the rented boat back where it belonged, it took more than two hours to write up a statement and get it signed and notarized. The only good part of the ordeal was that Dick managed to sneak out when finished without encountering anyone from the media.

Of course, the interrogation from his wife still loomed before him.

As an ex-football player, ex-Army Ranger, pretend wastewater treatment consultant, and senior agent for a super-secret spy organization, Dick had a lot of expertise. Apparently, none of it extended to understanding women, especially his wife.

As he'd expected, Melanie was waiting for him when he arrived back at their room at the Hyatt Regency Chicago, but not with the foot-tapping, accusatory glare, type of impatience he'd anticipated. Not that she was lounging in a negligee ready to pounce on him and fulfill his every sexual whim, but she did rush to him as he entered with a concerned, even solicitous, look on her always pretty face.

"Are you okay? Did you get shot? Did you get hurt?"

It was as close to a "my hero" moment as Dick had experienced since his football days; cops and Army Rangers aren't gushy no matter how many times you save their lives.

Dick had some bruises and scrapes from the fight and the explosion, but he wasn't about the ruin the mood by admitting not only that he was human, but getting older.

"Got a bit too much sun waiting for my ride. Should have worn a hat." He looked down at his feet, clad in cloth slippers a nurse at the hospital had given him when the Coast Guard insisted on taking him in for a medical check-up on the way to de-briefing. "Lost my shoes in the fight."

Melanie's brow creased. "I can't even begin to imagine how that could happen." She held up a finger before he could respond. "And I don't want to know. I don't need the details." She grabbed hold of his beefy paw and held it to her. "I've never needed ... never ever really wanted ... all the gruesome details about what you do. I just need to know that you're safe and that you trust me."

He leaned into her. "I feel safest when I'm with you." They shared a warm, lingering, contented kiss. When they'd finished, Dick opened his eyes and glanced around the sitting room to the two-bedroom suite. The entire trip was, after all, on the Subsidiary's dime.

Melanie guessed at the question his eyes sought an answer to. "Seth left to take a stroll along the River Walk. Said he wanted to go see the lock where the river meets the lake."

"He's a good kid." Dick didn't know if Seth was genuinely curious to see the workings constructed by the Army Corps of Engineers, just wanted to go for a walk, or was purposely making himself scarce so his mom and dad could have some alone time. Probably a bit of all three, not that Dick was going to hang a sock on the door to the suite to warn the kid away from a too early return.

Melanie pulled him toward the master bedroom. "I just need to know one thing."

"I love you," said Dick. "You know that. You've always known that."

He saw her trademark one-dimpled smile for the first time in a very long time. "But always good to hear." Her smile faltered. "I just need to know that this ... today ... your heroics. That was all just happenstance." She sighed and looked away for an instance. "Not just an accident, I know. It took quick, smart analysis to figure out something was wrong and ... well ... bravery to act so decisively to stop it." She met his eyes. "Nobody could have done that but you."

The signals were coming in so mixed and so fast, Dick wished he'd taken the time to learn semaphore, but before he could say anything, Melanie made her meaning clear.

"I just need to know this wasn't a mission. You didn't take me ... your son ... on a mission for the Subsidiary without telling us."

"God, no, honey," he rushed to reply. "This was all dumb luck. Seth pointed to the water crib and I just thought it would be fun ... and educational ... to take a look. I had no idea—" He trailed off as he noticed the tears forming in her eyes in relief. He said what he, as clueless as he could be, suddenly knew what she wanted to hear. "I would never bring you on a mission without telling you. Never."

She hugged him tighter than he'd ever been hugged in his life. What happened next wasn't half-bad, either.

Suddenly, because of some scum-bag terrorists, his family vacation was going a whole lot better than he'd dreamed.

#

He awoke feeling very good. Refreshed, relaxed, rejuvenated, and reconnected with his wife and son.

Room service breakfast, including four extra orders of bacon, was better than expected, too. His mood held until both Melanie and Seth retreated to their respective rooms to shower and get dressed for a day of shopping and sight-seeing and Dick took a minute to check his texts and emails while he sipped dark coffee and munched on the last of the bacon.

A simple text from an anonymous number harshed his mellow: "We need to talk. PN"

While Dick hadn't really expected Nerevsky not to find out about his encounter with bad guys on Lake Michigan, he'd fooled himself into believing it might take a while for him to ask for a debriefing. Or maybe, just maybe, he'd hoped the mirthless bald goon would hold off asking for a report until he was back from his trip with the family to Chicago. But, deep down, Dick realized Nerevsky probably knew about the water intake incident even before Dick had been picked up by the Coast Guard, because Internal Audit knew everything about everybody they made a point of monitoring. Worse, Nerevsky probably thought he'd shown admirable restraint by waiting until the wee hours of the morning before demanding a report.

He let out a sigh. Both showers were running. Probably best to get it over with.

"Call," he texted in reply.

The phone rang within seconds. He thumbed it on.

"Thornby."

"Not exactly maintaining a low profile," said the cold voice he'd come to hate.

"Just doing what I'm trained to do when bad shit is going down."

"Fine work, but I don't want your sudden celebrity to complicate another matter."

Dick let out a long, slow breath. "How soon do you need me?" He glanced at his watch. "It takes a bit longer to get places when I'm making my own arrangements and flying commercial."

"No panic," came the terse reply. "Wrap up family time over the weekend and head home. No doubt the authorities will have a few follow-up items in the meantime, and there's no need to raise any suspicions with them or your family by rushing off."

"You say, I do."

"I'll text with details for a meet Tuesday evening in Philly, but not at the office."

"Understood."

"I've also authorized a deposit as a bonus for fucking over the Lake Michigan terrorists."

"That wasn't work-related—"

"It should have been, except we were caught unawares. That won't happen again."

Somehow Dick knew every person his terrorist opponents knew was suddenly under constant surveillance.

"Sounds like a big op."

"Don't worry, we're saving money elsewhere, so it's all within budget."

Dick knew Nerevsky didn't give a shit about budgets. It was the goon's way of saying somebody's head was rolling for the intelligence screw-up that had almost allowed terrorists to poison the water supply of a major metropolitan area. Internal Audit was a master at carrot and stick motivation, but they relied so heavily on stick Nerevsky almost couldn't help but show stick even when he was dangling a carrot.

"Always happy to fuck over the bad guys."

"That's what I'm depending on."

The line went dead.

Dick took a moment to power up his laptop and maneuver the cursor to check his bank balance.

Hot damn.

Maybe Seth could switch over to a four-year college in the fall, after all. He'd have to figure out how to explain the windfall to Melanie, but he'd do so as honestly as possible as soon as he could. Things were going well in his marriage for the first time in a long time. He wasn't about to screw that up by lying unnecessarily. That's how things had gone bad in the first place.

"Ready to go, dear?" called Melanie from the master bedroom.

"That's my job," answered Dick, "to always be ready for anything."

Chapter 4

A park bench, maybe a parking garage like Deep Throat, or a booth in a diner serving up Philly cheese-steaks. All would have been acceptable places for a meet in Dick's mind. But the Head of the Subsidiary's Internal Audit division was not a man who was conventional or routine in his methods.

That's why Dick was on Fox Street north of the Allegheny West neighborhood, outside a shitty warehouse with broken windows. The building said Kelly Corner on the side—at least that's what the remaining letters suggested. But, more importantly, for Dick's purposes, a smaller sign at ground level near an entrance confirmed it was the home of Penn Jersey Roller Derby, which included both the Hooligans and the She-Devils. Yep, his ex-KGB handler had invited him to a meet at a roller derby workout session.

The sounds of skates and cursing from inside confirmed the workout was already in progress. They also confirmed what everything he ever knew about KGB spooks suggested, the solidly-built vixens of the She-Devils were the team currently training. Russians loved their vodka, but they also couldn't resist a good catfight between muscle-bound dames.

He let himself in. It wasn't like the place had security. Hell, it didn't even have decent seating for spectators—this was a decidedly low-budget operation even if it was, as one sign proclaimed, a proud member of both the WFTDA (Women's Flat Track Derby Association) and the RDCL (Roller Derby Coalition of Leagues). A placard also declared the She-Devils had won the MADE (Modern Athletic Derby Endeavor) National Championship at the Battle of the Bank in 2014.

Funny, he didn't remember a parade.

He wandered past the flat track laid out on the warehouse floor to the banked track erected in the center of the crappy warehouse space. Pyotr Nerevsky stood at the near turn on the left, watching the circling bevy of buxom bruisers skate by and making an occasional note in a small, spiral-bound notebook.

As Dick approached, Nerevsky spoke without looking back at him. "I see you found the place without a problem."

"How could there be a problem?" replied Dick with as little enthusiasm as possible. "Is there a man, woman, or small child who doesn't know the home ... track ... of the Penn Jersey Roller Derby?"

"Some prefer the Philly Roller Derby over on Belfield Avenue," responded Nerevsky. "But they only compete on a flat track, which lowers speeds and requires less skill than the banked version."

"Good to know," said Dick. "When I think of skill sports, roller derby is the first thing which pops into my mind."

Nerevsky finally turned and looked down his nose at Dick. Even though the former Russian agent was only a few inches taller and the setting was, to say the least, informal, he still managed to convey cool superiority. "No doubt you prefer the professional athletes of the National Football League or professional wrestling."

"I don't think you invited me here to discuss my preferences in violent sports."

"Not the kind with rules, anyhow." Nerevsky glanced around as he continued. "It's a good place for a meet. Noisy, too noisy for effective electronic surveillance. Not much of a crowd, so a professional tail would stand out."

Dick nodded. "You got that. All amateur tail here."

Nerevsky bristled. "No need to be crude. The skaters here work hard handling difficult tasks with a level of showmanship that is both effective and impressive." His thin lips formed a tight smile. "But I think it is fair to say that no one here is likely to overhear our talk about international events ... or care if they do."

"You're right, of course. So, let's get to it before some rocketing babe flies off the track and body-slams me. I don't want to have to explain broken ribs *and* smeared lipstick to my wife."

"Of course." Nerevsky tilted his head to the side, then ambled toward the nearest warehouse wall. "I almost forgot how important explaining things to your wife is to you."

Dick followed without comment.

Nerevsky turned and leaned back on the warehouse wall when he got to it, staring back at the sweaty gals working out on the track. Dick took up a similar position, as if the thrill of roller derby, or skating wannabe models cross-checking each other, gave him a hard-on. His handler ... actually, if he told himself the truth, his new boss ... launched into the briefing as if giving color commentary on the mayhem on the oval.

"On May 28, 1993, there was a flash and accompanying ground disturbance in the Outback of Western Australia. The flash and seismic signature was in many ways consistent with the detonation of an atomic explosion. That flash was followed up with a pulsing red-orange hemisphere of light visible at great distance at the epi-center of the flash. Local ranchers, peasants, indigenous natives, and transportation jockeys driving at night all witnessed these events, along with various light displays preceding, accompanying, or following in the wake of the flash, along with rumblings compared to an outsized mining explosion. You'll find a more complete report in a manila folder in the trunk of your vehicle when you leave here."

Dick whistled a long, low tone, drawing a dirty look from one of the broads coaching the team. "A possible nuclear test in the middle of fucking nowhere in 1993? I can see why you needed me to get on that right away."

Nerevsky shifted his head almost imperceptibly to glare at Dick. "Incendiary at every opportunity, as always." The man's cold, dark eyes flicked back to watching the flashing elbows and knees on the track. "Official reports determined with certainty the flash was not a nuclear test. No crater. Radiation consistent with the presence of uranium, but uranium ore mines dot the area. None of the nuclear powers of the time appeared to have operations in the vicinity."

"The Israelis, maybe South Africa or Japan, might have wanted to test a small nuke at the time, but keep it under wraps. Maybe a terrorist group with access to fissile materials from a real nuclear power—"

"Not exactly original thinking, Thornby. But, of course, your *forté* is action, not analysis." The man paused, but Dick knew better than to respond. "In fact, the epi-center of the flash ... explosion ... or whatever was located quite near a half-million-acre sheep station called Banjawarn Station that was in the midst of being purchased by followers of Shoko Asahara."

Dick forgot the pretense of watching babes skate and fight for a moment, swiveling toward his companion. "The guru at the top of the Aum Shinrikyo cult? The doomsday fanatics who gassed the Tokyo subway in the mid-nineties with sarin?"

Nerevsky kept his eyes forward as he responded in a low, calm voice. "Mind your cover and your volume. Sarin is not a word to be bandied about, even here." He tipped his head toward a tall, bountifully bosomed skater clambering over the track's rail. "Zaftig Zelda is majoring in business and minoring in international affairs at the local community college."

"Sorry," Dick muttered as he resumed his stance eyeballing the rolling parade of female flesh. "I should have noticed she has a brand-new pair of roller skates and you've got a brand-new key."

"The press and the various conspiracy theorists and paranoid fantabulists that always flock to these things like ... well, like a moth to a nuclear flame ... jumped all over the Aum Shinrikyo connection. Their property had some small uranium deposits on it, which, according to the real estate broker who showed them the station, they tested before agreeing to buy."

"Okayyyyy. But you don't build a nuke with a small deposit of naturally occurring uranium ore. You need purification, centrifuges, blah ... blah—"

"You don't say."

Dick thought back to his last several missions. "You're right. It doesn't take much to get those guys going, even if the science doesn't really work out."

"They just need something sinister to latch on to. In this case, it was a small number of sheep dead by way of sarin gas."

"Bloated, wooly corpses and a mention of chemical weaponry is enough to make one's blood run cold."

"Thank you."

"Thank you?"

"I got the idea from *Close Encounters of the Third Kind*. You know, when the military types were trying to keep Richard Dreyfus away from Devil's Tower?"

Dick's mouth fell open. He would have closed it to maintain his cover as a roller derby enthusiast, but he expected most of the spectating clientele drooled during workouts. "Whaddya mean, you got the idea?"

Nerevsky's shoulder twitched, as if he was too subtle ... too cool ... to shrug. "The KGB ... well the Federal Security Service by then ... was most interested in keeping a lid on possible tests of clandestine nuclear weaponry. Russia did not have control of all of the former Soviet Union's deterrent forces after the latter's collapse."

Jesus. Had a top ex-KGB/SVR operative just admitted to Dick there were missing Soviet nukes floating around then? Now?

Nerevsky continued. "The first cover story, that there had been a meteor strike, was neither compelling enough for the conspiracy buffs, nor consistent enough with the eyewitness accounts to satisfy the press and official inquiries. As always, the usual UFO crazies spouted their usual crazy theories, but nobody takes them seriously. They cry 'wolf' every time a mylar birthday balloon reflects a bit of light."

"So, you ... you, personally ... just made up a story about Aum Shinrikyo."

"Along with their other outlandish beliefs, the cult was fond of Nostradamus, so making up a grandiose story after the fact to fit random bits of unrelated information seemed to be fair play. I used some convenient tidbits of information, a bit of poison, and the bloat-inducing impact of the hot Outback sun on wooly carcasses to point away from what really happened."

"Which was what?"

Nerevsky sighed. "That's the problem. I don't know. Almost three decades later and no one really knows what happened that night in the wilderness. After I covered up the incident, I tried to find out what was really going on, but my superiors thwarted my efforts."

"Boxing you out? Covering their asses? Couldn't care less? Or, just being cheap?"

"Hard to know their motivation for icing my efforts without knowing what happened."

Dick laughed out loud. "And you want me to find out? That's the mission? That's the job? Pick up a cold trail in the middle of nowhere by interviewing surviving geriatric witnesses whose accounts have been so messed up by re-telling and misinformation that any resemblance they might have to the truth would be entirely coincidental?" He folded his arms across his chest. "You're more obsessed with something that could be no more than a freak electrical storm than the UFO nerds are every time there's ball lightning."

Nerevsky's face hardened. "This is a standard briefing. In accordance with the usual protocol, you get background information, then you get the current situation, and the assigned mission parameters."

Dick stopped smiling. "Yes, sir."

"There was another incident in the same general area a week ago."

"Didn't hear about it in the news. Of course, I've been on vacation."

"You didn't hear about it in the news because, one, American news organizations don't give a crap about what happens elsewhere unless an American is involved. Two, nobody cares about what happens in Australia if it doesn't involve Lara Bingle or Hugh Jackman with their shirts off. And, three, I know how to do my fucking job. And, if that means suppressing local reports of strange lights in the sky, bright flashes, rumbling explosions, and domes of pulsing red lights, I suppress the fucking reports. Just like you, I do whatever it takes to do my job."

The rant was inconsistent with the cold, detached demeanor the head of Internal Audit was known for, but Dick didn't think it was phony. That meant Nerevsky really thought the strange flashes in the godforsaken countryside of Western Australia were real and somehow important. It also meant there were probably a few more suspicious deaths in Australia than average in the past week.

"Understood. Mission parameters?"

"You need to go to Western Australia with your family and find out what is really going on."

Chapter 5

"Whaddya mean I'm supposed to go to Western Australia *with my family* and find out what is really going on?"

"What part of my *orders* do you not understand?"

Dick wanted to spit out a few choice expletives at Nerevsky, but he swallowed them. "I mean, *I'm* the agent. *I'm* the operative. *I'm* the goddamn spy." He jerked his thumb over his shoulder. "Not my wife. Not my kid. Me."

Nerevsky stayed silent.

Dick couldn't. "How'd you like it if the Subsidiary ... or the fucking KGB ... sent your wife and your kids out to do your dirty work?"

"I don't have a wife or kids—"

"Color me shocked—"

"—anymore."

Logically, Dick knew both the KGB and, later, the SVR were ruthless organizations which had few qualms about using whatever methods needed to control and motivate their personnel, and that life was tough in the Soviet Union even without that. There were a million different ways in which an ex-Russian operative might have lost his wife and kids—their cars were crap in crashes, for one thing—but he didn't want to ask. Not only would it be awkward, but he didn't really want to temper his loathing of Pyotr Nerevsky by anything approaching sympathy. Nerevsky was a cold, heartless bastard and Dick didn't want to think family tragedy had forged that steel; he preferred to think the guy was such an institutional prick he had sent his own family out to the Gulag in Siberia so they wouldn't distract him from his patriotic duty.

Dick fluttered his hand to dismiss the topic. "Doesn't matter. It's stupid to take family on an op. Terminally stupid. They're a distraction. Keeping them safe is an even bigger distraction. Their presence could give the bad guys leverage. And, they're not trained agents. They don't know what to do and say. They don't know how to lie."

"That last part isn't your strong suit, either, Thornby. That's why you got in trouble at the Subsidiary. That's why you're here. That's why you have to do whatever I want you to do."

"Whaddya going to do? Off me at the roller derby?"

That last remark drew a smirk. "No. But understand this. If I 'off' you, you won't be the only casualty."

Dick felt his face flush with anger, but Nerevsky held up a hand to shut him up before he erupted.

"Think it through. You insist upon telling your wife where you are at all times. Your family knows who you work for and what you do. And, it's not like you're being sent to take out a hardened facility or assassinate a rising political figure. You're being asked to check out what most people think is a meteor or lightning storm or friendly UFO. Your family going along supports that cover. Besides, they don't have to be with you every single second during your actual investigation. They can sun themselves poolside, take in the local sights, surf the waves, and eat prawns and drink a few beers like any sensible family would while dear old UFO-obsessed dad chases strange lights in the sky. I hear Swan Lager and Emu are popular local brews; they should give them a try. There are no 'cover' names to remember—I send you out under your own identities as if on a further, extended vacation. To bolster your UFO credentials, I've even arranged for you to make a stop in England on the way there. You can check out the site of the Rendlesham Forest incident. Kind of a pilgrimage for anyone serious about UFOlogy."

"I dunno," Dick temporized.

"I wasn't giving you a choice."

"Trust me," said Dick. "I understand that part. You can order me around and I have to dance when you wobble the puppet strings, but you don't understand something."

Nerevsky arched one brow, but said nothing.

"I dunno if I can sell this to the wife. Seth—hell, he'd go along in a minute. But Melanie doesn't push easy. And Seth coming along makes that an even bigger push than it already is."

"Not my problem."

"Sure, it is. If I have a problem, you have a problem. That's how handling an agent works."

Nerevsky chuckled. "You know nothing about handling agents. Look, I don't care about your relationship with your wife. I don't care if you convince her, force her, or lie to her. I'm not Glenn Swynton. I'm not going to hold your fucking hand. But I'm not Dee Tammany, either. I'm not going to give you shit about blowing things up if they need to be blown up. You pride yourself on doing what needs to be done. Well, I'm the guy telling you this needs to be done." He squinted his beady, dead eyes at Dick. "Go get it done."

#

Business class.

Nerevsky might be a world class dick, but he didn't skimp, at least not with counterfeit mileage points.

Seth stowed their carry-on luggage in the overhead bins and settled into the window seat in the row behind them. Melanie took the window seat in their row, with Dick in the aisle seat. Sure, it was a routine flight on what was supposed to be vacation, but he always liked to be able to move quickly and take action without clambering over someone in the event of trouble. Being able to easily access the contortionist boxes that passed as restrooms on a commercial airliner didn't hurt either. If having a kid about to start college didn't make him feel old enough, having to pee more often did the trick. It wasn't fair. Jason Bourne only went into restrooms because the abundance of porcelain gave him something to smash bad guys' faces into.

Melanie settled into her seat, but even though Dick was pretty sure she'd never flown anything but coach before, she didn't look happy. Not quite a scowl—not full-fledged pissed—but not happy.

Dick snatched the small blue pillow he'd stuffed into the seat pocket in front of him and held it out to her. "Want a spare pillow? Might as well get some good sleep on the way to merry olde England."

"I don't know why I let you talk me into this."

"What? A European vacation? Gladys, down the street, was practically drooling with envy when you gave her a key so she could water the plants."

She flashed a faux smile at him. "You know what I mean."

Dick glanced around. "Look, I know you're not that interested in Rendlesham—the whole UFO side of the trip. But you and Seth can see the sights. See the Crown Jewels and the Tower of London. Visit a local pub—Seth's legal to drink in England, you know."

"Teaching my kid to drink beer—"

"—warm beer."

"—is not exactly a point in favor of this ... this ... expedition. You know what I mean."

Sure, Dick was on a mission probably no one in the world cared about except his surprisingly obsessed ex-KGB boss, and he was in a situation where the chances anyone listening would give a damn what he said was infinitesimal, but he didn't, he wouldn't, break character. Not even if he was playing himself, albeit himself in somewhat fictionalized circumstances.

"Look," he said, "I know you're Scully to my Fox Mulder." He fluttered his hand upward. "You don't think there's anybody out there. Or, if there is, that they would bother coming to this insignificant, watery planet to play hide and seek with some hairless apes living on the rocky, dry parts of the planet. And, that's okay."

Melanie's facial expression slid from unhappy to very unhappy, tending toward aggravated.

"But, for me, it's like being an armchair detective or putting together a jigsaw puzzle upside down. It's engaging, even fun."

To his surprise, Melanie played along. "So, what's the big puzzle about Rendlesham?"

"Well, these security guards at the East Gate of this RAF base there see some lights descending into the forest east of the base and, thinking it might be a downed aircraft, they go investigate. They see strange lights in the woods and hear weird sounds. The next day, they investigate more and find some depressions in a clearing and some broken branches and shit.

"Compelling," replied Melanie, her tone droll. "And when did this happen?"

"Late on Christmas in nineteen eighty. Well, three in the morning afterwards—Boxing Day."

"Isn't the British m1ilitary known for drinking heavily on Christmas? Isn't that why Washington crossed the Delaware? To surprise them when they were drunk?"

"That was Hessians," said Dick.

"Hessians?"

"Hired mercenaries from what is now Germany. The British hired them to fight the American revolutionaries. Besides, I think that happened on Christmas Eve."

"Goodness knows a bunch of young soldiers on holiday would never go on a three-day bender. Is that it?"

"Well, one of the higher ups, he checks it out another day later and finds radiation levels in excess of customary background levels. Then there's more flashing lights in the woods and stuff."

"Flashing?"

"Periodic."

"Like Morse Code?"

"No. Every five seconds." Dick hesitated before continuing. "At the same periodicity as the lighthouse five miles away."

Melanie snorted.

"Wait, there's more."

"There always is."

"They also saw hovering lights in the sky at a distance."

"Hovering. In the distance. You mean, like stars?"

"Brighter than the average star."

"Like a planet? Or maybe the North Star?"

Dick smiled. "You're a great skeptic."

Melanie smiled. "The most unbelievable part of all this is that it turned into a cornerstone of UFO belief. Doesn't seem to be that much there ... there."

"Probably wouldn't have been as much interest, except the one higher up at the base, he sent a memo to the brass, which has since gone public. He also made a mini-cassette recording in real time when they were out in the woods investigating."

"Uh-huh. Just don't start making mashed potato sculptures of Devil's Tower."

Dick said nothing. Apparently, his wife and his boss had the same taste in movies.

Melanie patted his arm on their shared armrest. "Well, you have a nice time wandering through the woods listening to scratchy audio from the disco era."

"I think disco stopped being great in the late seventies."

"Wrong," said Melanie, with a smirk. "Disco was never great. It was just popular."

Dick knew better than to argue about something he didn't give a damn about. He scrunched up his nose. "You and Seth just concentrate on having a great time in London while I make the side-trip up to Rendlesham. Then we'll be off to the beaches of Australia in just a few days. This gives you guys a great chance to travel you wouldn't have had otherwise."

Melanie's light expression evaporated. "This trip isn't a great chance at anything. Don't oversell."

Dick's heart sank. "I know it's not the vacation you always dreamed about. Just think of it like any other business trip where the family comes along. You do the tourist thing; I do my thing. It beats sitting at home in New Jersey wondering what I'm up to, doesn't it?"

Melanie's expression softened, almost imperceptibly. Dick pressed his advantage by repeating the selling point—okay, the white lie—he'd used to convince his wife to go along with Nerevsky's family spy fun scheme. "Seth deserves something special—so do you. Treat it as quality family time. An opportunity not to be missed, you know, with Seth headed to college in a few months now that I got that special bonus from work for this project."

He had, after all, gotten a bonus. He didn't need to tell Melanie it was for thwarting the Lake Michigan sleazebags. He told her it was for bringing her and Seth along to vacation while he did a simple historical investigation for work using a phony interest in ancient aliens as cover. Seth was enthusiastic about college, and Melanie was laser-focused on higher education for her only child. So was Dick.

Dick also thought it would be good for his son to have a dad ... and a mom ... and a life. So, he lied.

He felt guilty about it, but not too guilty. After all, this whole, stupid mission was probably the lamest and least dangerous thing he'd done since high school. Wandering around, asking people about lights they saw in the sky years and years ago. Asking silly questions. No, *probing* questions.

He smiled at his own joke.

What could possibly go wrong?

#

Yuri Lemarov looked at the thin communications file and leaned back in his desk chair, his lips forming a sour pucker as he contemplated the situation. "So, it begins, Pyotr. You think of yourself as an Arctic Owl, sitting cold and motionless, seeing and hearing everything, ready to swoop down without a whisper of sound, and snatch up what you desire. But you are no true predator. You are a mouse, hiding in the shadows, feeding on crumbs and larvae, scurrying away should a true predator come your way. True, you have aspirations ... no ... more like naked ambitions. You wish to be more. But you are still a mouse, a mouse studying to be a rat. A starving mouse too hungry not to take the bait."

Chapter 6

People think the life of a spy is never boring. They're wrong. Espionage is almost always snooze-worthy. It's just that the long run-on sessions of sitting in a car on stake-out or hiding motionless in a tree waiting for a convoy of black Suburbans carrying an assassination target, are punctuated with bursts of unspeakable violence and underlined by bold-faced stress. Worse yet, there are few markers—no real clues of what is to come—between the endless hours of internal introspection amidst unchanging, bland scenery and the sudden onset of staccato bursts of action, blood, and dropping bodies.

Dick expected—no, he knew—his late evening stroll along the Rendlesham Forest Trail was just an exercise to cement his cover for his probably equally pointless Australian expedition, but he tried to make the best of it. Forestry England had made a pleasant family park out of the place, with a triangular metal placard at the beginning of the broad, level path. The signage referenced the incident and suggested kids look for strange symbols along the route, which they could decode with the help of the "Alien Leaflet" available in the nearby Forest Office. According to his map, a variety of other, longer, hiking and biking trails wound through the woods which surrounded the old RAF airstrip on three sides. But with light fading as the sun set, almost all the hikers and bikers were packing up and leaving the pay-and-park lot at the edge of the woods.

He'd picked up an LED flashlight—torches, they called them here—on the drive up. He grabbed it and headed west without yet turning it on. A right, left, and a right brought him to the East Gate of Woodbridge Airfield, where the security guards who instigated the whole UFO search had been stationed. Yep, looking at a rusty chain-link gate is what passed for tourism for the aliens-please-abduct-me crowd. Barbed wire along the top, but the fence wouldn't even slow down anyone seriously trying to breach the airstrip's security.

He took a few photos in low-light mode with his phone—it's what his cover personality would do—then turned east, skirting the side of the airfield and, after a quick jog to the left, continued east into the forest. Darkness fell as he meandered along, but he kept his flashlight off. The path was wide and clear of debris; there was no reason to ruin the moody ambience of the place. Besides, always best to keep your night vision tuned when you were looking for aliens creeping along in the woods out to get you. Another minor jog to the left, then eastward again to the edge of an open field and a quick loop back into the woods to the supposed landing site of the alien craft. Originally, three wooden posts had marked where the slightly radioactive indentations in the ground had been found, but the site was now graced with an artist's rendition of a black alien craft, complete with bizarre markings on the side of the shiny, squat object.

He stretched out his arm to take a selfie with the craft in the background—it would be a crappy, dim shot in the now almost complete darkness, but he had to go through the motions of building his cover. It's not that anyone was here to see him—to gauge his compliance with the histrionics of Nerevsky's background set-up—but it was important for him to feel like the character he was portraying on a mission, and that meant doing things to establish the character in his own mindset.

He dialed up a smile and hit the button on his phone to snap the picture.

A blinding white light assaulted his eyes.

Crap! He must have accidently thumbed on the auto-flash setting before he took the shot. Well, his night vision was worthless for at least a half-hour now. He blinked to clear the after-image of the flash, then closed his eyes completely to speed their readjustment to darkness as much as possible. When doing so, he realized that the amorphous blob of color burned into his retina actually showed a shadowy outline of his extended arm ... and the phone.

What the hell?

The light hadn't come from the flash; it had come from *behind* the phone.

He pocketed his phone with one hand and brought his flashlight up with the other simultaneously. Probably some kids playing tricks in the dark—the same kind of punks who flew drones into the airspace at Gatwick Airport in London a few years back, disrupting air traffic for days. But Dick didn't like anyone getting the drop on him, no matter what his cover was. Instincts kicked in; adrenaline coursed through his arteries. He held up the flashlight to the side and slightly forward of his face and flicked it on, then did a slow, steady sweep from right to left into the woods.

Nothing.

Then his subconscious mind finished the geometric calculations his high-school-self had told him he'd never need. The bright light hadn't come from the woods; it had come from the sky. Higher than the trees, on his left, in the direction of the open field. He pivoted left, and raised his gaze, automatically shining the light uselessly into the night sky.

At the same time, he heard ... almost felt through the soles of his feet ... a deep bass thrum just above subsonic range. Impossible to source, but there was a slight rhythmic pulse to it.

What the fuck? The map he'd picked up from the Forestry Service didn't say anything about an ersatz UFO experience at the sculpture site.

He didn't see anything as he scanned the sky, but then he realized that, itself, was a clue—a big, fat, scary clue. It was full-on dark now, but he didn't see stars where he was looking. He spun about, keeping his eyes to the sky. There were stars aplenty to the north, west, and south, but a blob of black blocked the stars in a patch to the east-southeast above the open field. He trained his flashlight at the edge of blackness and, just for a microsecond, a glint of light reflected off something flat, shiny, and edged hovering silently in the sky above the field.

No. Not silently. The thrum notched up ever so slightly.

Abruptly, five red lights burst out of the black hole, arcing into the atmosphere, dripping sparks.

Flares?

Before he could answer his own question, he heard a faint *zuzzing* sound, like a zipper being zipped too fast ... or ... rope rushing through rappelling gear.

Shit.

At the same time, thin lines of green laser light cut through the night, shifting left, right, up, down. Multiple sources, crisscrossing one another as they bounced through the area, dodging trees, snaking down paths, all converging on him. He heard several soft thumps and then bright white light exploded all around him, searing new, confusing images on his retinas.

A sudden wind whipped up, buffeting him from all sides and pelting him with dirt and debris. He knew what was coming next.

He felt himself being lifted up. Soon he would be on the strange, silent, black craft in the sky.

Fucking Lightning Teams. Somebody was having way too much fun at his expense.

Somebody? No, fucking Nerevsky. He couldn't just call for an update, he'd sent a fucking Lightning Team in their whisper-quiet black Bell ARH-70 helicopter to snatch him up for a status report.

Before his vision cleared, he felt a canvas bag slide over his head. Jesus, these guys were taking this much, much too seriously. He didn't blame the Lightning Team crew. They just did what they were told. Besides, he had a soft spot for the guys since they'd saved Seth by rushing him to a hospital after Pao Fen Smythe had sent a hitter after him. But he'd have a few choice words for the Head of Internal Audit when he saw him.

He started picking his swear words carefully in preparation.

#

After way too much travel and too much rough handling, Dick was slammed into a metal chair and the canvas hood yanked away from his face. Bright lights again blinded him, but he worked to focus on the dark blob nearest his face, his lips forming invectives, ready to spew forth the instant he confirmed his ex-KGB target.

Instead, his blinking eyes made out the bland face of Glenn Swynton, the guy who oversaw operations at the Subsidiary. Another blob coalesced into Dee Tammany, the Director of the entire damn Subsidiary. He was looking at his boss and his boss's boss from back in the days when he was in the Subsidiary's relatively good graces.

"What the fuck?"

Glenn flashed a forced smile. "Good evening to you, too, Agent Thornby."

"We needed to talk," added Dee Tammany, who was standing behind Glenn and leaning in over his shoulder, her face wrinkled in apparent concern for Dick's well-being.

"And," picked up Glenn, "we figured UFO abduction would make a good story should Nerevsky question you."

Tammany stood up straight and took a step to the side. "Whether chemical or bio-response activated, Internal Audit's methods of discerning truth versus fiction are impressive. But if you tell him the details of your ... abduction ... he will simply be impressed you are integrating your character personality so effectively."

A million thoughts raced through Dick's mind, but one stood out. "So, you're not working with Nerevsky." He stated it as fact. "You know he's running a black op without sanction, an op using me ..." He hesitated before continuing. "... and my family."

Glenn sniffed, as if the adrenaline and sweat his own operation had caused was offensive to his gentlemanly sensibilities. "That's the dead giveaway the op is unsanctioned. We would never involve your family. Frankly, your family is much too involved with your activities for the Subsidiary for our taste already."

"That's why we still keep tabs on you," volunteered Dee. "On all of you." She fixed him with a steely glare. "That's how we tripped onto Nerevsky's frolic and detour."

Glenn took over. "We had a high-altitude surveillance drone track him to your meeting in Philadelphia, hoping to listen in on the briefing. But, of course, our Kestrel couldn't follow you into the building, and the roller derby practice bollixed up any effort to listen in through vibrations on the glass panes in the structure with its high-gain microphone."

"Tell us everything," said Dee, grabbing a spare chair and sitting next to Glenn. "Everything."

Dick had been through a lot of interrogations during his career: Psych Ops interrogation resistance training in the Rangers; lying to dirt-bags and drug dealers when undercover while in the Chicago Police Department; even fibbing to Melanie about where he'd been when he'd gone on missions before she found out he was a spy. There was no comparison; this was his favorite interrogation of all time.

They softened the lights, asked questions, and sought clarifications in pleasant, even voices, let him take bathroom breaks, and avoided any semblance of threats of physical violence. All that, and they let him rat out the man he most despised in the world: Pyotr Nerevsky.

Fuck you, Pyotr. This one's for you and all your goons in Internal Audit.

It occurred to Dick that this all could be a test, that Nerevsky had asked—more likely forced—Glenn and Dee to do his bidding and find out whether Dick was loyal to him. But Dick didn't think so. He never knew anyone to push Dee around—at least nobody outside of the Subsidiary's oversight board of national representatives. And Glenn, well Glenn couldn't help but sneer in that barely effable British way when unhappy, and Glenn seemed perfectly happy to hear every unkind thing Dick had to say about his dealings with Internal Audit. Of course, it could be he was just happy to have a chance to pick up a few new bespoke suits while in England, but Dick didn't think so.

So, he told them everything.

When he was done, Dee and Glenn didn't even take a moment to confer before putting his new mission on the table.

"Thank you for your cooperation, Thornby," said Dee. "We want you to continue with your mission for Nerevsky, but we want you to report to us not only what you find, but what he asks you to do."

Glenn smiled. "We want you to be our inside man."

"You want me to do something kinky like that," said Dick, "you'll have to at least buy me dinner first."

Glenn got up and went over to a side table, picked up something, and came back, tossing it into Dick's lap. "Have a snacky doo."

Dick looked at the bag; it was a packet of Walker's Crisps—what Dick would call potato chips—but the label said they were "English Roast Beef and Yorkshire Pudding Flavoured."

"You must think I'm a pretty cheap date."

"You're not a date," responded Glenn. "You're just here to—"

As Glenn trailed off, Dick finished the thought. "—get fucked."

"Not at all," broke in Dee. "Maintaining operational control over the entire organization is a critical task for any covert agency. We think ... most particularly, the Russian representative of our oversight board has hinted he thinks ... Pyotr Nerevsky needs special scrutiny. Nerevsky's recently taken a number of odd actions for reasons unknown. We need a double agent within his operation to find out what is going on and why. That's where you come in."

Ahh. Spying on another spy for your own spy agency. It was so meta, Dick couldn't help but laugh. "Sign me up. Just promise me if you stick it to Nerevsky at the end of all this, I get to watch him go down."

Dee chuckled. "Well, we're not about to slow down taking him out when the time comes just so we can assemble a live studio audience, but we'll do our best to let you experience as much of what happens as is feasible—"

"—and operationally prudent given our security parameters," added Glenn.

Dick snorted. "Spoken like a true Director of Operations."

"We are what we are," replied Glenn.

Dick said nothing, but he agreed. Glenn understood how Dick operated and certainly had good reason to expect his cooperation. And Dick had no illusions about what he was ... who he was as an agent, a husband, a father, and a partner, not necessarily in that order.

And, at the moment, he was a double agent searching for hot clues and ancient aliens in a mystery more than a quarter century cold.

Truth was stranger than fiction.

"Just one more thing," said Dick to Dee.

"I'm not giving you weapons of mass destruction," replied Dee, "no matter how much you say you need them."

Dick flashed a quick, wry smile. "Yes, it's related to Denver, but no, not that. I just need some information for my trip to Australia I wasn't about to ask Nerevsky for."

Chapter 7

The sun had risen by the time Dick got back to the hotel in the center of London where Melanie and Seth were sleeping after a long day seeing the sights, including the Tower of London. Melanie woke as Dick climbed into bed.

"Hello," she said as she squinted at the bright light trying to penetrate the thick hotel curtains. "You're hours and hours later than you said you'd be. If you knew anybody in London, I might worry you were having an affair." She took a deep breath. "Of course, for all I know, you know scores of people in London."

"True," Dick said, then leaned forward to give her a kiss on the forehead. "But, in order to have an affair, I'd need to be dashing, debonair, and know how to engage in witty banter." He wrapped his arms around her. "Seems like a lot of work when I've got the perfect woman waiting in bed for me right here."

Melanie actually blushed at that, but continued on, her tone still light. "And yet, you were out all night. Get lost in the woods?"

There was no point to hiding what had happened from her. She was part of the team for this mission. Well, for Nerevsky's mission, anyway.

She was silent as he explained. When he finished, he simply asked "Well?"

Melanie pursed her lips a few seconds before responding. "I'm not sure I like being in the middle between feuding factions of a behemoth organization filled with operatives and weapons that could kill all of us at any moment."

"You could think of it that way," Dick replied. "Or, you could focus on the fact this intra-agency rivalry means we have twice as many people watching over us at each and every moment."

She pursed her lips again, and then a twinkle came into her eye. "If someone ... multiple someones ... is watching us at each and every moment, then let's give them something to look at."

For the first time in his life as a spy, Dick felt like he was actually in one of those fade-to-black moments in the always suggestive, but ultimately PG-13 rated, Bond films. Except in this case, the morning sun was streaming in along the edges of the drapes and Dick could see ... and enjoy ... *everything*.

#

The rest of Dick's stay in England was operationally uneventful. He strolled around parks and cathedrals, visited various squares, circuses, and houses of parliament, and doffed a few warm beers at pubs featuring huge bars made of polished, weathered wood and very little in the way of ambient light. The family even caught a showing of Agatha Christie's *The Mousetrap*, which was nearing seventy years in a continuous run—more than forty of those years at The St. Martin's Theatre. The best part was Dick didn't even try to cipher out the whodunnit. For once, figuring out who the bad guy was and stopping them wasn't his job. He relished his night off.

Once they'd all boarded the plane for Perth, though, his mind reverted to work mode. Remarkably enough, Qantas flew the Kangaroo Route non-stop from Heathrow to Perth using a Boeing 787-9 Dreamliner. Departing at 6:55 p.m. local time, Dick would have sixteen hours and forty-five minutes traveling at eighty-five percent of the speed of sound to wonder whether any of the other two-hundred-plus passengers was tailing him for Nerevsky ... or for Swynton and Tammany.

He wondered, but he didn't pace up and down the aisles trying to figure it out or anything. It wouldn't do to look like he thought he was being tailed for one thing. For the other, it would be inconsistent with his cover. With windows sixty-five percent bigger than standard airline fare and the plane cruising above forty thousand feet, a real UFO-ologist would take the window seat and stare into the skies, most especially during the dark hours over water or unpopulated areas when everyone else in the plane (possibly including the pilots) was getting some shut-eye in the hopes of making the long flight tolerable before arriving in Perth at one in the afternoon on the next day.

This time Dick decided it was best to stay more in character for the seating arrangements, giving Melanie the aisle seat and easy access to the restroom for the long flight despite his normal operational protocol. Seth settled into the row behind them and had his earphones on before their plane, which their flight attendant Annie had gleefully pointed out was named the *Quokka* after a small wallaby that frequents Rottnest Island off the coast near Perth, took off. No doubt the kid was binge-watching something or online on one of his video games. Dick didn't really try to regulate his kid's computer usage—he was practically an adult at this point—just as long as he didn't engage in any more espionage on the now resurrected remnants of Reality 2 Be, the criminal-ridden virtual reality world Dick had taken out in Denver several missions back.

Dick did his best to quiet his mind—about family, about work, about little green men—but he was a responsible guy. And with great responsibility comes a great amount of apprehension about one's lack of power to control anything the universe or your job wanted to throw at you.

After take-off, Dick joined Melanie in having a nice glass of Australian wine and let the alcohol join the drone of the plane and the darkening skies in dampening his concerns, or at least making them seem as though they were half a world away—which, of course, they were. It's just that they were getting closer every single minute.

#

Dick finally drifted off to sleep, just about the same time the aircraft re-entered the light of day and most of the rest of the passengers started to wake and fumble about for restrooms and fresh orange juice. He missed breakfast service altogether, but discovered when he woke that

Melanie had saved her bacon and a small packet of honey for him to snack on. This trip might be a complete waste of time for everybody in the Subsidiary, but if it got Dick and Melanie back into the groove of marital bliss, it was a godsend to him.

It was a good thing Dick started out in a good mood, because international travel was never the glamorous delight portrayed in fiction, especially when you were traveling with your family on a long trip with a substantial amount of luggage. Thank God, Seth was grown up and could schlep his own stuff—taking a baby or a toddler on an extended flight was probably one of the featured tortures in some circle of hell. But still, after most of a day and night in the air, they had to get their passports hand-scanned because the automatic Smartgate system was down, trudge to baggage claim, wait for bags, haul them off the carousel while a throng of impatient passengers stood in their way, then trek to the back of the hall and stand in line, awaiting their turn for a bored Border Force officer to either wave them toward the exit or play twenty questions with them in a mumbled, yet delightfully accented, monotone.

Having gone through this same routine more times than he could count—and a whole lot more times than Melanie knew about—Dick shuffled along on auto-pilot, barely paying attention to the routine questions. The inspector finished up, murmured: "Have a nice stay Downunder," as he handed Melanie and Seth their paperwork, but held back Dick's.

"Is there a problem?" asked Dick, suddenly alert.

"Not at all, sir," replied the inspector. "You've just been randomly selected for supplemental screening."

Supplemental screening sounded to Dick a lot like some bureaucrat's euphemism for cavity search, but he kept his cool. He turned to look at Melanie, whose eyes had gone wide, and inclined his head toward the exit. "You go ahead to the currency exchange in the main terminal and get some cash—including small bills ... or coins or whatever ... for tips. I'll be just a couple minutes behind." He turned back toward the inspector. "Right?"

The bland, bored man gave him a bland, bored smile. "Tipping is not customary in Australia. In any event, supplemental screening is generally completed in less than ten minutes barring any complicating factors."

Dick didn't know what complicating factors meant. Customs guys like the Australian Border Force were usually looking for people with balloons of drugs up their ass or down their throat, non-native reptiles hidden in their pants, or fellow terrorists on their speed-dial. Dick was clean of anything like that. He didn't even have a weapon—not that he needed one to deal with most one-on-one or even one-on-three encounters. But alarms were going off in his head all the same. Border Force would never separate just one person from a party traveling together for supplemental screening. Contraband could be hidden anywhere in the group's effects, for one thing.

No, nothing about this situation was normal.

Still, he trudged along behind the Border Force agent who had come to fetch him to the private screening room, waving at his clearly distraught wife and bewildered son as they shuffled reluctantly toward the exit from customs into the main terminal.

As soon as they were out-of-sight, the escorting agent opened a door into a small interview room with white walls, a white plastic table, and three white plastic chairs. Too soft to be intimidating to Dick, though the fact his quick survey located no security cameras to record his supplemental screening was less than reassuring. That his escort dropped him in the room, then left Dick alone, also made his spy-senses tingle.

After about five minutes, the door to his private room opened and a small, rabbity man entered carrying a cord-handled shopping bag with the image of a stylized multi-color kangaroo leaping in front of a large, yellow sun.

"Greetings, Mr. Thornby, from your *friends* at Quartermasters, a *subsidiary* of Perth Tourism Centre." The bloke actually winked at him. Jesus. He'd heard a tourist on the flight remark that Australia was a half-century behind the United States in terms of attitude and atmosphere, but he'd always known Australia's espionage agents to be both modern and competent. This guy's spycraft was neither; it was on par with *The Man from U.N.C.L.E.* ... no, make that *Get Smart*. Certainly, he had to be a plant of some sort, but Dick didn't know if he was some out-of-work actor freelancing in response to a last-minute casting call put out by Nerevsky or just a newbie shoved into position in a hurry by Glenn Swynton's local, obviously less demanding, equivalent.

Dick played dumb. It wasn't difficult. "I'm just waiting here for 'supplemental screening.'"

"Of course, you are."

Ye Gads! The twit winked again, then reached into the shopping bag.

"Well, here in Western Australian, supplemental screening just means having special, extra strength sunscreen to protect you from the harmful ultra-violet rays of the sun." He screwed off the top of a plastic tube of HyperBlok 85 and held the open end out toward Dick's face. Dick saw the green sheen and smelled the unmistakable aroma of almonds which identified the contents as Nobel 808, a form of plastic explosive common during World War II, but long since overtaken by Semtex, Demex, PVV-5A, and Seismoplast 1, among others. Given all the mining done in Western Australia, they must have RDX, the explosive agent in C-4, coming out the wazoo, yet this guy was giving him Nobel 808 and winking while he did it. Dick wanted to ask why, but he didn't think this guy would know ... or tell him if he did.

"The cap is a detonator. Simply use a piece of the bag's handle as a fuse and light it." The contact waved one hand at the tourist board bag. "The rest of the contents, including a new pair of aviator sunglasses, are ... self-explanatory. Compliments of the *Subsidiary*."

Jeez, the guy was about as subtle as a West Hollywood hooker. Dick expected the guy to flash his boobs any second.

"Understood," Dick intoned. "Thanks."

"Do you have anything for us?"

That was a dangerous question to ask a double-agent, especially when the double-agent didn't have any idea which faction had sent this clueless clerk. Fortunately, in this particular case, the answer was the same for both sides. "Not a thing," said Dick. "What do you expect? I just fucking got here."

A minute later, Dick had donned his Subsidiary-issued sunglasses and was striding with the tourist bag toward the terminal lobby currency exchange, where Melanie stood looking anxious, while Seth inspected the personages adorning the colorful and partially transparent currency.

"Any trouble?" asked Melanie, her voice low, but her distress visible from a mile ... er ... one point six kilometers ... away.

"Nah," replied Dick. "Routine."

She pointed at his bag. "What's that?"

"Welcoming gifts."

Before he could stop her, Melanie reached out with one hand and peeked inside the bag, where a 9 mm laid on top of other gadgetry. She gasped.

Dick put his arm around her. "Apparently they think that because Australia was populated with British criminals as a penal colony back at the end of the eighteenth century, it's still a dangerous place."

Chapter 8

Plenty of taxis in the queue, so it didn't take long to load up and head for the hotel, even with the family luggage far exceeding Dick's normal travel style. Still, he got chilled while helping the driver play Tetris with the assortment of suitcases which needed to fit in a trunk significantly smaller than the one in his Oldsmobile back home. The breeze and the light mist being blown in despite the overhang above the cab stand didn't help.

He clambered in the front seat of the Swan Taxi with the driver and turned to talk to Seth and Melanie in the passenger compartment. "Might be a bit nippy for surf lessons today. Maybe better to rest up, shake off the jet lag, and get the lay of the land at the hotel."

Seth snorted. "You don't think I'm actually going to take surf lessons while I'm here, do you?"

Dick's eyes darted side to side, as if he might find something to suggest why his kid wouldn't want to surf in Australia. "Uh ... okay ... so maybe lessons aren't your thing. Self-taught can be cool, too."

Melanie chimed in, maternal concern obvious in her tone. "I'm sure you can do it if you try. It's just like the balance exercises the physical therapist used to have you do."

"Sure, but—"

Melanie kept going. "And you don't need to be embarrassed about the burn scars on your legs, you know. Long board shorts are in style these days—"

"Besides," added Dick, "all the scars show is that you were a hero during a fire."

Seth flushed. "I tell most people they're from a shark attack." He let out a sigh. "Just kidding. And I don't care about my scars. That's not why I'm not going surfing." Seth waved his hand at the spattering of droplets on the passenger window. "Didn't you guys look up the average temperature for Perth before you packed? Not only are we in the midst of rainy season, we'll be lucky if it breaks seventy degrees while we're here. Nighttime lows could go into the forties."

Melanie frowned. "I thought Australia was hot. You know, deserts and tropical rainforests."

Seth rolled his eyes. "Parts of it are, but the place ... the continent ... is huge. And the farther down south you go, the closer you are to Antarctica. And while it might be summer break back home, it's the middle of winter here." He sat back and looked out the rain-spattered window. "I don't think you're going to need any sunscreen while you're here."

Dick pictured the tube of Nobel 808 in his goody bag. He certainly hoped Seth was right.

#

They took their time getting settled into their suite at the resort. As it turned out, surfing wasn't really an option in any event. The Crown Metropol Perth was located on the Swan River, not on the ocean. It was, however, within passable distance of the local zoo, as well as Kings Park and Botanic Garden. But then, of course, Perth wasn't really oceanside altogether. The beaches in Freemantle were as far from city center as their hotel was from where they just landed at Perth Airport.

Still, it was a nice resort. Large pool outside, but indoor swimming and a hot tub, too. Well-appointed, modern, and spacious, with some nice architectural touches—though the sheets of white sail furled high in the spacious enclosed lobby reminded Dick just a bit too much of Denver International Airport. And, with more than twenty restaurants within a half-kilometer, Dick was sure Seth and Melanie would have a pleasant time while he was engaged on his irksome tasks and toilsome responsibilities.

For tonight, they decided to dine at the Bistro Guillame on site. Nice view and excellent ambience, though most of the patrons seemed to be more interested in making eyes at each other. Apparently, the Bistro was a popular place for proposals, anniversary dinners, and romantic trysts, which would have been fine for Dick and Melanie, but made them feel a trifle out of place with Seth as a third wheel. Melanie had the twice baked cheese soufflé as an appetizer, followed by barramundi with caper and raisin beurre noisette and shaved cauliflower for her main course. Both Seth and Dick opted for a main course of Rangers Valley sirloin, accompanied by crispy kipfler potatoes, watercress salad and béarnaise sauce. Seth tried out the escargot for an appetizer, while Dick stuck with tried and true onion soup. Melanie picked different wines by the glass for the adults, while Seth limited himself to water. They shared desserts, including profiteroles with vanilla bean ice cream and warm chocolate sauce, a lemon tart, and vanilla bean crème brûlée with rhubarb. Service was attentive without being fussy.

The bill caused Dick to blanch for a moment—even though he knew the Subsidiary was picking up the tab—before he realized everything was in Australian dollars. Once he did the math, he was content. The rest of the patrons had it right; this was a great place for special occasions and vacations, but not an everyday kind of restaurant unless you didn't have to worry about money.

The family walked to a promenade in the hotel overlooking the river, along with views of the city and the ocean to the west. He stood with his arm around Melanie as the sun set. The colors were spectacular enough Seth even looked up from his phone, but Dick was too keyed up to let the deepening tones of mauve and orange comfort him. He was going through the paces of being on a family vacation, albeit one with a side helping of UFO fetish, but he couldn't help but focus on the mission and any danger it might entail.

Dick didn't know if this entire escapade was a fool's errand or a cake walk, but it certainly didn't have the feel of a regular mission. There was no discernible bad guy to target, no list of witnesses to interrogate, no insidious plot to thwart, nothing to blow up, and nobody to capture, maim, kill, or kidnap. He had next to no support services since the mission was off the books, but he still had not one, but two, sets of overseers second-guessing every move he would make, plus a family to keep safe while he dragged them from place to place. He'd worked hard over the years to compartmentalize everything—keeping work and family separate and turning his emotions on and off as necessary. But the compartments he had thought were so strong were really just nooks in a house of cards. That house was falling, and the contents were all spilling out in a jumble. He always did what had to be done, but right now he didn't have a clue what that was.

Still, Melanie felt and smelled good nestled under his arm, her bright eyes reflecting the pastel glory of the sunset as she smiled her infamous one-dimpled smile.

For tonight, that was enough.

#

Literally half a world away, Pyotr Nerevsky adjusted the shade in his chauffeured car to block out the glare from the rising sun. Ignoring his Subsidiary-issued phone, he reached into an inside pocket of his suit jacket to retrieve his second phone—his "black" phone. Though it didn't have all the features of his official device, it was far from a cheap burner. In fact, the encryption and security features were probably even better than the one he was supposed to use, especially the algorithms designed to prevent tracking, tracing, and tapping by the IT dweebs at the Subsidiary. He'd acquired it from a contact in the MSS. China's Ministry of State Security might not be the best at inventing, but they stole tech on a scale nobody else in the espionage business could come close to matching. They not only seized hardware and software on a routine basis, they placed agents in every university, tech company, Silicon Valley startup, and black hat hacker collective in the world. If it existed, they had it. If it was on some drawing board somewhere, they were monitoring progress and downloading the specifications as they were developed. So many people, so much effort, just so he could reach out and touch someone whenever, wherever he wanted.

He texted Thornby a time and place for a virtual meet. Time to get moving. He needed to know if current events had any connection to that mysterious flash a quarter century ago.

Chapter 9

Seth navigated through the streets and alleyways of Shangrilyfe, his fingers nudging the controller with a rush of taps, twists, and bumps. When he introduced the Shangrilyfe virtual reality platform to his dad, who, despite what he said, paid more attention to his online habits since the Reality 2 Be fiasco, his dad had marveled at how quickly Seth could maneuver online. Seth had responded that teenagers have quicker reflexes, rather than point out it was really just a matter of practice. Of course, unlike touch-typing or sending or receiving Morse Code, practicing online was fun, not work.

This particular foray, however, was all business. No time to shop or play games today; he had plans in real life. But he did want to stay in touch with his friends back in the states, even though they were twelve hours behind.

Shangrilyfe was a vivid, photorealistic world of saturated color and hyper-sharp visual detail, but ultimately a less sophisticated virtual reality than Reality 2 Be. At least as Reality 2 Be had been back when Seth frequented it both with his gaming pals and with a squad that was helping Chinese freedom fighters. In Shangrilyfe, there was lots to see, but less to actually do. Not just fewer games, but a less internationally diverse user-base, at least at this point in its development and expansion. That was okay; getting mixed up with international espionage via Reality 2 Be had taught Seth some very painful lessons. He didn't do that stuff anymore. He didn't even use bizarre monikers for his online avatar.

Here in Shangrilyfe, he was just Seth3D. His best friend, Brian, was just Netsurfer; there were way too many Brians on the system by the time they joined. They didn't do anything sinister; mostly they just chatted. Yeah, they could have just as easily texted, but it was more pleasant to chat with their avatars sitting on an ersatz beach watching the sparkling waves crash methodically on shore.

Netsurfer was already waiting at the beach, a virtual blanket spread out on the ersatz sand a bit closer than necessary to a couple of hot girls virtually sunning themselves. Seth swiveled Seth3D's head to bump up the volume on the girls' conversation ... about some romantic reality show or another. Of course, virtual reality being ... well, whatever you wanted it to be ... the eye-candy could actually be a couple of grandmothers connecting from their respective retirement homes, but that was okay. The view was the view. Shangrilyfe's three-dimensional rendering was one of its strong points. And, of course, there were no scars in Shangrilyfe, not unless you wanted them. Both Seth's and Brian's avatars were free of those in virtual reality.

"What did you do on vacay today?" asked Netsurfer. "Hit any topless beaches?"

Seth3D shook his head. Seth wanted to roll his eyes, but if the avatars could do that, Seth hadn't figured out how to make his perform the maneuver. "First off, it's too cold here for anyone to be running around topless. Second, my day—your tomorrow—is just starting."

"Oh, yeah. Any big plans? Or are you stuck with the 'rents?"

"Dad's doing some stuff on his UFO quest. Hoping he'll let me tag along." Seth actually didn't give a damn about ancient aliens crap, but he and his mom knew that was part of his dad's cover and his mission, and Seth was more than a little interested in that. Not only was it exciting to possibly see his dad in action for longer than it took to jump out of a boat, but helping with an actual covert operation for a secret organization beat the hell out of shopping for t-shirts and petting kangaroos at some billabong.

"When did he get into that stuff? Always seemed ... I dunno ... boring and business-like when I ran into him at your place or whatever."

"Not exactly sure," replied Seth3D—better to be vague than have to remember the specifics of a lie. "He travels a lot for work. Flies a lot, too. I think that kind of stuff gets more coverage on the news overseas than back home. That probably provoked his curiosity about flying saucers. I think the U.S. military finds UFOs all kind of embarrassing 'cause they can't explain 'em, so they downplay everything."

"Yeah, a lot of the YouTube things I've seen about strange lights in the sky seem to be foreign. Not sure why."

"Less blanketed by radar, less military, so not as easy to debunk, I guess."

"Maybe, but that doesn't explain why they have more video. The U.S. has a bajillion cell phones in people's hands."

Seth3D laughed. "Yeah, but everyone's looking down at them, not up in the sky. More light pollution in America, too, so harder to see the night sky. Besides, a lot of the foreign YouTube videos on UFOs are from dash cams. They're just not a big thing in the states."

Netsurfer craned his neck to ogle the side-boob on display next door for a moment. "Not sure why dashcams are popular elsewhere."

"Apparently people make a living in third-world countries by leaping in front of cars, especially nice cars, then jumping up and rolling across the hood. Then they claim to be more injured than they are and ask for cash to settle the matter. The dash cams show what really happened—at least that's what I've read. So, if you are worried about accident scammers, you set up a camera to record the view out your front window at all times. If something freaky happens, like a real accident or a shooting star or a ghost or whatever, you've got footage to download to the net."

"Easier to get an editing app and make crap up, I'd think."

"Maybe," replied Seth3D. "Supposedly experts can tell the difference."

"Yeah, I guess." Netsurfer frowned and Seth manipulated his avatar's controls to see that the beach bimbos had gotten up and sashayed away. "Hard to say why anyone believes anything on the internet in the first place."

"People believe what they wanna believe."

"That's a little simple, don't you think?" replied Netsurfer.

"Dude, you just ogled some virtual hotties for, like, most of our conversation, even though they could be someone, something completely different in real life. Hell, they could be part of the beach background programming or some add-on programmed by a kid in Sri Lanka with too much time on his hands. It's like the bimbo in the red dress in *The Matrix,* a subprogram set up to distract you from ... I dunno ... a flicker in the wave generator when it resets to repeat or something. Yeah. People believe what they wanna believe."

As if to make Seth's point, his screen flashed bright white for a second, then coalesced back into focus, but with a reddish tint which faded out before the full color palette flickered back into existence.

"What the hell was that?" exclaimed Netsurfer.

"You saw that, too?"

"Yeah. The whole simulation was wiped out by a white flash. What do you think it was?"

"Well, I don't think it was paparazzi." Seth scanned the screen looking for anything out of place, but saw nothing.

Netsurfer answered while Seth was still looking. "You think Shangrilyfe doesn't have avatars with flash cameras?"

"No. They say almost anything from real life can be simulated in Shangrilyfe ... if you have the bucks to spend for rendering and programming. I just don't think a paparazzo would snap a clandestine photo of the two of us on the beach ... and the cleavage cousins have already left."

"I dunno," replied Netsurfer. "The six-pack on my avatar looks pretty awesome in my humble opinion."

"Maybe, but it would be more accurate if your avatar had a six-pack *in* its abdomen, assuming you're still hiding beer in the crawlspace where your dad can't find it."

"Shhh! Not so loud."

"Not to worry," said Seth3D, "since you're keeping your stash of weed somewhere separate." Seth studied the screen a bit more, but saw nothing out of place. Finally, he spoke again. "Probably just a hardware glitch."

"Maybe a power surge?"

"Or a reboot of a software subroutine which interacts with the main user interface."

They talked a while longer, but Seth had accomplished what he came to do. Chat with his best friend, but, more importantly, support his dad's cover. He was going to help with this mission whether his dad wanted him to or not.

#

"I don't need my wife or ... for God's sake ... my kid to come along on this part of the trip," growled Dick at his computer. The avatar of a Saudi Arabian sheik stared back at him from the screen.

"No," replied the sheik in an Arabic accent which did not entirely hide the subtle influences on syntax and sentence structure Dick associated with a Russian accent—or, at least, the clipped Russian accent of Pyotr Nerevsky. "What you need is to, one, do as you're told, and, two, place a bet so our presence here doesn't look suspicious." The voice chat feature of the website was staticky and prone to random increases and decreases in volume, but apparently met the ex-KGB officer's standards of security encryption ... or, perhaps, was sufficiently crappy and obscure no respectable security apparatus would bother to monitor it.

Dick glanced at the upper left of the screen, where a betting board listed odds and names for the next race. He'd gotten a text from his nemesis to meet at this virtual betting site for, of all things, camel races. But not just camel races—camel races where the camels were ridden by robot jockeys. Apparently the rich and super-rich residents of Dubai and Qatar and Bahrain had poured petro-dollars into developing camel riding robots to replace slave children as jockeys in high-stakes camel races, as well as to maintain more direct control of their desert mounts.

The "camel jockeys" apparently did not trust actual camel jockeys to ride fair. The rein-holding and whip-wielding robots, however, could be controlled by remotes wielded by owners and trainers playing with joysticks in a traffic jam of high-end SUVs careening along next to the track during a race.

Dick temporized while he reviewed the odds. "I guess it's good they don't use kids for this anymore, but I don't understand why they dress the robots in racing silks."

"The camels prefer the illusion of human riders. They also spray human scent and cologne on the silks to maintain the pretense," answered the faux sheik. "Would you want an inhuman, unfeeling automaton riding you?"

Dick did have an inhuman, unfeeling automaton riding him—one by the name of Nerevsky—so he decided the question was rhetorical and let it slide.

"Come, come. Make a decision. It is almost post time."

Dick placed a small wager on the favorite while the sheik being controlled by Pyotr placed several bets, including a significant bet on a high-odds exacta. Dick didn't know why the Head of the Subsidiary's Internal Audit Division had a hard-on for bizarre games. Dick, who played college football, understood the attraction of sports, but he didn't ... couldn't ever ... understand the attraction of robot jockey camel races.

"Your betting, like you, lacks imagination," noted the sheik. "I've explained how the family supports your cover as a tourist interested in strange atmospheric phenomena. And I explained that their participation incentivizes you to perform. Of course, it also provides you with additional manpower for anything that may come up—manpower which is not otherwise available for this mission for reasons of which you are aware. This is not a matter for debate."

"But—"

"But nothing. Everybody spies. Everybody lies. Everybody goes. Now shut up and watch the race. Maybe a few more. It's a delightful sport, once you learn all the ins and outs."

Dick shut up. He knew about ins and outs. He was on the outs at work. And, with Nerevsky forbidding him from letting Melanie and Seth hang at the hotel while he investigated strange historical phenomena closer to ground zero, he was about to be on the outs with Melanie, too.

Chapter 10

"Think of it as an adventure," said Dick as he turned onto Route 94 and headed east past the airport and out of Perth.

"Yeah, Mom. It's not just a job, it's an adventure," Seth chimed in.

Dick could have lived without the smart-alecky reference to the Army slogan, but right now he was all about family harmony. Besides, he didn't think Seth was grouching at him; the kid had seemed absolutely thrilled when told the whole family was headed into the Outback to interview people about strange lights in the sky. Melanie? Well, not so much.

"I looked at the map," said Melanie. "I'm not sure why we couldn't fly there. The concierge said it was a seven hour plus trip."

Dick glanced left toward the passenger seat in the large rental car. The steering wheel being on the right side didn't bother him. Neither did driving on the wrong side of the road, but he did tense up a bit every time he saw a traffic circle—a roundabout—coming up. It wasn't that he didn't have plenty of experience driving on the opposite side of the road as a seasoned international traveler, or that he didn't know what to do. It was just one of those things about being outside the United States—like getting served reasonably sized portions at restaurants—that always felt wrong. Melanie was staring out the window as the last vestiges of the city's suburbs gave way to long since harvested wheatfields as they progressed east.

"Flying is faster, sure, but we need a car—"

"I'm sure you can rent a car in Kalgoorlie—"

"—and, well, it's not just an adventure. It's a job ... a mission, to be precise. Flying limits what you can take and announces where you're going. That's just bad spycraft. Take this car." He continued the thought with an unspoken Henny Youngman "Please." He tapped out a rimshot on the steering wheel as he pondered which of his automotive criticisms he wanted to pass on to his family. He didn't have the luxury of the Subsidiary's Quartermaster arranging his trip, so the late model SUV was lighter and smaller and painted with a brighter, primary color than Dick would have preferred. It also would be too slow in a chase. He kept all that to himself, as he continued with: "I went out of my way to rent it from a place that doesn't have GPS tracking of their vehicles, just in case someone tries to track exactly where we're going."

"I thought today's outing was just historical research," said Melanie with a slight edge to her tone. "Why would anyone want to track us?"

"I don't think they would," Dick rushed to say, "but it's always good to maintain professional operational practices. It doesn't hurt to expect the unexpected." Before Melanie could respond, Dick swiveled his head to look at Seth in the back seat.

"Speaking of expecting the unexpected, Champ, what's the guide book say about touristy spots along the way?"

Seth grabbed a guide book from the seat next to him as Dick returned his attention to the Great Eastern Highway—a paved road which stretched ahead to the horizon.

"There's a cool rock formation called "The Wave," because it kind of curls and looms over you ... but it's well off the main road to the south and I'm not sure we want to make the trip longer."

"I'm sure," muttered Melanie.

"Yeah, that's a hard pass from the front seat, Champ. What else you got?"

"Some places where you can get panoramic views from granite outcroppings or check out the pipeline paralleling the road. Get this, it's a water pipeline for bringing water from Perth to the gold mining districts around Kalgoorlie. Seems like it might be a place which would warrant a quick stop given your ... you know ... professional water treatment cover."

"Wastewater treatment ... but, yeah. What else?"

"Several national parks, but that's not for a while. Mostly woods and fields for the time being."

"Well, we'll make good time, then," said Dick.

"Once we get to Kalgoorlie, there's the Super Pit, this gargantuan strip mine where they dig and haul out gold ore."

"Some huge trucks in that kind of operation," mused Dick. When Seth was a kid, Dick had taught him the names of all sorts of construction equipment. Somehow the prospect of watching trucks with tires taller than their house back in New Jersey gave him a warm family feeling. "Anything else?"

Seth turned a page. "There's a brothel museum."

Dick glanced over at Melanie. "That's a hard pass from the front seat again."

They drove for more than fifty miles without further comment. Melanie gazed out the window, while Seth had his nose buried in the guidebook. Finally, Seth spoke again.

"Wow! Did you know Australia has more than thirty creatures that can kill or paralyze you if you don't get immediate medical care? There's blue-ringed octopuses and salt-water crocodiles and funnel web spiders and all sorts of snakes—"

"Delightful," mumbled Melanie.

"It's a big place," cautioned Dick. "I'm sure it's not that bad here, where we are. After all, we're not going in the ocean, so you don't have to worry about sharks or jellyfish or octopuses, or poisonous fish. And I think the funnel web spiders and a lot of the snakes are just in the eastern rainforest, so those don't count."

"Yeah, I guess." Seth sounded disappointed. "But the Inland Taipan lives in the arid interior. It has a neurotoxin that paralyzes and kills in forty-five minutes. And the Mainland Tiger Snake is found throughout southern Australia. On the spider side, the Red-backed Spider originated in Western Australia, but it mainly hangs out where there are lights and people."

"So, we'll watch out for snakes and spiders when we're walking and shake out our shoes before putting them on," Dick said. "Doesn't sound too bad."

"Yeah, maybe."

Dick heard a page turning, then a few miles ... okay, kilometers ... of silence passed, before Seth spoke up again.

"Hey, they also have this nettle plant called a gympie-gympie that has a neurotoxin on its almost invisible, hairlike spikes so excruciating people commit suicide ... like even years later ... because they can't stand the pain anymore."

"And it's found where?"

"Mostly rainforests in Queensland."

"Then nothing for us to worry about." Dick took a deep breath. "I think it's great you're interested in the local flora and fauna and ... well ... goodness knows the scenery and the drive aren't all that compelling. Just try not to scare your mom too much. Okay?"

"Yeah. I just want to be as helpful as I can to, you know, your job and all."

Dick grinned a tight smile. "I appreciate that, even though I wish you didn't have to come along on this part of the trip at all. But, don't worry. We're just going to be talking to some old-timers about stuff which happened a quarter century ago and some other locals about more recent history. We won't be chased by goons with guns across the desert while we forage for food and water. Most of my work is just research and waiting around to see something or somebody."

Melanie suddenly pointed at the side of the road. "Camels."

Dick flashed back to his last meeting with Nerevsky as he turned to see where she was pointing. "Camels?"

No camels. No camel jockeys, human or robotic. Just an animal crossing type warning sign. Three actually. One for kangaroos. One for some large rodent like creature that reminded Dick of something out of *The Princess Bride*. And one for what was clearly a camel—the one-humped variety. Apparently, they all frequently crossed the road, presumably not together, over the next ninety-six kilometers.

Okay. Well, now that they were well east of the coast, the land was flat and trees were getting sparser. If a kangaroo or a camel or a rodent of unusual size approached the road, Dick figured he'd see it coming.

After all, he was always on the lookout for trouble. And bacon. Dick liked his bacon.

"Any good roadhouses for food coming up soon?"

#

They arrived in Kalgoorlie later than Dick had hoped. Driving the Great Eastern Highway wasn't like cruising through Montana on an interstate, except for the long stretches of emptiness. Huge tractor-trailers lumbered up even minor grades with maddening slowness at times, frustrating the flow of traffic around them. Things slowed even more after they left Route 94 at Coolgardie—which Seth informed them was the original location of Kalgoorlie before people moved forty miles east-northeast to get closer to the gold—to take the even more rustic Route 49 into town. Of course, truth told, Dick kept his speed more in check with his family in the car, both for their safety and to preclude any complaints from Melanie about his driving. Just another reason to hate Nerevsky for making him bring everyone along on this investigation.

Given the time and the lackluster roadhouse food hours and hours ago, the evening consisted of nothing more than finding a decent hotel and an acceptable meal. Seth was disappointed not to see any sights (and, Dick guessed, not to see any espionage action), but Dick promised him tomorrow would be more exciting. He certainly hoped it would not be *that* much more exciting, of course, but part of parenting was managing expectations even when you had no idea what to expect.

Chapter 11

They began the day with shopping and sight-seeing. Not only did Dick need to keep his family happy, he needed to maintain his tourist cover and ease them into helping him out on his fact-finding mission. They started at a place that sold clothes and camping gear, as well as the usual assortment of trinkets and postcards. Plus, they had rocks—mostly chunks of opalized rocks too low-grade to be worth much, but some sparkly quartz and glittery feldspar, too. Melanie wandered over to take a look at the opals while Dick and Seth perused the hats.

Seth tried one on. "How come Aussie hats always have one side of the brim tucked up?"

Dick knew the answer, but he turned the question back on his son. "What do you think?"

Seth took off the hat and held it at arm's-length. "I dunno. I'd say it was maybe so you could leave the brim down on the side that faces the sun ... you know, to shade your face ... and put it up on the other side for better distance vision. You know, like pirate eye patches, which they'd switch from one side to the other."

Dick didn't know and he couldn't imagine. "Huh?"

Seth waggled a hand. "Well, not because of where the sun is. But a pirate captain goes from up on deck, where it's sunny, to down in the hold, where it's dark all the time. So, they wear a patch up on deck so one eye is always kept dark—that way when they go below, they can flip up the patch and their night vision is unimpaired from the get-go."

"Interesting. I didn't know that." Truth was, Dick hadn't thought about pirates much in his adult life, except for that one incident in Reality 2 Be.

"Obviously," Seth continued, "this isn't *quite* the same." He turned the hat back and forth as he looked at it, then frowned. "And that doesn't explain why only one side has a snap to tuck up the brim. Not both sides."

Before Dick could respond, a clerk strode up—happy, no doubt to have an early morning customer looking at something higher-end than postcards. "That's because these hats mimic our Army hats. One side is tucked up so the brim doesn't get in the way when the soldiers are shouldering arms during drill. Started back in the 1890s."

Dick dialed up a broad smile. "Funny, you don't look that old."

The clerk chuckled. "Only sixty, though the sun and wind weathers you right fast 'ere in the Goldfields. And, I've been here nigh on thirty years."

Exactly the opening Dick needed. "So, that means you were here back in '93 when there was the big flash up north and all the weird lights in the sky."

The shopkeeper sighed almost imperceptibly, but Dick purposely ignored the conversational signal, pushing on with enthusiasm like any true believer would. "What did you see? What do you think it was? A missile? A nuclear test?" He paused for effect. "Aliens?"

"Didn't see dingo scat," the clerk replied. "All that was out woop woop ... out in the middle of the Outback, a hard day's trek from hereabouts. And I was sleeping ... stuffed from working flat out the whole day b'fore."

"Ah," said Dick.

"Too bad," added Seth. "Heard it was pretty pyro—"

"Oh, the town was all abuzz about it in the aftermath. Some drongos thought it was a nuclear test, especially after all that hoo-ha came out about the Jap cult people killing sheep with sarin up at Banjawarn Station." He sniffed. "Not me. Like those Asian hippie cult freaks could cobble a nuke out of sheep shit and low-grade uranium ore. Nah. More likely just a shooting star or a mine explosion or ball lightning. Couldn't be a meteor impact. No crater. Couldn't be a nuke. No radiation to speak of."

Seth interrupted. "That doesn't rule out a UFO." Dick was proud of the kid for helping with the mission task, stupid as that mission might be.

"That always sounded a bit iffy to me. Half those hoons driving road trains that night were more'n likely stuffed themselves. Or they had a slab of Swan—"

Seth interrupted again. "You eat swans here?"

The man looked at Dick's son as if he were an idiot. "What? No, we don't snack on fookin' swan. It's behr—"

Seth grimaced. "You eat bear?"

The man huffed. "Not bear ... behr." The words sounded identical, but Dick knew what the guy was saying. "B ... E ... E ... R. Behr," the man continued. "Most truckers keep a slab ... that's a carton, four times what you Yanks call a six-pack ... in an igloo in the back of the cab for a trek that hearty. Those half-arsed witnesses were likely half-pissed or more."

With the local slang, Dick didn't understand everything the guy was talking about, but looking at the guy's belly, he figured there was good reason why they had slabs instead of six-packs in these parts. In any event, Dick got the gist of the tale. Besides, the clerk wasn't a first-person witness. This convo was all just background and cover maintenance.

Seth seemed satisfied, too, though he went ahead and purchased a hat. Dick didn't know if Seth really wanted one or he just had a natural instinct for ponying up for information on the job. Since this was all on Nerevsky's tab, he didn't really care, either.

Outside the store, an elderly, gap-toothed Aboriginal man sitting on a makeshift bench in front of the store's window spoke up as they exited. "You want tales of times past, you need to talk to the people of times past."

Dick studied the old man. A dirty handkerchief on the ground by his feet had a few coins scattered on it. Dick stopped. "You can tell me about the past?"

"I can tell you of the Dreamtime, when the land was formed and the People came to be."

"Much as I'd like to hear that story, my interest is not so far into the past." Dick glanced up toward the sky before continuing. He dropped a local ten-spot into the handkerchief. "I'd like to hear about the lights in the sky."

The man grinned, his tongue peeking out between his missing front teeth. "Half of half of a century ago, a bright light trailed high in the sky from over the horizon in the southern waters, then across the land. Deep in the desert, at the edge of the world, it stopped, and there was a flash of bright white, brighter than the day, and a rolling thunder bellowed out of the sky and shook the earth beneath the feet of the People. A spirit orb the size of a small mountain glowed north of here, the color of the setting sun before a storm at sea. Lightning flashed around the edges and a deep, low sound thrummed at the edge of hearing. Many, many of the People saw. Dingoes howled, cattle lowed and turned their backs to the unnatural light—a red moon upon the surface of the earth—and birds flew away in terror. Eventually, the pulsing light went dark and the earth once more was at peace."

The old man closed his eyes and leaned back against the window of the store. "That is my story."

"Is it true?" Dick asked in a soft, warm tone.

"As true as you want it to be," came the response. "Like many of the People, I have seen the min-min lights on many nights, guiding my journey."

"The min-min lights?"

"Bright lights that hover in the sky during sojourns in the bush."

"And have you and others told this story to those asking questions?"

The man opened his eyes. "Many times."

"And did they pay you?"

"Of course. Old men like me, we have nothing to sell but stories. The People have a hard life. Men like you, they pay for stories. We tell stories men like you want to hear. We get along."

Dick dropped another ten into the dirty handkerchief. "You tell the story well."

"I have had much practice."

"May you practice many more times."

As he finished his conversation, he looked over and saw Melanie approach a pudgy woman in bright clothing coming out of a beauty salon two storefronts down. The woman held up her hands in front of her, her fingers splayed, obviously admiring her fresh manicure.

Melanie held out her hand. "Hi. Do you mind if I ask you a few questions?"

The woman looked Melanie up and down, a sour look on her face, and did not take her hand, whether from hostility or to protect wet fingernail polish, Dick didn't know.

The woman's upper lip twitched. "I don't give money to strangers and I don't sign petitions."

"Very wise," replied Melanie with a smile. "I don't do those things either. I'm just asking some of the local experts about whether they saw the lights in the sky and the bright flash that occurred back in 1993. I thought if you lived around here then you might remember from when you were a small child."

Dick thought the "small child" reference might be laying it on a bit too thick. The woman, whose coifed hair had an unmistakable artificiality in its shade of auburn, was well out of college back in those days.

"Oh, you mean the space debris?" said the woman.

Melanie obviously knew what she was doing. "Space debris?"

"Oh, yes," said the woman. "The so-called 'superpowers,' they always aim their crashing space junk our way, where nobody important might get hurt. When SkyLab fell from orbit, they said it would fall in the ocean. But then it 'missed' and left debris strewn all over a huge area down by Esperance along the coast south of here, back in 1979 ... er ... so I'm told."

"How terrible," replied Melanie. "But this was later, in 1993. What would have fallen then?"

"God only knows," said the woman, who then looked around conspiratorially, as if someone might be watching. Dick quickly averted his gaze and pretended to study a store window before her search got to where he was standing. "The Yanks and the commies, they have all sorts of military spy stations up in the sky, watching us. Watching everything we do." She lowered her voice and Dick could barely hear, but he thought she continued with "I never use the outdoor shower. You know, in case those pervert commie spies are watching."

"I see," said Melanie. "I mean, I understand. But, how does that explain the bright flash of light after the fireball of debris streaked across the sky?"

Dick turned his head back to watch the scene continue.

"Well," said the woman with a huff. "All those space stations are nuclear-powered, you know. When it hit, the nuke went off."

"A nuclear power reactor isn't the same thing as a nuclear bomb," replied Melanie.

"Of course, it is—"

Dick strode toward his wife. "There you are, honey. Time to get back on the road. Lots to see."

They left off making inquiries at that location, but he and Seth and Melanie repeated the basic formula as they traveled around town stopping at roadhouses, restaurants, tourist traps, and even a couple of retirement villages looking for people to chat with about lights in the sky, both in 1993 and more recently.

And, while the rest of the day was mind-numbingly the same, the theories for the lights in the sky varied considerably. Lightning. Ball lightning. Meteor impact. Cache of mining explosives. Minor earthquake followed by escaping methane from an underground pocket set off by an illegal campfire. Black helicopters with spotlights followed by flares illuminating special forces training missions. Secret nuclear testing by the Japanese ... the British ... the Russians ... the

South Africans ... the aliens ... or the mole people or the lizard people or Aum Shinrikyo. Yadda, yadda, yadda.

Seth even got into a discussion with a retired miner about whether it was simply a rare sighting of the Southern Lights ... the South Pole equivalent of the Aurora Borealis.

"They dance in the sky most often down in Tasmania," said the leathery-faced local. "But you get a big enough magnetic pulse and they light up the sky all about southwestern Oz. Damn dark out here, so they shine bright and colorful."

"Sure," said Seth. "I understand that. But the Aurora Australis would be in the southern sky ... not up north where these lights were reported."

"You callin' me a liar?"

"Not at all. I just—"

"I hauled ore for more'n twenty years. Don't be tellin' me I don't know which way from sideways." He stomped away. "Damn Yanks!"

Despite the old-timer's damnation, Dick and the rest of the family pushed on, pressing local raconteurs, tourist huskers, and meandering Alzheimer's patients about the events around the Banjawarn incident in 1993. Young, old, Black, white, and various mixes of races and nationalities. They asked everyone. Over the course of the day, their questioning became honed and routine. And the answers became repetitive. Almost all were secondhand or worse, which was not helpful. Sometimes Dick could tell which people reciting the details of the 1993 events had read the same reports or news sources. Actual eyewitnesses either were sparse or not talking.

Those who experienced recent events had varied stories. In most of those, the light traveling across the sky—which had occurred farther west, closer to Perth and the rest of Australia's coastal civilization—was not described as a pulsing orb, but as a flaming light from which small sparks or flames would drop off and down. While that spectacle was associated with a thundering, roaring, or locomotive sound before the large, concussive explosion at the end, the end explosion was not accompanied by a bright flash of light, nor a pulsing orange-red hemisphere or mushroom cloud. That much seemed consistent, but there were also a lot of tangential threads to sort out.

Asking about "lights in the sky" seemed to bring out the storyteller in people. Enough so that Dick thought some of them were just making things up for sport or, worse, to fuck with him. The younger witnesses were also much more likely to grab for their cell phones when questioned Not to film them, but to show off something they'd seen or heard about. These folks eagerly shared YouTube clips of objects in the sky over the suburbs of Perth that could have been anything from Mylar balloons to windblown trash bags to untethered kites and weather research flights.

One fellow pulled up a site about the Marree Man, a five-kilometer long geoglyph of an Aboriginal warrior "rivaling the Nazca lines" more than two thousand kilometers to the east. Dick tuned out when the fan mentioned that, although originally discovered in 1998, locals had recently restored the drawing after the image became difficult to view, even from the air. In Dick's mind, using road-graders to "restore" the drawing was evidence it was not only of recent origin, but likely created in the first place simply to boost local tourism.

Another enthusiastic teenager pulled up a website speculating about the Cervantes/Badgingarra Triangle Mystery and strange impact sites north of Perth, on the way to Geraldton. Interesting ... until a five-minute Google Earth search by Seth showed the strange shadows and markings looked to be nothing but a turbine wind farm not so far off a well-traveled roadway. Dick's guess was the original satellite photos which sparked interest were taken when the hulking three-bladed behemoths were in the initial stages of construction.

Between stops, Dick also asked Seth to do some online searches about the "min-min lights" the Aboriginal storyteller early in the day had mentioned.

"Says here that the Aboriginal stories go back prior to European settlement and that they're blobs of light that seem to hover and bob in the air, sometimes moving along with people. Some of the Aborigines believe them to be spirits of their ancestors, but modern research says they're more likely an example of *Fata Morgana*."

Melanie turned toward Seth in the back seat. "What's the legend of King Arthur have to do with Australia?"

"Uh," replied Seth. "Wrong Morgana, Mom. The *Fata Morgana* is a kind of optical illusion, a mirage created by an inversion—a layer of warm air sitting in the upper atmosphere above cold ground air. The inversion creates a refraction and reflection that can cause an image from far away, beyond the horizon, to appear to be hovering in the sky. It's how sailors can sometimes see cliffs or cities or other ships hovering in the air far out to sea, nowhere near where those things actually are."

"I guess that makes sense," said Melanie, "but nobody reported seeing anything like that."

"True," replied Dick, "but think about how that kind of optical illusion would work if it happened out in the middle of a lot of empty ground in the black of night. A single source of light—a campfire, a mine complex, or even a brightly lit residence—might be the only light source for miles and miles. So, if the conditions are right for a *Fata Morgana* to occur, there might not be anything to see except a single blob of light in the black sky, like a mirage, always out of reach in the distance no matter how fast or what direction you travel."

"Oh." Melanie leaned back into her car seat. "It sure feels like we're chasing a mirage, that's for sure."

They kept at it, but learned nothing new. In short, despite having rented a four-wheel drive SUV for the trip out to Kalgoorlie, the entire day was spent spinning their wheels.

"Well, that was a complete bust," complained Seth as he plopped into the back seat after yet another frustrating stop quizzing store clerks. Dick agreed, but it also made him think of one more stop they should make as evening fell and they headed back to the hotel.

Ostensibly, Dick pulled into the sprawling roadhouse and truck stop complex to fuel up and replenish their stock of emergency water, as well as grab a few tasty snacks and sugary beverages to stave off crankiness until they got dinner. He put Seth in charge of the fueling and Melanie in charge of the supply run while he wandered toward the portion of the lot where the semis, B Doubles, and road trains parked so the drivers could catch some shut eye ... and spend some quality time with the lot ladies who prowled between the behemoth semis looking for an invitation to join the operator in the cab (more accurately the bunk perched behind the cab of most cross-country tractors) for a fee. With evening falling, the big trucks were lumbering to life. The big truckers and their fuckers were doing the same.

Dick avoided the shady ladies—they spent too much time staring at the ceiling of a cab—and concentrated on catching a trucker ambling in to breakfast from his rig. Those were the guys who spent hours ... nights ... at a time staring at the starry sky as they rolled across the continent in the relative cool of the night.

He kept a folded twenty-dollar bill in his right hand and held it out as a grizzled specimen slammed the door of his cab and clambered down into Dick's path.

"Looking for some information."

The trucker looked at him hard, but did not reach for the bill. "Haven't seen your daughter ... or your sheila ..."

"Not looking for a girl."

"Then, you're in the wrong part of the lot." He inclined his head toward a darker section, nearer to the back of the building. "Boys and the like be back there."

"Not looking for a guy."

He tilted his head to the north. "Plenty of sheep round about Menzies and Leonora."

"Not looking to wet my whistle at all. Interested in some information about lights in the sky."

"That so? You guv'mint?"

"Nah. Just an open-minded researcher."

"Hah!" barked the trucker, his leathery face wrinkling even deeper at the corners of his mouth. "Open-minded. Bull crap. You're one of them believers in E.T. and ancient aliens and all that stuff and nonsense."

"Maybe. Just wanna know if you've ever seen anything." He straightened out his already extended right arm, bouncing the twenty a couple times as he did. "Willing to pay; eager to listen."

The man sucked on a tooth, then reached out and snatched the twenty from Dick's hand. "Sure. Told my story to the cops for naught. Might as well run my mouth to you for scratch."

"Start with when."

"The big brouhaha, that was back in early winter of '93, north of here a piece. Everybody haulin' that night saw it. Light traveling from south to north, mayhaps angled a bit to the east. Blue-white light, not trailin' sparks or nothing. Not fallin', either, mind you. Tracking along more or less parallel to the ground, pulsing a bit as she flew, but moving at a steady rate. Eventually, lost out of sight behind the hills at the north-northeast horizon, but still showing a glow from behind the hills. Then, all sudden, there's a flash of bright white light like you never seen before. Brighter than the sun on a cloudless summer day. Seared into the retinas. Had to stop my road train on account of losing my night vision. Once the flash had subsided and the darkness imprinted on the back of my eyeballs finally started to fade, I looked back north, where the bright light had been, but holdin' my hand so to shield my eyeballs if need arises. Big ol' dome of red peeking out above the northerly hills and looks to be a terrifyin' ginormous cloud above. You know—" The man looked about, as if the word he was searching for might be on the side of one of the massive vehicles surrounding them. "—you know ... a ... shiitake cloud–"

"You mean a mushroom cloud?"

"Yessir, that's the moniker. A mushroom cloud, hanging over it like death on a stick."

"Like a nuclear explosion."

"Yes and no."

Dick frowned. "What's that mean?"

"Same kinda shape like you see in the pictures of tests and crap, but narrower, with a lot more lightning in the cloud than in a regular nuke cloud."

"You've seen a mushroom cloud from a nuclear explosion in person?"

"Nah, but plenty on the news. Telly ran a documentary on the Maralinga tests here in the WA by the Brits, from back in the mid-fifties. My gramps, he was in the indoctrinee force sent to witness the Red Beard test during Operation Buffalo. Gave him the cancer later in life, it did." He spat on the ground. "Big blow and radioactive fallout in the middle of our fuckin' country, and what did we get outta it? A big nothin'. That's politicians for ya." He spit again.

"So, you don't think the light in ninety-three was a nuclear explosion?"

"That's what the investigation later decided, not like I trust the guvmint to tell sheep shit from paydirt. But it don't make no sense whatso' it would be an A-bomb. They don't test those things by flyin' missiles from somewhere in the sea betwixt here and Antarctica over half a continent and droppin' them on a sheep station run by a bunch of Jap terrorists. Testing's a military operation, like my gramps took part in. They use towers and bunkers and shit. And what I saw soarin' through the heavens weren't no rocket exhaust, it was a pulsing orb of light. And a nuke, it don't put up no red-glowin' sphere like some damn forcefield in the movies. It goes boom and rolls out in all directions."

"So, a UFO?"

The old-timer guffawed. "That's my choice? A nuke explosion by a rag-tag group of subway sarin terrorists what barely showed up in-country before it happened or a bunch of big-eyed cattle mutilators come to play Star fucking Wars 'cause they didn't want us to live long and prosper?"

Dick spread his hands, palm up. "Then, what?"

"Energy weapons. Tesla energy weapons. Testing whether they could induce earthquakes from a distance."

Dick furrowed his brow. "Say again?"

"Hellfire, boy. You come Downunder talking about lights in the sky and you haven't read Harry Mason's Bright Skies treatise?"

"Uh ... I guess not."

"Always thought you ancient aliens chasers were bonkers. Proof's in the pudding and so's your head." The man fluttered one hand at him and turned to be on his way. "Yanks. Too stupid to believe, but big believers in stupid things." He started to walk, then turned back. "Just so you know, yes, a dingo did eat her baby."

What the fuck? "Whose baby?" Dick yelled after the departing trucker.

The man shook his head, but kept walking. "Meryl Streep's, you uncultured bogan."

Dick stared after the man for a moment, then hustled back to the SUV, where Seth was helping Melanie load up a case of water and several bags of other consumables.

Like the open land of Western Australia, there was an endless supply of unanswered questions. Questions which had no answers. Just plenty of driving, plenty of interviews, and plenty of online research ahead, all with his family in tow. Ahh, the glamorous life of an international spy.

#

Less research than he'd thought.

When he'd asked Seth to search for the references he'd just gotten from the trucker, Melanie had interrupted to explain that Meryl Streep had played the lead in a movie about an Australian woman who was accused of killing and burying her baby during a camping trip to Ayers Rock—or Uluru as it was now called in adherence to its historic

Aboriginal name. She maintained her innocence through a widely-publicized trial, claiming a wild dog—a dingo—had carried off her baby. Seth chimed in to let Dick know that Dingoes Ate My Baby was also the name of the fictional band one of the characters on Buffy the Vampire Slayer played in.

Dick didn't think either reference was relevant to the mission.

More importantly, though, Seth made short work of finding Harry Mason's Bright Skies treatise online. The fact Dick's laptop had an internalized satellite connection to the internet had proved invaluable in doing so, however, even this close to what passed for civilization in Western Australia. Mason was a surveyor for the gold mineralization industry who had taken up investigating the supposed nuclear explosion at Banjawarn sheep station in 1993 as his life's calling. Seth volunteered to read the report aloud as they headed in for the day, but it was quickly apparent it was too long and rambling for Dick to parse while driving.

"So," said Melanie as they headed for the hotel, "this is what you do?"

Dick shrugged. "Sometimes. I do end up asking a lot of questions while I pretend to be somebody I'm not. But, no, not really. This mission is bizarre, almost comical. I've been sent off to gather evidence of something that's already been investigated to death by everyone from the *New York Times* and the U.S. Senate to the Australian government and a bunch of locals who like to spin theories on the internet. Usually I'm doing something very specific for a very specific reason. Here, I'm casting about randomly with no particular goal in sight—at least not one the powers-that-be have bothered to tell me."

"An *Expedition Unknown*."

"Huh?"

Seth spoke up. "It's a TV show on basic cable. This guy—"

"Josh Gates," volunteered Melanie.

"—yeah, Gates. He goes around the world looking for lost things or strange puzzles to solve. Everything from the tomb of Genghis Khan to pirate treasure and lost Incan cities and all that crap. Oh, and aliens and Bigfoot, too. Mom watches it a lot."

Melanie blushed. "Well, he's very—"

"Handsome?" asked Seth.

"—personable," replied Melanie with a glare at her only son. "And even though he rarely really finds anything important, he's very enthusiastic about the history and the puzzle and the hunt."

Dick smiled. He was glad Melanie found their bizarre hunt for information in Australia a pleasant puzzle. He didn't even mind she apparently found the host of a cable television show "personable." He just liked her to be happy. She seemed happy today and he didn't mind she found some joy when he was away from her, off saving the world or sitting around waiting for something to happen.

"Maybe we'll try to find an episode on the TV back at the hotel after dinner," said Dick.

"That seems unlikely," mused Melanie.

"Duh, guys," said Seth from the backseat. "You don't need to scroll through channels and try to ... I don't know ... set up your VHS recorder blinking twelve o'clock to see a show anymore." He thumped Dick's laptop. "You've got high-bandwith streaming. You can watch anything you want online at any time."

"Oh," said Melanie.

"Oh, yeah," agreed Dick. "Headed back to the CBD."

"Huh?" said Seth.

"Central Business District, where our hotel is. Aussie slang. I can learn new things from people other than my very clever son, you know."

Chapter 12

Seth turned around in his seat to grab a bottle of water as they headed back into the CBD of Kalgoorlie. The car behind them was familiar; he was sure he'd seen it at their first stop in the morning. And, now, here it was, hours later, still going where they were going.

"I think someone's following us."

"Good eye," replied his dad. His mom angled her head to try to get a look via the passenger side mirror, but his dad's head never wavered.

"You already knew," said Seth. It wasn't a question, but it wasn't really a complaint. It was simply a matter of fact.

"Pegged that particular dusty silver sedan a couple of hours ago. Showed up too many times as we moved from one location to another quizzing the locals. From time to time they trade off with a gray panel van with a small machine repair shop logo on it, so they're at least making an effort not to be noticed. Still, hard to follow someone in such a small town with just two vehicles without being made. If we were on a long trip, having the same car in the rear view for a half-hour wouldn't be too unusual, but when you're just tooling around town, hard to imagine someone else has the same itinerary."

Seth slumped down in his seat. "I don't even remember seeing a gray van."

"Don't beat yourself up. I'm a trained professional. You're—"

"An amateur?"

"—still in training. Besides, it's not like you were assigned to watch for tails and failed. You picked up on something by sheer instinct and good situational awareness."

Seth decided his dad was being sincere, not patronizing, so he took the compliment. Then another thought popped into his head.

"So, are we going to try to lose them?"

His mom turned to his dad, her eyes wide. "Are we going to get involved in a car chase?"

His dad reached over and patted his mom's hand. "Nah. What's the point? We're headed back to the hotel. They probably already know where we're staying. And it would let them know we know they're tailing us."

His mom's face softened, but she still stared at his dad while he drove the last couple of blocks toward the hotel. "But … but who are they?"

"Excellent question. Since they started following us long before our inquiries could have attracted enough attention to warrant a response by some ... cabal ... covering up for any close encounters of the third kind, my guess is a couple of low-level guys at the closest office of Catalyst Crisis Consulting were tasked with keeping an eye on me and rendering any required assistance."

His mom's brow furrowed. "That sounds odd."

"At the very least," Seth added, "it sounds suspicious and redundant."

"Suspicious and redundant!" His dad chortled. "Welcome to the world of international espionage, where the paranoia is only exceeded by the expenditure of effort. If this entire mission to track down what happened a quarter century ago and how it relates to recent events doesn't say 'paranoid' and 'too much time and resources on hand' to you, nothing will."

They arrived at the hotel, but instead of pulling into the self-park garage for guests, his dad pulled up to the valet. "Keep it in sight," he said as he got out and flipped the keys to the bored valet. "I didn't take the rental insurance and I don't want it to get dinged up."

No, Seth thought, you don't want anyone messing with the car or installing a tracker on it. His dad might not think so, but Seth knew how to think like a spy.

#

Dick was pissed. Not just because persons unknown were shadowing his family as they tooled about Western Australia, but because he'd just lied to his wife and kid about it. Whoever was following his movements wasn't sent by the Subsidiary or their cover organization Catalyst Crisis Consultants. Glenn and Dee were keeping knowledge of his actions on a tight rein to make sure Nerevsky didn't find out they were aware of his off-the-books op. And if Nerevsky had the spare manpower to follow him around the boondock wilderness of Australia, he wouldn't have needed Dick to do his bidding in the first place.

That meant somebody else actually cared enough about what Dick was doing here to expend effort and manpower to keep tabs on it. That what he was doing wasn't just placating Nerevsky's paranoid conspiracy theories was mind-boggling and more than a little worrying. Seth was a bright, capable kid, and Melanie had the kind of stoic strength and will all good mothers have, even if they don't necessarily give themselves credit for it. But that didn't mean he wanted them to do-si-do with bad guys—even with low-level spooks who were probably under strict instructions not to engage. Still, he didn't know what their instructions were, and he couldn't begin to fathom who might be giving them.

Best to get them out of the picture as best he could without drawing Nerevsky's ire. He was going to have to do precisely what every fan of horror movies and every player of *Dungeons & Dragons* always said never to do. It was time to split the party.

He'd deal with that in the morning. In the meantime, they had a nice dinner at the hotel and Seth streamed an *Expedition Unknown* episode about the Japanese "Atlantis" on Dick's computer, hooking it into the hotel room television screen for convenient group viewing. Dick didn't really care about whether the underwater features were natural or man-made, but he did think the host had balls to plummet down the hot metal conveyer roller slide he found along the way. At least, he used to have balls before the slide pummeled them.

He begged off when the rest of the family went to bed. Not only did he want to stay awake for a bit, just to make sure their tail from earlier wasn't going to bother them overnight, but he had some reading to do. He called up the tab on his computer which Seth had found earlier in the day and started digesting the long, long Bright Skies posting.

Like a lot of internet conspiracy theories, the six-part Bright Skies treatise was a mix of detailed points of information which aligned with the author's worldview of the situation and a lot of conjecture. The basics were consistent with what Nerevsky had told him and what the later U.S. Senate investigation had established. Lights on the 28th of May in 1993, rumbling sounds associated with it, an earthquake (in an earthquake stable area) measuring three point nine on the Richter scale with an epicenter near (but not at) Banjawarn sheep station, a half-million-acre ranch in a semi-desert region dotted with mulga bushes, scrub, gum trees, and spinifex grass amidst the sand and rock. It gave detailed reports from various groups about the ground shaking with the explosion, the apparent distance traveled by the light arcing parallel to the surface of the land for more than two hundred fifty kilometers—one hundred and fifty miles—and other fireball events at other times in Western Australia. No big crater to indicate a meteor impact or a nuclear detonation.

That made sense. You can't hide a big impact crater. Sure, there were lots of small craters in the WA, like on the moon, which parts of the WA resembled. The reason was simple. Because there was little in the Outback to disturb a crater once made, they persisted for decades, maybe centuries. That's why, Dick knew, Western Australia was a great place to search for meteorite fragments. Not only did the dark sky make even small meteors visible for great distances, there wasn't much to hide the detritus they left behind. The oldest crater ever found on Earth—a two-billion-year-old, forty-mile wide scar known as the Yarrabubba impact structure—was, Dick found out during one of his tangential internet searches, located in Western Australia.

He stopped musing and went back to reading.

The treatise also contained considerable detail about the notion that the Aum Shinrikyo sect, which had just purchased the Banjawarn sheep station before the event, was involved in some manner. Dick discounted much of this information—Nerevsky had basically admitted that the sarin-poisoned sheep found on the ranch had been a Russian cover story, and Dick doubted the doomsday sect ever had access to nukes, even though they apparently tried hard to get one or more. But the treatise didn't really rely on the sect's access to nuclear weapons to explain their involvement. Instead, it made much about the nature and the use of probes and equipment to test the uranium ore at the station by Aum Shinrikyo personnel handling the land purchase. Supposedly, this was somehow connected to Aum Shinrikyo's potential involvement with energy and earthquake generating weapons, designs for which the Russians were supposedly developing with the Japanese at the time. Proof? A lot of contact between the Russians and Japanese members of the cult and the remarkable fact that Shoko Asahara, the founder of Aum Shinrikyo, predicted an earthquake in Kobe Japan nine days before it occurred in January of 1995.

Of course, like most internet conspiracy theories, the later parts of the treatise were less detailed and more speculative, attempting to connect the Banjawarn incident to myriad catastrophes. Everything from a freak storm and explosion in Mansfield, United Kingdom in 1987 to the destruction of Flight 800 off New York City in July 1996, and the bombing of the Murrah Federal Building in Oklahoma City in 1995. It even mentioned a high-density energy slug shot into space from Western Australia as warding off an alien craft in 1991, as documented by a Space Shuttle video. It all struck Dick as farfetched and paranoid, but he knew from his own experience there were at least some small grains of truth hidden in many of the internet's wacky and/or paranoid conspiracy theories. And, he noted that the speculation about Tesla designed energy weapons, remote earthquake inducers, and the like had a Russian connection ... and so did Pyotr Nerevsky.

Chapter 13

Dick dipped the end of an impressively thick piece of bacon into a glob of honey, then bit off a chunk. Like many Aussie buffet breakfasts, the hotel dining room had stations for guests from various locales. Dick had hit up the American station, with bacon, an omelet post, and waffles with syrup, chocolate nibs, and whipped cream. Melanie had picked up some oatmeal there, then headed over to the Asian station for fruit and various things Dick couldn't identify. Seth got a little bit of everything from everywhere. That's what kids do, he knew; they experiment. Dick, on the other hand, already knew what he liked and he liked what was familiar.

"New plan for the day," he announced as the waiter walked away after refreshing his cup of coffee.

"Don't tell me you're canceling the tour of the Super Pit," complained Seth, who then lowered his voice and continued. "You said it was a good way to maintain our visibility as, you know, tourists."

"I already got tickets from the concierge," added Melanie.

"No, no," replied Dick. "That's still on ... but just for you guys. Look, the best way to get this research done is for you both to maintain our—" He tilted his head toward Seth, "—tourist profile and finish making inquiries about the more UFO sightings in Western Australia. In the meantime, I'll pop up north to Banjawarn Station. You know, do the whole pilgrimage for an obsessed fan of UFO phenomena, then come back and meet you here."

It was a stretch, but Dick guessed he could persuade Nerevsky that as long as the family was helping with the mission, they didn't necessarily have to be in the same place with each other each and every moment. Besides, he also thought that given the manpower shortage yesterday's botched surveillance implied, he could pull the team monitoring them up north to keep tabs on him, leaving Melanie and Seth out of danger. Well, except for the short list of killer Aussie animals Seth had identified as actually being local to where they were.

He doubted Melanie would go anywhere near anyplace a respectable snake would hang out—that just left Red-backed Spiders, if he recollected correctly. And Melanie wasn't afraid of spiders. She was a strong woman. She had to be to put up with him.

Seth typed something into his phone. "Banjawarn Station, that's quite a distance. No way you can pop up there and be back here tonight."

"Not by car," Dick replied. "Not even by air if I'm going to have time to do anything while I'm there. I'll stay overnight and get back tomorrow afternoon. I'm leaving the car for you to use. You can drop me off at the local airfield. I've arranged for a light plane and a local bush pilot to take me." He turned to his wife. "The concierge is quite helpful." Of course, he'd used the concierge. If he was going to draw surveillance off of his family, he had to make sure they had time to make their own arrangements to follow him through the skies.

Melanie frowned. "I don't like the idea of you flying in one of those little planes."

Dick chuckled. "Then thank goodness you don't know how many times I've done it ... and how many times I've jumped out of them."

Melanie pressed her lips together, then sighed. "Sometimes I think I liked it better when I thought you were a wastewater treatment consultant."

Dick reached out and covered her hand with his. "Sometimes I think you never really believed that I was." He patted her hand. "What is undeniably true, however, is they are both shitty jobs." Shitty jobs that keep a lot of people from dying.

#

After his family dropped him off at Kalgoorlie-Boulder Airport, Dick checked in at the Goldfield Tours and Outback and Back Services counter. A fit-looking man in his early fifties with a graying, curling beard and hair to match checked his identification, charged his credit card, and motioned for Dick to follow. Instead of handing him off to someone else or taking him to a gate, the fellow simply headed past a Pilatus PC-12 sporting the logo of the Royal Flying Doctor Service toward a Cessna 172. He opened the door and motioned Dick inside, then followed and took the pilot's seat. He began going through his pre-flight checklist as he spoke.

"Connal Westerton, at your service. Next stop, Banjawarn Airport at Lake Darlot, Western Australia." He looked at Dick. "No bags, no camera equipment, so—"

Dick held up his cell phone.

"—no *sophisticated* camera equipment, so am I correct in assuming you are looking for a direct flight with panoramic vistas *en route*?"

Dick wrinkled his nose. "Happy to see any sights along the way, but you can skip the broad vistas. Prefer to be low enough to see anything interesting on the ground, but not so low you have to dodge anything along the way. Got you for an overnighter there and back, so I may ask you to deviate a bit along the way if something catches my eye."

The pilot nodded. "I'll slip over the Super Pit on the way out. Can't really miss a hole that awesome and gargantuan, even if I tried. Then head north, paralleling Route 49 on the east side til we get to Lake Marmion. Most interesting sight along the way. Will crossover to Lake Ballard as the road jogs east and show that off a bit, before tacking to the north-northeast past Leonora. Eventually, the main road will wander northwest and we'll leave it behind and head straight in to Banjawarn." He smiled. "All, of course, subject to any detours you care to take, as long as they're within conservative flight range parameters." He waved vaguely to the north. "Bad place to run out of fuel."

Dick hmmmfed. "Worse place to run out of water, I imagine."

Connal shook his head. "Not when you're in a plane."

Within a few minutes, the flight check procedures were history, all the appropriate switches had been toggled, and the Cessna had lurched into the blindingly blue sky. Almost immediately, they were over the Super Pit. Dick gazed out at the massive strip-mining operation in awe.

"The Fimiston Open Pit is one of the largest open-cut gold mining operations in the world," intoned Connal, on auto-pilot in terms of tour guide mode, even though he was handling all the controls manually. "Three point five kilometers long, one point six kilometers wide, and six hundred meters deep. More than fifteen million tonnes of ore are extracted annually, broken up by regular blasting and long-reach drills to probe and collapse underground voids, whether natural or resulting from shaft and tunnel mining in olden days." He gestured at the series of switchbacks climbing from the depths of the pit to ground level. The road was already dotted with scads of trucks climbing out with ore and heading back empty. "Trucks make their thirty to forty-minute roundtrip trek to and from the pit twenty-four-seven each and every day of the year, excepting World Cup Finals. A typical truck will consume eight million dollars Aussie in fuel and three million in tyres over the course of their expected lifespan, hauling two hundred and sixty tonnes of ore to the mill on each trip."

Dick wished he could be playing tourist with Seth today in the Super Pit instead of, well, playing tourist in some macabre pilgrimage to the site of a Japanese cult's practice yard for a terrorist attack, but that was the job. Someone had to do it.

The Cessna banked only slightly as they headed north out of Kalgoorlie into the desolate, lonely wilds of the Outback. The view was expansive, even impressive, but desolate beyond belief. Horizon to horizon of reddish earth, brownish-tinged scrub, and scattered rocks and outcroppings. The few roads and trails looked artificial, as if imposed on a Martian landscape where they didn't truly belong. The rhythmic thrum of the Cessna subtly reminded Dick he was not part of the ecology of the land, but a mere observer in a contrivance which was as foreign to this place as the prisoners plunked down on the coast when the continent was colonized by the British.

The farther they got from Kalgoorlie, the fewer human impositions Dick saw. Some smaller scale mining operations, windmills, metal water troughs, and ramshackle farmhouses associated with sheep stations, but damn few sheep per acre, especially compared to the flocks he'd seen grazing contentedly on the green-soaked hills of New Zealand when he was there. Still, he searched the vista with the patience and systematic shifts of focus of someone who'd once had to look for enemies or for squad members in need of rescue during combat operations. At first, every sighting of a bounding kangaroo or slinking dingo distracted him from his quest, but before long he'd trained his mind to ignore the wildlife and focus for something different ... something else.

He kept at it, but broke the conversational silence without looking at Connal.

"Ever seen anything strange?"

"Saw a two-headed snake at a reptile sanctuary when I was a wee lad, but I 'spect that's not what you're asking."

"Yeah. Not what I had in mind." Dick tilted his head forward. "Weird things in the desert. Odd lights in the sky."

"The mines, near everybody from the Fimiston Pit to the small time scrabblers, blast on a regular basis. So, you get sudden plumes of dust snaking up into the sky ... some of 'em two-headed. Seen yahoos—tourists most likely—driving off-road at night, shining spotlights and shootin' at critters. The occasional bush fire or dust devil. Some spectacular lightning displays, but mostly in the distance—too dry away from the coast. A couple of meteorites burning green, then white, then red before they burn up or disappear over a ridge or the horizon."

Dick perked up, but kept looking out. "Anything especially odd about the meteorites?"

Connal harumphed. "Beggin' your pardon, you being a person interested in Banjawarn Station and all, but nothing like glowing red hemispheres of light or inexplicable flashes or mushroom clouds." There was a pause. "I do encounter drones from time to time, especially after notable meteorite events, whether one I've seen personal or heard were reported via the telly or hanger chit-chat."

"Drones?"

"Yep. Figure they're mostly from the DFN."

"What's that? Military?"

Connal chuckled loud enough to be heard over the pulsing engine thrum. "Not hardly. The Desert Fireball Network, part of the Global Fireball Observatory effort."

"There's a Global Fireball Observatory effort?"

"Oh, yeah. Started here, as I recall. They've got operations all around the globe now, but mainly where there are people with computers and ... well ... too much bloody time on their hands. They put up cameras which take long-exposure shots of the sky at night every thirty, forty seconds, then feed the information into a data dump and the computers analyze it and spit out any indications of anomalies, so people can see 'em and track 'em. Some of the science blokes, they try to figure where the meteor came from. But at least in the WA, most of the regulars are more interested in where the meteorites land. They send out drones to try to find chunks of rock what fell from the sky. Prolly well below any airspace I'd like to share, but you never know. Just in case, I keep an eye out when they're buzzing around like crows over a fresh dingo kill."

Dick sat up straight and finally glanced over at his companion. This could save him a lot of time. "So, there's an organization that can give me truckloads of information about the night sky over this area?" That would be incredibly useful.

"Ahhh, nah. Not to say they don't have terabytes and terabytes of information. But they put up their cameras close to home, which means the coastal areas back toward Perth and north from there, or the populated areas east and southeast. Not to say wankers aren't out and about hereabouts looking for meteorite fragments, either by foot or using drones, but they don't have further guidance from the DFN cameras once they get way out here."

Dick's posture slipped back into a hunch and he refocused his attention on the ground flowing beneath the Cessna.

Time passed as monotonously as the ground beneath the droning plane.

Then a glint off to the right ... east ... caught his eye. He pointed. "Can we swing around there? Just short of that trail skirting the edge of the gray ridge."

"As they say on the brothel tour: 'Your dollar. Your desire.'" Connal eased the small plane into a shallow clockwise curve, dipping the starboard wing in the process. "You'll have to guide me as we get closer, so keep your eye fixed on the spot you want a better view of and I'll do my best to keep it on your side of the plane as we come around."

While the glint of sun on metal had disappeared as their angle to the spot changed, Dick had no trouble maintaining the position. A short spur ran from the trail at the bottom of the ridge, poking out at a right angle and ending maybe a klick westward. The end of the spur was where he'd seen the glint, in an indistinct jumble of reddish-brown protuberances at the bottom of a minor hillock. Probably just a flat face of shiny quartz or a bit of glass detritus in some rocks—God knows people littered wherever they went—but the detour was a break from the unrelenting, dusty nothingness which extended as far and wide as he could see in every direction. He pointed out the front windscreen as the Cessna straightened and approached the spot.

"See the darkish clump, right there? Is that just a pile of rocks or something man-made?"

Connal raised his left hand up and shielded his eyes. "Man-made, I'd venture, but sanded in by the drifts caused by that bump-out next to it. Don't recall seeing it before. Might have been completely covered by and by, but recent winds shifted the sands."

"What do you think it was?"

"Hard to see. Harder to say. Hoist for an old mine shaft. Wind generator for a well-water pump." The shape of the protuberance became clearer as they got closer. "Looks angular at the base. Might have been taller, but the top got knocked over by wind or rusting out. Path suggests it was maintained at some point, but not regular and not for a while. If you look close, you can see a rectangular outline around it—maybe fenced at some point, not like a fence would stop anybody ... or anything ... out here what wanted to take a closer look-see." Connal set the plane at a light bank, circling the point.

"It's not a ... navigational ... thingy?" asked Dick, his mind unable to come up with the real words he meant to say.

"A navigational thingy? That a technical term?"

Dick flushed. "Had some neighbors over for a barbecue in New Jersey, years back. They'd been on a road trip to the western United States, crossing the prairie along where the covered wagons took the Oregon Trail to the northwest. Kept seeing these small, squat, low buildings with what looked to be a steeple in the center. No windows. No markings. Surrounded by a square of chain-link. They were just sitting there out in the middle of the prairie or poking up from a cornfield or whatever. No real road to 'em. Just an overgrown path. Started calling them Children of the Corn Shrines. Asked around, but nobody seemed to know what they were until finally a real estate agent told them they were some kind of radar or some shit used to track planes at cruising altitude. You know, when they weren't near an airport or landing or taking off."

"I dunno. Maybe some old VOR stations or somesuch."

"VOR?"

"VHF Omnidirectional Range. It was used for navigational before—" He tapped a small screen in the dash. "—GPS became commonplace. Had a steeple-like tower atop a squat receiver. Nobody needed on site to run it."

Dick jerked his thumb toward the unknown clump on the ground. "Could this be that?"

"Not likely. Aside from mine surveying and sightseeing trips, not much in the way of flights hereabouts. None justifying ground station navigation out woop woop ... ah ... beyond the black stump."

"Out where?"

Connal screwed up his face. "Out, you know, in the never never ... ah ... the middle of nowhere, I guess you would say. All same same, just different phraseology." He seemed to regain his composure. "What do you want to do? We're most of the way to where we're going and, far as we can tell from the air, there's nothing there, mate."

Dick frowned. "Can you give me a GPS location? I'll drive out and see for myself while I'm on the ground."

"Your dollar. Your desire."

Chapter 14

Dick left Connal behind, seeing to refueling his aircraft for return, as he bounced out of Banjawarn Airport in the location's only rental, an aging Range Rover. His plan was simple. Complete his pilgrimage, then take a detour to the location of their mysterious "find" in the desert, which he had tagged with the name "The Steeple of Woop Woop" in his mind. He'd do the stop at Banjawarn Station first, then head into the never never. He didn't know how long either stop would take, so he brought enough water and other simple supplies to allow him to sleep in the vehicle, if necessary.

Banjawarn Station wasn't much to look at, but then nothing on the dusty ride out to it was exactly bursting with color or beauty, either. A star picket fence, weathered, but newer than most any he'd seen since the airport, paralleled the road as he approached the entrance to the fabled station. Still, it took some time to get there—the Aussie equivalent of a ranch was composed of half a million acres—the same size as the Ponderosa if he remembered correctly from the reruns his mom liked to watch when folding laundry. A bevy of trucks even more weathered than the fence huddled near the main entrance. Out here, you might not fix a piece of equipment that shuddered to a halt, but you never got rid of anything which conceivably could provide parts to fix something else. It's not that the station owners in the Outback were poor—though neither the global economy nor global warming were helping their prospects—but it was just too far and too much trouble to get something new when something old and worn-out would do.

He pulled into Banjawarn Station and simply turned off the ignition. There was no need to go to the door of the farmhouse or the entrance to the shearing barn or anywhere else. The noise of his vehicle carried over the dirt and spinifex grasses which dominated the landscape. The dust billowing up from the wake of the Range Rover still wafted lazily upward in the long line of his approach. Decades after the fact, now owned by people who weren't at the Station at the time of Aum

Shinrikyo's ownership, Dick didn't really expect any new information. He was just doing what he needed to do and happy to take any data that came his way without pushing.

Nigh unto ten minutes passed before a wrinkled woman in a faded sundress appeared at the door to the house. She pushed open the screen, shadowed her eyes with her hand and squinted toward Dick, then turned her head to face back into the house. "Just another weirdo," she hollered, before turning back and striding out toward him. The screen door slammed and bounced twice before settling in place behind her.

"Got nothin' for you, mister," she called out as she got close. "All that fireball nonsense is unadulterated bullshit. Saw nothin' then; got nothin' for you now. Just mindin' my cattle, my sheep, my dogs, and my own damn business. Suggest you do the same."

"Don't care about any of that," replied Dick through the open window of the Range Rover. "But I've got a hundred local if you give me permission to take a couple pictures."

"No one wants a picture of me," said the woman.

"I doubt that," replied Dick with an easy smile, "but I don't need you in the picture in any case. Just want a picture or three of the ranch ... er ... station."

Her brow furrowed. "You a reporter? Don't need no more retrospectives on the Aum Shinrikyo or flashes or earthquakes or glowing red lights or uranium ore ... or dead sheep. Long as the water flows, my sheep do just fine."

"I'm not a reporter." That much was true, but he couldn't exactly tell her he was a spy. He paused. "I'm on what you might think of as an old-fashioned scavenger hunt, excepting I don't have to collect things so much as prove I've been to various places."

She approached the vehicle, but stayed at arm's length. She reached out her hand. "Money up front." Dick reached into his wallet and took out the necessary currency. He folded it and held it out to her. When she took it, he reached for the door handle.

"Stay in the car," she barked out, before calming her tone. "No need for professional quality shots if this really is for a scavenger hunt."

Dick withdrew his hand from the door handle and held them up, as if she were a rookie cop who might get spooked and do something stupid and deadly. "Fair enough. I do have one question, though, while I'm taking my shots."

"Of course, you do."

"Answer or not. Up to you."

She took a deep breath. "Ask your question. Not like you weirdos ever ask anything not asked and answered a hundred times before."

Dick held up his phone and snapped three quick pictures of the entrance and the buildings and vehicles nearby, then lowered it and looked the woman in the eye. "Seen any Russians up this way?"

She started and then squinted hard at him. Obviously, this was not a question asked and answered a hundred times.

"Back then, when we acquired the place after the Aum Shinrikyo skedaddled, or recently?"

"Ever."

She tilted her head and squinted some more. It seemed like she was studying him, but the squinting might be due to the bright sunlight for all Dick knew.

Finally, she seemed to make up her mind about something. "Yes. Then and now. The Aum Shinrikyo, you know, had more Russians as members than Japanese, back in the day. Heard tell there were groups of them around about, back before the Station got raided. In the cleanup and aftermath, likewise. Still see some, usually two, three guys traveling together, from time to time. Folks say they ask about uranium ore and mining concessions and the like, but it's not like the Russkies don't have plenty of that shit without coming way out here to dig up a bunch of low-grade dirt."

"So why do you think they're here?"

"Dunno, really. Used to think maybe Aum Shinrikyo, they hid something the Russians are looking for. You know, like a treasure hunt.

But that kind of quest gets old and tired pretty quick. Nowadays, I just figure they're headed for a ridge where they can monitor the ULF broadcasts from Exmouth." She tilted her head to the west-northwest. "Or, maybe, the Jindalee Radar Network." She tilted her head east-southeast. "Eighty or so klicks the other way." She arched an eyebrow at him. "Why do you think they're here?"

Dick jinked the Range Rover into reverse. "I haven't a fucking clue." He waved, then backed up. He cut the wheel sharp to the right and drove out the entrance and back into the dusty embrace of the never never.

#

"Sometimes," said Netsurfer as they watched the waves and the bikini-clad beach bunnies, "I think Shangrilyfe is better than real life."

Seth3D laughed. "You're just saying that because hot women don't lounge around your basement in New Jersey, even though it's way nicer than the one in your old house."

"There's that, but it's not just the babes. I mean, think about it, in Shangrilyfe you don't need to work or sleep or take care of yourself. You don't even need to shower."

"Not true, dude. I've been gaming with you in your basement before and I can personally attest to the fact you need to take more showers."

"You know what I ... Hey, look at that!"

Seth looked up at the screen as a particularly fine female specimen walked out of the ocean in a wet white T-shirt.

"That. That right there. That never happens in New Jersey." Netsurfer's tone was almost wistful.

"That. That right there is why you need to take a shower ... a cold shower ... IRL."

"Nuh-uh," replied Netsurfer. "Games are real life. Your mind experiences reality as a series of electronic and chemical stimuli which input to your brain. Places like Shangrilyfe, they're getting better and better at creating the same types of stimuli. As the tech gets better, the distinction between virtual reality and physical reality will blur, then fade and eventually disappear."

Seth3D snorted. "While you lay on the couch in your basement, putrefying in your own sweat, wasting away from lack of nutrition, hooked up with wires and electrodes like Neo's cocoon in *The Matrix*."

"Not at all, dude. There are already interfaces that let people play rudimentary games with their minds, that let paraplegics use robotic arms with their minds, that let blind people see with their minds, that—"

"—that let pervs like you jerk off with their minds."

"Look," said Netsurfer, "if you add all that cutting-edge interface tech to the computing power behind a virtual reality like Shangrilyfe and layer in a bit of augmented reality tech, the day will come when you can go about the real world and it will look and feel and taste and sound and smell like a virtual reality world. Music will play in your mind and all of the chicks will be hot—"

"—and all of the dicks will be big."

Netsurfer sputtered. Seth guessed Brian had let a big swallow of soda go down the wrong tube while they chatted online.

"And what's wrong with that?"

Seth3D shrugged his shoulders. "Nothing, I guess. And, once that happens and enough time passes, people might even forget they're in an augmented reality. They could think they're actually IRL."

"So?"

"I dunno. Seems kind of sad somehow. Some serious dudes, you know, science guys, could be trying to figure out the nature of the universe never even knowing it was fake."

"Yeah, I suppose."

"And every glitch and random bug would cause wonder and confusion and grand searches for an explanation when ... well, when it was nothing but a random power surge or a cosmic ray hitting an optic cable or a cockroach in the circuitry."

"Yeecch. No talking about cockroaches in Shangrilyfe. The place is bug-free as far as I can tell."

They fell into companionable silence for a while.

Finally, Seth3D broke the silence. "You know what my dad says he dislikes the most about the internet?"

"That's a tough call," responded Netsurfer. "It's a close race between (a) it's got too much porn on it, and (b) you spend too much time on it. Of course, the two are related."

Seth3D laughed. "No, that would be why your *mom* dislikes the internet."

"True dat."

"Nah. He says all the usual stuff about how all the world's knowledge is on the internet, but people spend time looking at cat pictures, scrolling through click-bait, and arguing with strangers. But the absolutely most disappointing thing is that here, for the first time, you have the means to interact with everyone without anyone knowing if you're young or old, white or Black or Asian, straight or gay, male or female or other, fat or thin, beautiful or mutt ugly—a means of eliminating all superficial bases for discrimination—but, instead, people use it to bully, demean, and harass each other about the same old prejudices. He just wishes the internet had lived up to its promise."

"I guess," said Netsurfer, "but your dad does know the internet is just a bunch of connections between people, right? It's just a tool for people."

"Yeah. So?"

"So, people are dicks. The internet just allows them to demonstrate their basic dickishness more efficiently."

"That's deep," said Seth3D.

"That's just the facts of life."

Seth3D stood. "On that sad note, I guess I'd better book. Going on a tour of a giant gold mining pit. They've got these humongous excavators and trucks as tall as four-story buildings."

"Awesome," replied Netsurfer. "Your dad taking you?"

"Nah, he's running some errands. Mom is going along."

"Bummer."

"It's okay. Mom likes the vacationy parts of vacation."

"Still," said Netsurfer. "Women just don't get monster trucks. I mean, they've got great equipment, but they just don't appreciate great equipment."

"Shut up, dude. You're talking about my mom."

Chapter 15

Even with GPS coordinates and an off-road capable vehicle, it took Dick more than three and a half hours to find the drifted-in equipment he and Connal had spotted from the air shortly before landing at Banjawarn Airport. Every single outcropping from the edge of the ridgeline got his hopes up, but the GPS didn't lie. Despite some misgivings, he ventured farther and farther from what passed as a main road ... which meant a single lane rutted dirt track ... out in the never never. Finally, late in the afternoon, he edged the Range Rover around yet another spur jetting out from the ridge and found the jumbled outcropping of dirt and half-buried equipment he'd seen from the air, a rectangle of weathered chain link guarding it on all sides, but so buried by dirt and sand he could step across it at will.

Though the fence was so short as to be an afterthought, the scale of the equipment itself was much larger than he'd expected. The view from the air had been at a safe distance and, with no known objects to scale against, had appeared relatively tiny from such vantage. Up close the fallen main tower looked to be at least eighty feet plus, though most of it was obscured by dirt. The only portion really exposed was parts of two sides of the tower's superstructure, which was comprised of an open, but surprisingly dense, tangle of Erector Set style riveted steel girders and braces. The tower narrowed at a regular angle from the base toward the top, then, based on the much wider knob of dirt bulging out, appeared to end in some kind of bulbous round top. A spherical shield protecting radar components? Dick had no way to know without a lot of digging.

Fortunately, he'd thought to make sure the Range Rover carried a shovel. It wasn't surprising it did; including a scat shovel to cover your shit when camping was basic equipment for a responsible outdoorsman. A smaller head and shorter handle than he might have liked for moving a substantial amount of dirt, but it and a lot of sweat would do the job.

Dick got to it. He always did what needed to be done.

He made good headway at uncovering the buried portions of most of one corner of the tower before the sun disappeared over the ridge line and he decided to quit for the day. A good choice, since it got real dark and surprisingly cold fast out woop woop. Cold air on sweat-damp clothing wasn't pleasant. Dick retreated to the supple leather seats of the Range Rover to rest, drink more than a liter of water, and chow down on his food supplies.

At some point he dozed off.

He woke in a state of hyper awareness, his senses in overdrive, his mind racing to figure out what had jolted him from his slumber. Without even looking at the time, he knew it was late, that he'd been asleep for hours. Not only was there a gummy crustiness at the corners of his eyes, but the dark of the Outback was stark and velvety black with pincushion pricks of light scattered liberally across the sky.

He turned first left, then right, as far as he was able, gazing out through the windows at the blackness, able to discern the behemoth tower he'd been digging out and the dirt and rubble enshrouding it only by the lack of diamond pinpricks in an uneven configuration at the lower portions of his field of view.

New moon. Pitch dark.

Excellent time for an invasion.

Only when he relaxed straining his eyes to see into the void did he notice an almost subsonic thrum vibrating through his bones. Earthquake? Or was something approaching? Something big?

He fumbled for the door handle and jerked it, bailing out of the car as he swore at the courtesy light flashing on in the passenger compartment as the door opened. So much for surprising whoever or whatever might be out there.

He stayed low, doing a somersault roll as he leapt from the passenger seat, using one arm to swat the door back shut as he went by. He came to a halt in a crouch, then slowly pivoted three hundred and sixty degrees until he had peered into the starry abyss in all directions.

Still nothing, but the thrum was louder, more prominent outside the relatively airtight confines and rubber tire cushioned comfort of the vehicle. He felt it in the soles of his feet, but he also felt it in the air, a buffeting fluctuation in pressure from some source unknown. The hairs on his arms, already standing from the leap from the body-heat warmth of the SUV to the stark cool of the desert night, pulsed with the sluggish, steady beat. He even felt it on the top of his head, a staccato drumbeat from somewhere out of sight, hitting the entire area from some unseen height.

Fuck! That's when he thought to look up, not for something, but for nothing, for a void in the glitter that was the southern sky. For the fucking, whisper quiet black helicopter that had bedeviled him at Rendlesham Forest. For the assholes from the Subsidiary's Lightning Team, coming to swoop him up for another damn report. For the next smug Subsidiary representative who was looking for a report, but was really looking to get punched in the teeth. Rinse and repeat.

But, when he looked up, he didn't see anything and he didn't see nothing. He saw the full panoply of stars studding the sky unobstructed by clouds or helicopters or ...

FLASH!

A bright whiteness blinded him, leaving nothing but a forked, jagged afterimage on his retinas.

BOOM! A thunderclap instantaneously deafened him and threw him down onto the hardscrabble earth. He instinctively flattened himself upon the ground as his mind reeled with adrenaline and questions.

FLASH! BOOM!

Again, he was assaulted. He closed his eyes tight and put his hands over his ears to protect his fragile eardrums. Then it came again and again and again.

FLASH! BOOM! FLASH! BOOM! FLASH! BOOM!

Though measured in milliseconds, the delay between the flashes and the booms seemed to somehow be decreasing as if whoever was pounding him with flash grenades was getting closer, or whatever pissed-off cousin of Thor atop the ridge tossing lightning bolts was zeroing in on their aim.

Lying flat on the ground helped protect him, but it wouldn't save him from a direct hit. He tensed, then waited for the next strike.

FLASH, BOOM!

The strike and the thunderclap melded into one as Dick leapt up and, in a low crouch, sprinted for the black void that represented the wider portion of the downed metal latticework of the strange tower ... The Steeple of Woop Woop. He held his arms out—one high to protect his head, one low to protect his knees and shins—until he felt the cool metal of one of the steel crossbeams. He stopped and felt about until he found one of the larger voids in the gridwork, where a piece had twisted and broken in the fall. He slitted his eyes, then held for the next flash, using it to sear an afterimage of the pattern of steel and open area on his retinas.

FLASHBOOM!

With his retinal map he contorted his body and stepped, twisting and ducking, into the void between metal pieces. Once inside, he angled to the left where the tower narrowed and quickly wriggled as far up and into the partially sand-entombed structure as possible, praying one of the Inland Taipans Seth had warned them about wasn't curled up in the dark, waiting to strike. Even aside from unwanted encounters with deadly wildlife, part of Dick's mind screamed that this retreat was about as smart as swinging a nine-iron on a golf course during a thunderstorm. But the other part of him hoped that between the grounding capabilities of the enshrouding sand and the lattice work of metal now completely surrounding him, he was effectively protected from the bolts of searing electricity as if in a Faraday Cage. He remembered seeing some old black and white documentary with some guy sitting safely as high voltage electricity zapped and crackled across the surface of a protective cage of metal lattice. He also knew a small Faraday Cage pocket protected his Subsidiary cell phone from disruption or surveillance when he was carrying it, but not using it, on a mission.

FLASHBOOM! FLASH, BOOM! FLASH! BOOM!

FLASH!

BOOM!

As suddenly as it started, it stopped. Still, he wasn't stupid. He waited for ten minutes to be sure. Then he crawled through the utter blackness of his entombing structure toward fresher, cooler air, and the star-sparkled expanse of the Outback night.

All was quiet on the Western Australian front. A faint odor of ozone lingered in the clean, cold air, but whatever it was, it was over. Whatever had attacked him was gone.

What the hell?

He drained the lizard, made his way back to the Range Rover, and fell into a sleep punctuated with dreams of lights in the sky, big-eyed, gray aliens, and uncomfortable probes.

He woke at dawn finding he'd shifted into an awkward sleeping position atop the gear shift. Embarrassing, but less embarrassing than telling someone you were abducted by aliens. He'd leave this particular detail out of his reports to both Swynton and Nerevsky.

#

Come morning, the only evidence of the previous night's events, other than his own dreams, were several glassy spots on the ground, where bolts of electricity from the sky had fused the sandy soil into crystalline form. He pocketed a few pieces for later study, ate a couple of granola bars, swigged some water, then got back to digging.

By noon, he'd reached the end of the steeple-like superstructure and began shoveling dirt away from the rounded device atop it. He'd expected some kind of white plastic dome or curved, solid sheets, like protected many radar antennae. Instead, he found that, after a relatively narrow collar of shiny metal extending maybe one-fifth of the way up from the bottom, the spherical top to the tower was also an open grid of metal parts. This material, however, was narrower and more fragile, almost electrical in its look. It definitely wasn't structural; it wasn't supporting anything or holding things together. Instead, it looked as if an outer mesh-like surface comprising the entire middle and top portion of the slightly flattened globe perhaps collected energy. A more conical series of electrical parts perhaps conveyed such power through an open circle at the top to the sky.

He took a rest from his hard labors and tried to envision the entire setup in his mind's eye. The Erector Set Steeple of Woop Woop standing tall, holding a gleaming disco ball high above the bleak landscape of the Outback, soaking in ... what? Energy? From where? Radiation from the uranium ore common in these parts? Solar power?

Then, what? Neither the topography, whether from above or the ground, suggested any kind of cabling or wires for transmission to or from the site. Did the power somehow collected get transmitted into the sky? Perhaps to a geosynchronous satellite array? Or was the device merely passing along what it received to the next apparatus in an entire series, like the Beacons of Gondor in *Lord of the Rings*? If so, what was it signaling? Who was it warning?

And, then, in a flash as bright as those of the night before, it came to him. He'd seen this kind of tower before. Not at a military base when he was in the Army Rangers. Not in a communications array he'd infiltrated while on a mission for the Subsidiary. Not even on a drilling platform far out to sea. No, in a documentary long, long ago about Nikola Tesla.

Wireless electricity or generating dynamos or who knows what, but this ... this tower ... was something out of the discarded electrical engineering schemes of Tesla.

Long seconds after that flash of insight came a rumbling, grumbling roar of a throaty boom as Dick also recollected that somewhere in the lengthy ramblings of Harry Mason's Bright Skies report about the Banjawarn Station incident was a long, dissembling discussion of Tesla energy weapons, earthquake generators, Tesla fireballs, orange-red Tesla shields, and Magnifying Energy Transmitters.

Truth told, he'd skimmed through those parts pretty quickly because ... well, because it was late at night and he typically didn't give too much credence to internet conspiracy theories. And, it was highly speculative and even more fantastic. But he should have known better; he should have paid closer attention. If his work in Denver had taught him anything, it was that even the most outlandish internet conspiracy theories can have some small, core kernel of truth. And if the Canary Islands had taught him anything, it was that bad guys will do monstrously outlandish and unbelievable things.

He had a lot of re-reading to do.

But, for now, he had to make sure to get back to Banjawarn in plenty of time for his pick-up back to Kalgoorlie and his family. After last night, he thought they might be in a whole lot more danger than when he believed Nerevsky was a nut-job with a fetish. Okay, Nerevsky was a nut-job with a fetish—at least for bizarre sports—but he also might be on to something the Russians or maybe others had been covering up out woop woop. And, just maybe, Dick should give a big fucking woop woop about whatever that was.

Chapter 16

Seth and Melanie were waiting for Dick at Kalgoorlie-Boulder Airport. Melanie greeted Dick with a kiss which lingered long enough for Seth to suggest they "get a room." For his part, Seth practically bubbled over with excitement about the tour they'd taken the day before at the Super Pit. Facts and statistics poured out of him so quickly Dick had no real opportunity to digest them; he was just happy his kid had enjoyed at least part of this misbegotten adventure.

"What about you, Dad? Anything cool happen up at Banjawarn Station? Any new leads?"

Dick ran his tongue over his front teeth while he contemplated how much to say.

"Banjawarn Station was pretty much the boring place I expected it to be. I don't think they really appreciate tourists or ... researchers ... bothering them." He paused. "Did have to take cover from a pretty intense lightning storm overnight out at a ridge line I was camping below."

"That's funny," said Melanie. "No lightning here. No rain. No thunder. Didn't see or hear a thing. Nothing."

Dick waved her off. "No reason for you to have. Banjawarn Station's over four hundred kilometers ... two hundred fifty miles ... away from here. Sure, you can get huge lines of thunderstorms associated with a weather front, but you won't see hide nor hair of a lightning strike more than thirty or so miles away."

"Er ... not true, Dad," said Seth. "At least, not necessarily true."

"Really? You become an expert on lightning storms at some point?"

Seth wrinkled his nose. "Not really. It's just that Mom and me, well we, you know, kept asking people we met while you were gone about lights in the sky and shit ... er ... stuff ... and one guy suggested the whole thing could have been a lightning strike with associated ball lightning or ignited methane gas escaping from an old mine opening."

Dick wrinkled his nose as he tossed his bag into the back of the SUV and headed for the driver's side door, then corrected himself and headed to the opposite side of the vehicle to the actual driver's side door. "Yeah. Heard some of that earlier from others. Sounds like a bit of a stretch to me."

Seth jumped into the back seat. "It did to me, too. So, I did some checking online once we got back to the hotel last night—I guess just about the same time you were taking cover from the storm up north—and I found out there's actually a recently documented case of a single megaflash of lightning in South America that covered four hundred and forty miles and lasted almost seventeen seconds. And there have been ones in Oklahoma that have been two to three hundred miles end to end."

Dick started the SUV. "Really?"

"Oh, my," said Melanie as she buckled in.

"Yeah. Of course, those kinds of strikes are only associated with what they call mesoscale convective systems. Really huge storms with a lot of energy and moisture in them, which affect a huge area all at one time."

Dick pulled out onto the road for the short drive to the hotel. "So, not what you have here in the arid environment of Western Australia, either last night or way back in 1993."

"Exactomundo," agreed Seth.

If one of his old partners at the Subsidiary had had this colloquy with him, Dick would have grouched that they had wasted his time, but he realized that was not the correct response. Not just that Seth was his kid and Dick wanted to treat him better than someone from work, but that Seth had gone above and beyond the call of duty. He and Melanie had kept interviewing in his absence, furthering both their cover and his research, and Seth had taken a bit of new information obtained, researched it on his own time, and debunked it as a possibility, but still presented it to Dick so he wasn't left out of the analytical equation.

Dick glanced to the back seat. "Good work. You're a whiz with that computer, Seth."

"Thanks," replied Seth, blushing. "I figure if you have the entire knowledge of the civilized world in your hands, you ought to use it for something besides playing games and arguing with strangers."

It was a fine, warm, bonding family moment for a few precious seconds, then Melanie spoke up.

"Or looking at porn—"

They drove in silence for several minutes.

Maybe it was the lack of conversation that heightened Dick's concentration on the road in front of him and the traffic behind, but his adrenaline surged when he noticed the same dusty, silver sedan he'd seen following them a couple days back. He kept an eye on it, watching more intently when it turned off and, sure enough, was quickly replaced in his rearview mirror by a gray van.

The good news was that whoever was tailing him and his family obviously hadn't managed to install a tracking device on the SUV or they wouldn't need to be following so close. The bad news was he still didn't know who they were.

Ultimately, Dick decided he didn't give a shit, at least not right now. They could follow him to the hotel, just like the other night, and he'd check in to see if anyone from the Subsidiary was keeping an eye on them. He didn't really think so, but he needed to eliminate that possibility before he began speculating on who was keeping tabs on this mission and why.

Unfortunately, his pursuers had something else in mind.

As Dick was cutting through a traffic-free side street on the way to the hotel, the silver sedan entered the block from the opposite end, then accelerated rapidly toward them. Less than eight car lengths ahead, the driver—a white male with beady eyes—cut the wheel sharply and the car slid sideways, blocking their path. At the same moment, Dick heard the pop of shots being fired from the van now closing in from behind.

Fuck!

"Get down! And stay there," barked Dick as his mind raced through alternative courses of action. If he was on his own, especially in his own car, Dick just would have plowed through the obstacle in front, trading fire with the would-be killers. But he wasn't going to crash head-first into anything with his wife in the front seat and his kid in back.

He wrenched the wheel hard to the left into the exit for a drive-thru bank deposit and ATM lane, blaring his horn to ward off anyone who might be turning into the lane from the opposite side of the cash-dispensing machines. He purposely clipped the back of the freestanding ATM one lane left with the passenger side mirror, which prompted a scream of terror from Melanie as the mirror tore off. Hopefully, it also triggered a tamper alarm which would draw the local cops to the area, thinking a robbery was in progress.

Unfortunately, he didn't have time to wait around for the Australian mounties or whatever they were called to come to the rescue. The gray van pursued them into the bank drive-thru and so did the gunfire. Short bursts; probably a MAC 10 from the sound of it. Not the weapon of a sniper, but plenty effective, and being wielded by someone smart enough not to fire bursts in full-auto mode. Their SUV thundered out of the entrance to the bank's parking lot onto a somewhat busier thoroughfare, drawing a horn blast because Dick had straightened out the vehicle on the wrong side of the street. Melanie gasped, but Dick didn't have time to reassure her.

"Stay down!" he barked.

He swerved into the correct lane and kept his eyes as much on the center rearview mirror as on the street ahead. He was still accelerating, one thumb pressing down to keep the horn blaring at all times. It cleared traffic, warned off pedestrians, and, hopefully, would draw the attention of any approaching patrol cars.

To his irritation, he saw no sign of Kalgoorlie's constabulary—no doubt checking out the historic brothel tourist district—but he did see the gray van lumbering onto the roadway behind him. A quick glance to the left as he sped through a four-way stop revealed the silver sedan racing parallel to his path, no doubt trying to cut him off, if not at the pass, then at an intersection two or three blocks ahead. He couldn't let that happen. If the cops wouldn't come to him, he'd have to go to them.

"Seth! I need directions to the nearest police station. Now!"

He felt a bit odd following the instruction always given to women driving alone if they think they are being followed by a predator or if an unmarked vehicle with a single Mars light is trying to get them to stop on a lonely piece of road. Still, only idiots would roll their pursuit and gunfight into the parking lot of a police station.

"Why?" shouted Seth.

"I need a place where the bad guys won't follow."

"Gotcha."

Dick glanced back and saw Seth poke his head up and look out the window.

"Stay down!"

Seth ducked. "Turn right and keep going straight."

Dick didn't know how the hell the kid could get a bead on the nearest police station in less time than it would take Dick to access an app on his phone, but you either trust your partners in the field or you die. He took his foot off the gas, jinked the wheel hard to the right, skidding around the corner at speed, then floored it again.

"How far?"

"What?" replied Seth.

"How far to the police station? Which side of the street?"

"No police station. When the road Ts, turn right again and head through the gate into the Super Pit."

"We need protection!"

"Guard station. Plus, trucks roll twenty-four-seven, so we know people will be around."

Dick gritted his teeth. The kid meant well and he got points for making a fast decision, but rent-a-cops weren't likely to scare off the bad guys, even if they were packing and he doubted they would be. Still, he'd back Seth's play. It was better than careening through

Kalgoorlie waiting to see if a zinging bullet or a high-speed crash would wound or kill his family.

Sure enough, the street ended at T-intersection with a broader road near the edge of the massive gold mining pit. Dick eased some extra speed out of the long gentle curves of the road, then spied the guard shack at the entrance. He'd hoped for a cement block redoubt, but it was a simple wooden affair, with no real cover, even if he managed to somehow get his family inside with the confused guards before the gray van closed on them.

Instead, he flew though, busting the gate, and sending one guard leaping, while another grabbed for a phone. At least now he knew the police would soon be on the way. Of course, he had no exit and didn't relish the thought of racing down the hairpin turns passing behemoth haul trucks blind as they lumbered up and down the hill in a constant cycle of replenishment. He cast about for some alternative before the road into the depths was his only option.

Seth poked his head up again, but before Dick could yell at the kid, Seth pointed to one side. "Pull into the boneyard. Maybe we can hide the car."

Dick looked where his kid was pointing. The boneyard was a sizeable lot to one side of the road with room for parking while tourists ogled cast offs from the Super Pit's history of mining. Big haul trucks with tires twelve feet tall, shovelers, graders, and the like, all abandoned in one spot to accommodate tourist photos and kids on holiday. Dick had no real choice. He pulled in, accelerated toward the spot holding the largest of the gargantuan cast-offs and braked hard, spinning the steering wheel and skidding through loose gravel to a stop with the passenger doors away from the pursuing van and close to the gigantic equipment.

"Out! Out! Out!" If Dick had learned nothing else in the military, he had learned any order was made more urgent by repeating it three times in rapid succession. Seth quickly bailed out of the back seat, slammed the door behind him, and crouched behind the car. Dick arched over Melanie's huddled form and grabbed the door handle, wrenching her door open and half-shoving her out as he awkwardly straddled the center console so he could follow her out her side of the vehicle.

Dick turned to Seth. "Is the kangaroo of many colors bag in the back?" Dick had left his complimentary gift bag of spy equipment behind when he went to Banjawarn Station, not wanting to have to deal with the hassle of explosives and unregistered firearms just in case either Kalgoorlie-Boulder Airport or, much less likely, Banjawarn Airport had any scanning or security equipment checks.

"Y-yeah, I think so."

Dick re-opened the back door and slid in, grabbing the tourist bag, and sliding back out as he reached in and grabbed the pistol he'd been provided. Melanie cowered, stunned and shaking, by the front wheel well. Seth crouched to one side, hugging her protectively. Dick searched for options, looking past them toward a giant shovel and an ore truck beyond. There was more of a gap between the shovel and the front of their vehicle than he liked, but he saw no other alternatives. They'd have to move fast.

Dick pointed. "Get behind that ore shovel, now!" he ordered. "Go! Go! Go!"

Seth half-lifted Melanie and urged her forward, both of them keeping low. Dick crouched at the side of the car, near where he'd sheared off the passenger sideview mirror, and extended his weapon with both arms over the hood of the car, loosing one valuable round of ammunition at the windshield of the rapidly approaching gray van to provide at least some minimal cover for his family's dash for the protection of the massive shovel. As he followed close behind, Dick caught a glimpse of the silver sedan entering the boneyard, too.

If these assholes had any smarts or training, they'd be flanking them from opposite sides within minutes. Dick rested his back against the hot metal of the shovel for a few moments to put together a tactical plan.

"Shouldn't we have stayed with the car?" asked Seth, his arm still around his mother, who had the pale appearance of someone going into shock. "We had cover on all sides and the chance to drive away if we got a break."

Dick kept thinking while he responded to what his guidance counselor in high school would have called a "teachable moment."

"A regular vehicle provides concealment, not cover. The bullet for a typical street weapon will penetrate through the sheet metal body and back out the other side, unless it hits the engine block or maybe the housing for the automatic windows. Best cover you can get aside from the engine is the wheel wells. Differential, axles, and brakes are all relatively solid." He rapped on the metal he was leaning against with the butt of his gun. "This stuff is super heavy duty. It'll stop anything." Dick tilted his head toward the old tires farther down the line of dusty, unused equipment. "Fuck, the tires are thick and resilient enough, they'd probably stop what these bozos have."

He focused in on the series of discarded gargantuan tires. "In fact ... take your mother and sneak down to those tires leaning up against one another. Stash her laying down in one and you take cover in the one behind her, then stay down. With all the commotion we've caused, the cavalry's bound to be arriving soon in a hell of a big hurry. We just have to stay alive until they get here." Dick knew Seth couldn't run as fast as before his burn injuries—he wasn't that long out of Physical Therapy—but Seth could still run as fast as Melanie, and that would be enough for this situation.

Seth gave a curt nod and grabbed his mom's elbow, urging her to go with him. Melanie looked at Dick, her eyes pleading with him to join them.

"Go!" said Dick. "Go with Seth, now. Go! Go! Go!"

Dick twisted back to the edge of the shovel and peeked out, his weapon ready to draw attention and provide cover if needed, but the yokels in pursuit hadn't yet gotten out of their respective vehicles. He turned back toward the retreating forms of his wife and son.

"Remember," he called after them. "Tourists. We're just tourists. We don't know who these guys are or why they are after us."

That last part was true, truer than Dick wanted it to be, but it could be handy in case anyone demanded a polygraph over this bizarre incident.

Dick didn't really want to start a gun fight. Not only was he outgunned, but explaining to the local constabulary why he had a weapon, and where he got it, would complicate his life. But he clenched it tight; better a complicated life for him than no life at all for his wife and his son.

Still, if he wasn't going to provide covering fire, he had to do something to distract their pursuers. He poked his head around the corner of the shovel edge, then ducked back. He smiled when he heard several rounds pound into the other side of the heavy slab of metal. They'd seen him; they were hoping to pin him down.

He couldn't let them do that. And, he couldn't chance they'd find and capture his family as a way to leverage him. He dithered for a few more seconds, giving Melanie and Seth precious time to hide, then made a decision. If these guys were after him, if they thought he had something they wanted, they'd pursue him. He turned, planting one foot against the solid edge of the shovel he was behind and tensed, as if setting for wind sprints in football training camp. Then he exploded out from behind his cover in a mad dash back for the SUV his family had abandoned. He threw himself inside, contorting himself into a low, awkward position behind the wheel, started the vehicle, and punched down on the accelerator.

He jammed the gear shift into drive so hard his hand twinged.

The SUV bolted forward and Dick spun the wheel hard to the left without bothering to look through the windshield. The vehicle spun, spraying gravel like shrapnel in a wide arc as it did, hopefully causing the bad guys to duck for cover. Then he straightened the wheel and adjusted his position so he could see the road. He left the parking lot for the boneyard by darting out the side and onto a roadway which, he prayed, would lead to the pit. After all, the tour buses got from here to there somehow and there weren't a lot of choices for which way to go.

He continued to pick up speed on a short straightaway, then curved left, T-ing onto a broader roadway wide enough to let two of the massive ore haulers pass one another with room to spare. He turned left, the direction of the massive pit, without stopping. He didn't want to end up in a maze of ore crushing equipment and potential dead ends. As he turned, he looked out the window and confirmed that both the silver sedan and the gray van were in hot pursuit. He wasn't sure what would happen next, but at least Melanie and Seth were away from the action and that was enough to give him a charge of bravado.

"Catch me if you can, fuckers!" he yelled, even though he knew they couldn't hear him. He floored the accelerator and raced down a sloping broad gravel roadway. Sooner than he expected, the roadway disappeared from view and he realized the first of many hairpin turns was fast upon him. He braked, jerked the wheel abruptly, then tapped on the accelerator again and took the first hairpin in a sliding drift that made him feel like he was in an action movie. Of course, the looming rear end of a behemoth ore truck, its tires three times as tall as his SUV almost ended the flick in the first reel. With no time to stop, he instead committed to a blind pass of the truck. He flew by the empty ore truck, drawing a thunderous horn blast as he did. Once well past the monster truck, he glanced into the rearview mirror, expecting the trucker to be flipping him off, but instead the worker had a radio handset up to his mouth, no doubt cautioning his fellows against the madman speeding into the pits of hell.

Dick slowed somewhat, vowing to be better prepared for the next turn. Control wasn't a problem. The road was well-graded, with long patches of dry gravel alternating with gravel which had been wet with spray to keep dust down. He took the second turn at a more controlled pace and again accelerated into the next straightaway sloped downward. Another glance back revealed that his pursuers were one level up on the roadway and trying to make up some distance on him.

Dick wasn't sure what he would do when the slalom course ended at the bottom of the pit. For now, he just needed to keep ahead and lead his adversaries farther from his family. The police had to be on their way by now, though there was no telling what their tactical approach might be.

Another massive truck loomed ahead. He moved over to pass, but a heavily laden ore transport was lumbering uphill too close to allow him to pass easily before it cleared. He braked and bided his time at what seemed like a crawl, his eyes flicking to the rearview mirror every few seconds. His pursuers were not slowed by traffic at the moment and gaining.

He couldn't wait. He rammed his foot down on the gas and jerked the car into the oncoming lane, fishtailing on a section of drier gravel as he pulled out. Fortunately for him, it seemed as if the oncoming truck had slowed, whether due to the grade or his presence, Dick had no clue. He accelerated directly toward the towering impediment, praying the empty truck he was passing would slow to give him room—and allow him a chance to avoid a head-on crash into an obstacle his puny SUV wouldn't even dent.

Probably should have buckled in when he was escaping the boneyard, but there was no time to correct that oversight now.

The truck to his side was his friend, slowing just enough that Dick was able to jerk the wheel and avoid the head-on collision, but still clear the massive tires of the truck he was passing—tires which would have easily crushed his vehicle if they had caught his bumper.

Unfortunately, his rapid switch back to his own lane was quickly propelling him off the wide road. In a moment, he would be sailing right out there, attempting to fly over the Super Pit as he had just a couple days before, but without wings this time.

He stomped on the brakes and spun the wheel again until the car pointed away from the void, then took his foot off the pedal just for a microsecond to boost his traction and popped his foot onto the gas.

Once headed in more or less the right direction, he was forced to again slam on the brake pedal to maintain control.

The SUV slid to the inside edge of the wide gravel road and bumped against the rock wall at the edge, crumpling the fender and jolting it to a halt. He braced for the potential impact of the truck headed downslope, but it didn't come.

That's when he noticed the two ginormous trucks had stopped abreast one another, blocking the road. A few moments later, he heard flying gravel as the vehicles pursuing him slid to a stop on the other side of the trucks. The fast-thinking and safety conscious teamsters of Fimiston Super Pit had prevented the pursuit from continuing.

Dick got out of his vehicle on the driver's side, which had the good fortune of being away from the rumbling ore carriers. He dropped his gun into a small depression on the side of the road and shoved some dirt over it with his foot so he wouldn't be caught with it should the police quite reasonably decide to search him and his vehicle when they arrived.

Just as he finished, he heard someone shouting. He moved to the center of the road and sighted between the two ore haulers blocking the road. A head poked out of the window of the silver sedan. He yelled toward Dick, his Russian accent thick and broad. "Ve are leaving, Mr. Thornby, but ve will be around. Just forget you ever saw the equipment and ve won't have to come back and finish the job."

With that, both the silver sedan and the gray van sprayed gravel as they spun around and high-tailed it back uphill.

Dick heard sirens approaching, but based on the pitch and volume, he doubted they would arrive before the bad guys got back up the hill, unless, of course, more vehicles conspired to block their way.

A Black man wearing a hard hat leaned out of the giant, idling truck facing Dick. "Stay where you are, bloke. The authorities are on the way and you don't want to make us stop you." The throaty idle of the behemoth ore carrier thundered up to a deafening roar to punctuate the demand.

Dick got the point. He nodded in an exaggerated fashion, then smiled and waved, to show he understood and would comply.

He doubted the workers would stop the men with guns fleeing uphill, but, like most of this mission, what happened next on that score was out of his control. He opened the passenger door to his vehicle and sat, his legs hanging out the open door, and considered his next move. His brow furrowed.

Forget he ever saw "the equipment?" People saw this equipment every single day. It was on a tour. The tour operator probably spewed out all sorts of facts and figures about it just like Connal had on the plane. It didn't make sense.

No, not this equipment. The Tesla coil in the desert.

Fuck, maybe there was something to this mission after all and he had accidentally stumbled upon it.

The sirens got closer. The chase, the defensive escape maneuvers, even the efforts to draw attention from the police, could all be explained as the instincts of a former cop and former Army Ranger. Why somebody would actually be after him was a harder thing to explain.

Fortunately, he didn't have to.

After the Western Australia Police Force arrived and retrieved him, his SUV, and his family, they were taken to the police station and placed in an interrogation room.

Seth started to ask him a question, but Dick shushed him. Even a mediocre cop in a small town knew enough to separate suspects for interviewing. No doubt they were being monitored to see if they'd talk amongst themselves before things got down to business. Best to just stay silent until they were asked for answers—he didn't even dare tell his family why they should stay quiet, but after that initial shushing, they did. His wife and his kid knew he was a spy. They knew not only that he would lie, but that he ... and they ... would need to lie to the police to escape scrutiny because they, like him, were on a mission.

They were a family of spies.

Finally, an officer ... Police Rangers they called them here ... came in and handed him his license, which he had surrendered at the Super Pit.

"Got to admit, mate. We had a bit of a go trying to figure out why two vehicles worth of armed blokes would be chasing a family on holiday with such vigor." He inclined his head at the license as Dick was returning it to his wallet. "Then we ran your name through our databases. Took a bit o' time, hooking up with both Interpol and the Yanks, but, of course, that's when we found out you were the "Hero of Lake Michigan" and all." He motioned to Seth and Melanie. "The whole lot of you, thwarting terrorists trying to poison the water supply and whatnot. No surprise you needed a holiday after that. And no surprise some bad elements have a grudge out for you." He smiled at Dick. "At least that's how we got it figured. That what happened?"

The detective's interrogation technique left a lot, a *whole lot,* to be desired, but Dick didn't imagine he got much chance to practice protecting the streets of Kalgoorlie. And Dick knew better than to look a gift-horse in the mouth. No, he would simply ride this horse to freedom.

He shrugged his shoulders. "Didn't have any time to *think* at all, detective. Just tried to get away with my family as best I could."

"Well, you did a fine job of it, by my reckoning. Drive pretty well for a Yank, from what I hear, too. Remarkable job." He reached out a hand to Dick. "I ... well, if you don't mind ... I just want to shake your hand, sir. I just want to shake your hand."

#

Yuri Lemarov flicked on the phone at the first chirp.

"G'day," said an Aussie-accented voice.

"Report," demanded Yuri.

"Message delivered. All very dramatic. Squealing tires, flying gravel, shots fired, cowering family members."

"And you and your men, all in the clear?"

"No wuckas, mate."

"And was the source of the message clear?"

"Da," came the response with a light chuckle. "It couldn't have been more obvious if I had asked for the location of the 'nuclear wessels.'"

Yuri didn't get the reference, but it didn't matter. The Aussie's faux Russian accent was so thick it sounded cartoonish to Yuri's ears, but the Subsidiary's American operative, like most Americans, was by all reports action-oriented and less than sophisticated when it came to the nuances of Mother Russia.

The next set of wheels in his complex machine could be set in motion.

Chapter 17

It was late by the time the family got back to the hotel and Dick finished giving them a version of events from his trip up north which had been sanitized for their protection. Seth and Melanie settled into bed almost right after, but Dick had things to do.

He called up Harry Mason's Bright Skies report and started reading. He skimmed past the sections of the document which dealt with the political affiliations of various Australian officials in relation to the Aum Shinrikyo movement. Figuring out whether the Japanese, the Russians, the North Koreans, or others were involved in some vast decades-long conspiracy to develop electromagnetic displacement weaponry didn't really matter … unless there actually was tangible evidence of EMD weapons capable of generating earthquakes at a distance on command and/or force field shields or pulse energy weapons. Harry certainly seemed to believe that such weaponry existed. He also suggested it had been tested and utilized repeatedly. In theory, the entire Banjawarn Station incident could be seen as a multifaceted test of Tesla Fireballs (basically slugs of infolded electromagnetic energy). Supposedly, slugs of energy plasma could be sent through the atmosphere and triggered to detonate by a second, faster-moving, slug of scalar-induced energy. This same kind of energy could be used to create a Tesla Shield, a hemispheric force field preventing anything from passing through.

The report recited numerous other incidents that had occurred in Western Australia in addition to the Banjawarn Bang. These included an October 1994 succession of plasma spheres witnessed by a great number of people. The spheres supposedly traveled from west to east across an area near Tom Price, a town east of the Naval Communication Station in Exmouth (on the northwestern coast of Australia, well to the north and west of Banjawarn) in Western Australia. There was also an incident in the skies above Perth in May of

1995, and another in Victoria exactly two years later, all allegedly headed more or less to or from Exmouth.

The examples of tests recited in the report were not limited to Western Australia. The most notable of these tests other than the Banjawarn Bang incident seemed to be the earthquake in Kobe, Japan, on January 17, 1995, which was publicly predicted nine days earlier by Aum Shinrikyo's leader to be imminent (by action of a foreign interest) and suggested after the fact by Aum Shinrikyo's science minister to have been activated by electromagnetic power.

There was more ... a lot more. The rambling report had some interesting observations about the locations of various places of interest along a great circle route. Starting at Exmouth, which uses an array of thirteen radio towers in a star-shaped configuration to communicate by very low/ultra-low frequency radio waves with submarines at sea, the route traced through Hong Kong to Kobe, Japan. From there, it bisected a supposed transmission station in Kamchatka, Russia, then traveled across the Arctic to Cutler, Maine (also a VLF/ULF transmission facility), and on past the gigantic radio telescope in Arecibo, Puerto Rico. Finally, it continued through Argentina and past several Antarctic research stations, then through Western Australia back to Exmouth.

The report also contained casual speculation about everything from the disappearance of Australian Prime Minister Harold E. Holt (allegedly while swimming in the ocean, although the body was never found) in 1967 to the disappearance of Flight 007 over the alleged Kamchatka base, and other even more far-fetched theories.

The more disparate incidents the treatise mentioned, the more fantastic it all sounded. While Mason no doubt thought he was offering more and more corroborating details, the added UFO sightings and speculation had the opposite effect on Dick. If one or more of the incidents could be debunked or explained, it tainted the entire thesis in his mind.

Still, Dick didn't know for sure what to believe and what to discount. Certainly, his natural skepticism and his prior experience with his Denver mission suggested he not believe everything he read on the internet, especially when it involved suggestions of massive underground facilities with restricted access. Still, he knew that many wild speculations had some connection with reality. He couldn't simply dismiss Harry Mason or his rambling report without knowing more.

#

Melanie laid awake on the soft mattress in the Kalgoorlie hotel. Dick had left the door ajar to the sitting room in their suite, but the light he was using to read at the desk did not bother her. She wasn't awake because of light pollution or Dick's sometimes overwhelming work ethic or even because of leftover adrenaline from the chase and gunfight earlier in the evening. No, she was consumed with the mission and a need to get more involved and to be more helpful in getting the mission done. It wasn't that she had any loyalty to Dick's employer, Catalyst Crisis Consulting, the front covering for the Subsidiary. The Subsidiary had almost wrecked her marriage and put her husband's life at risk more times, she was sure, than she would ever know. And it certainly wasn't because she thought this mission—this bizarre amalgam of UFOs and conspiracy theories and real people with real guns and real ammunition—really had anything to do with saving the world.

No, it was because, whether she liked it or not, she—and Seth—had become enmeshed in Dick's world of espionage and intrigue. She could tell herself she was an unwitting pawn, an unwilling participant, who deserved to be kept out of all the intrigue and danger and mystery of an international spy agency. She could tell herself all of this was Nerevsky's fault, even though she had never met the man who was making Dick and Seth and her jump to his puppeteer's dance, but that wasn't really true. She knew she had insinuated herself into Dick's secret life when he admitted to her what he really did for a living when she had insisted he always tell her where he was. She had inserted herself into the spy game. And, when Dick called, at the risk of his mission and his livelihood and maybe even his life, and demanded she pull Seth out of the hospital and flee inland and uphill during his Canary Island mission, that communication had tipped off the powers-that-be of her complicity, of her involvement. From that moment forward, she was a player in a game she didn't know the rules of and had never imagined.

The problem with playing a game you don't understand, though, is that not only can you never hope to win, you don't even have a clue as to what may happen next and you can't protect yourself ... or your family ... from any move any other player might make.

That's not the kind of position any woman, especially a wife and mother, ever wants to be in.

Today was proof of where that could lead: panic and possible death at the hands of unknown killers for reasons beyond her comprehension.

To hell with that. She'd pulled Seth out of the hospital against medical advice to save him from some impending disaster during Dick's Canary Island mission. She'd been strong and decisive and determined. She'd taken action. For too much of this mission—particularly today—she'd been passive and afraid and unhelpful. That stopped here.

Sure, she wanted to protect Seth; for one thing, she worried he found his dad's spy games a bit too exciting for his own good. And, she wanted to support Dick, who she realized with more certainty than she'd felt in years she was going to stay with through thick and thin. But she also wanted to fulfill her own destiny.

If she was going to be the wife of a spy ... no, if she was going to be a goddamn spy … she needed to heave to and do her job. No matter how hard, no matter how thankless, no matter how incomprehensible, and no matter that no one was actually paying her to do it. That's what mothers do; they do the work without a paycheck or a thank you and they save the goddamn world every damn day.

She got up and wandered to the door to the sitting room to tell Dick of her new commitment.

When she poked her head around the door to tell her husband everything she'd just decided about him and her and their life together, he was, of course, on the computer, chatting with another woman in the middle of the night.

Chapter 18

Ace Zyreb didn't interrupt as Dick set forth his request for assistance. It wasn't that she didn't want to know how he was or what the big lug was up to or where he actually was in the real world, but when your partner—or, at least, your ex-partner—from a prior mission contacts you and asks for help, you get down to business and quick. You don't know how much time he has, how much danger he ... or the mission or the world ... might be in. You just listen and agree to do whatever you can. Maybe even a few things you shouldn't do.

She was surprised when Dick contacted her, almost as surprised as he was that her sojourn in Eastern Europe was over and she was back in the United States. She wasn't surprised he knew how to get in touch outside of Subsidiary channels. Anyone who has ever had a partner in the spy business exchanged backchannel ways to connect if need arose. But she found it odd that he had instructed her to meet him online on Shangrilyfe. Using virtual and game worlds for clandestine chatting was, of course, now a standard way to try to avoid the massive data collection surveillance of espionage aggregators like Palantir and I2, but Dick had specifically directed they chat in the gardens of an online version of the Byodo-In Temple. Given the big guy's Type A personality and surly reputation, she didn't think he came to the place regularly to meditate. More likely the recurring deep thrums of the Temple's gong disrupted certain eavesdropping algorithms.

Whatever. Dick had saved her life more than once and, though almost no one knew it, millions of people along the Atlantic coast in Europe and America owed him their lives. So, when he said jump, she'd at least hop online for a chat.

"You know," she said, "when I heard you got called into Internal Audit, I wasn't so sure I'd see you again."

She heard Dick take a deep breath. "I'm ... I'm not sure you will."

Her brow furrowed, but of course Dick couldn't see her—just her avatar. "I figured you must still be their go-to guy after I heard about you breaking up that terrorist group attacking the water supply in Chicago." She paused. "Of course, the fact that it was in the papers probably was a bit higher profile than Glenn Swynton would have liked."

"I wasn't on the job in Chicago. Just the right guy at the right place at the right time."

"Sure, sure. Need to know and all that."

"What I need to know right now is some information about Nikola Tesla," said Dick. Apparently, the minimal pleasantries were over.

"*Kurva!* Is that all? You can find plenty on Wikipedia. Or, you know, you could go to an actual fucking library."

"I've cruised the online info, but I need more about his sketchier inventions ... his Death Ray and his Electro-Magnetic Displacement device ... his so-called remote earthquake generator."

"And is there some reason you don't get the research gerbils at Catalyst Crisis Consulting to do this for you?"

"I'm ... well, I'm not exactly on an official mission at the moment."

Ace thought a few moments, then let out a long sigh. "You're not freelancing for somebody else, are you? I know I owe you, but I don't want to get involved with someone who is working outside of the Subsidiary."

"No, no," Dick replied. "Nothing outside the Subsidiary. Just not something official. A quiet project for the powers-that-be."

"*Kecáš kraviny!* That sounds like bullshit to me, but I'll let it slip—"

"Let it slide."

"Slip, slide. Don't correct the idioms of someone willing to help you out." A sudden thought popped into her head. "*Ježiši!* I'm not the only person left at work who is willing to help you out, am I?"

"Of course not," replied Dick, a bit too glibly for her taste. "Given your geographic background—"

"In case you hadn't noticed, I'm assigned to the Philadelphia headquarters again, not to Eastern Europe."

"Either place could have worked for this project. Wardenclyffe, the location of his laboratory, is just over in Shoreham, New York. It's practically in the neighborhood."

"You Americans have very large neighborhoods."

"I just thought with you being Czech and Tesla—"

"What? You thought I'd have special insights on Tesla because I'm Czech? Tesla was a Serbian, born in what is now Croatia and educated in the Austrian-fucking-Empire!" She let out a huff. "Do they even teach that Eastern Europe exists to American students? Could you ... even you, Dick ... find the Czech Republic on a map if your life depended on it?"

"Sure. No problem."

"Because you're such a student of history and current geo-political affairs?"

A few seconds passed. "Probably not. It's just that—"

"—that you're willing to lie to me to get me to do research errands for you?"

Dick chuckled. "There's that. But, no, probably because there's not much I wouldn't do if my life depended on it. Or my wife's life ... or my kid's ... or yours—"

"—or some random henchman who's on fire on an oil rig about to be blown to bits."

She could almost hear Dick smile. "That? That's what you got out of our mission together? You'll do anything not to feel special won't you?"

She said nothing. Finally, he continued.

"Yeah. You're right. That's just how I roll. When it comes to saving people who can be saved, everyone is equal."

"But," she replied, "some are more equal than others. Ha! *Animal House!*"

"*Animal Farm,* actually. More obscure and of considerably less impact on American youth, I'm afraid. I'm surprised it's on the reading lists in the Czech Republic."

"We kicked the Russians out a long time ago, Dick. Read some fucking history about Eastern Europe when the mission is over and we'll call it even."

"An odd request. But, sure. We'll call it even."

#

Dick looked up from the laptop when done and was surprised to see Melanie leaning on the door frame to the bedroom with one hand hanging onto the top of the partially open door.

He blushed. Not because he was caught having a call with another woman, but as a spy he should have had enough situational awareness not to have been caught unawares by someone listening in on his end.

"I ... uh ... I was just asking my old partner to do a bit of background research for me."

"No problem," replied Melanie. "I ... well, I know I've not been as useful to you on this mission as I should have been."

Dick waved her off. "You were fine. You got Seth and you to cover when push came to shove. You're not trained for combat. Everybody is shocked when they first experience combat. They think they've seen it and experienced it and know what to expect from the movies or TV or first-person-shooter video games and all that crap, but they're wrong. You either have to be trained to deal with violence or ... or ... well, you're a sociopath. Then violence doesn't affect you because you have no empathy and no soul." He softened and lowered his voice. "I love that you have empathy and a soul. You're my soulmate."

"Forever and always."

"And if we can get through this mission in one piece, let's concentrate on that and let the world take care of itself."

She smiled. One dimple formed. "The world doesn't seem to do a very good job of that without your help."

He closed his eyes for a moment, then looked and she was still there, beautiful as ever. "It doesn't do a very good job with my help, either."

It was almost dawn, but there was time for the scene to fade to black before the sun rose again, creating shadows where danger could hide.

Chapter 19

Checking in with Glenn Swynton and, by proxy, Dee Tammany at the Subsidiary was relatively straightforward. Dick avoided the usual protocols and equipment to make sure Internal Audit wasn't a party to—or even aware of—the communication. But the procedures he received after his Rendlesham Forest incident were neither complicated, nor dangerous to implement. He reported everything, no holds barred and no shading his concerns, even if the lightning incident in the desert made him sound a bit paranoid. Glenn and Dee took it all in without comment, assured him he was doing a great job which they truly appreciated, and confirmed that nobody at the Subsidiary—at least nobody sanctioned—was following him, shooting at him and his family, or bedeviling him with lightning bolts beyond the black stump in the never never.

Reporting in to Pyotr Nerevsky at Internal Audit was considerably more complicated and, frankly, bizarre. Since his alleged mission was off the books, he couldn't just use the usual Subsidiary protocols here, either. And, since he didn't know if who in Internal Audit beside Nerevsky was in the loop on his little side trip to the Outback, he couldn't communicate with anyone else there, not even to leave a callback message. Nerevsky, of course, had established procedures to initiate and consummate contact. These involved calling a message service from a pay phone, which was itself a bit of a trick to find in Kalgoorlie, then waiting for a call back with instructions on when and where to meet. To Dick's surprise, he wasn't instructed to head to a local cyber cafe, so they could meet online. Instead, the big guy wanted to meet in person, back in Perth.

Though he always felt like he needed a shower after dealing one-on-one with Nerevsky in person, Dick was glad enough to tell his family to pack up for the journey back to their hotel in Perth. It's not that being in the big city made it any less likely he or his loved ones would get shot by whoever was trying to thwart this bizarre mission, but at least they would be in a metro area with decent health care facilities if bad things happened.

A day later, Dick left Melanie and Seth at the hotel in Perth while he headed off for his meet up with his boss and nemesis. Given the time differential and long flight undoubtedly involved, Dick figured maybe Nerevsky would be tired and subdued, maybe even a bit cranky. But, no. His shadowy puppet-master was positively hyper. It wasn't because he was happy to see Dick, though. It was because his team was winning.

According to the antiquated electric scoreboard in the gymnasium Nerevsky set for the meet, Brisbane A was beating Perth 17-7 on what looked to be a volleyball court. But, of course, it wasn't volleyball. First off, there were four guys on a side. Second, none of them were particularly tall, but then the net wasn't that high either. Most of the players looked to Dick to be of Hmong or Filipino ancestry. And there wasn't a volleyball in sight.

Just as Dick caught Nerevsky's eye and headed to the retractable bleachers on one side of the gym, someone blew on a shrill whistle and an odd yellow ball the size of an extra-large grapefruit flew over the net, which Dick now confirmed was definitely set lower than typical for volleyball. The ball looked like it was made of wide strips of something—bamboo? cane? plastic?—woven together, with gaps revealing a hollow interior. Dick stopped walking long enough to watch a point, discovering that while the back and forth looked a lot like volleyball in terms of sets and slams, the players apparently weren't allowed to touch the ball with their hands or arms. Just their feet, chest, and head. Maybe their butts, too. Dick didn't watch long enough to find out and he wasn't about to ask. Instead he made his way over to Nerevsky, who was pumping his fist in a rolling motion like he was at a rodeo disco.

"Watch much sepak takraw?" asked Nerevsky without looking at him.

Dick sat an arm's-length from the head of Internal Audit.

"Oh, sure," Dick drawled. "I've got it set up to record every single time there's a match on ESPN. It's absolutely takrawesome."

Nerevsky glanced at him for just a moment before redirecting his attention to the game. "You're lying. You probably don't even know the rules of the game."

"My job is all about lying. That's literally what I get paid to do." He looked up at the scoreboard, which now read 20-7 in favor of Brisbane A. "Match point coming up."

Nerevsky's eyes squinted. "You're guessing the matches are the same as volleyball, a much inferior sport which, like basketball, relies too heavily on genetic freaks of nature, rather than training and skill."

"Yes, I am. Yes, it does." Dick watched the baffling sport spectacle for a few seconds, until match point scored. Only a few of the scattered spectators cheered for the visiting team, but Nerevsky was one of them. When he stopped, Dick continued. "But, then, you're relying too heavily on my patience and good will. I don't like being kept in the dark and I don't like being followed. I certainly don't like being shot at. But way past that, I won't put up with my family being shot at by goons when I don't even know why anyone gives a good goddamn about what the fuck went on decades ago out woop woop—"

"Out where?"

"—the desert, the Outback, beyond the black stump, the middle of fucking nowhere."

Dick told Nerevsky the whole story—except for the parts about Glenn and Dee and Ace—starting with the interviews in Kalgoorlie and being tailed there, then continuing with the trip up to Banjawarn Station, the desert lightning, and the running gun battle on his return.

"*Gavno!*" muttered Nerevsky.

Dick didn't know what the word meant literally, but he'd been around enough pissed off people in his work to know when someone was swearing because they were pissed off.

"Exactly," he replied. "So, what the fuck is going on and who the hell is shooting at me?"

Nerevsky leaned toward him and lowered his voice to almost a whisper. "The KGB ... now the SVR ... must have gotten wind of my ... er ... our ... extracurricular activities."

Dick scrunched up his face. "The KGB. The SVR. You *are* the fucking KGB and SVR. At least, from all I understand, you used to be. Why would they fuck with someone working for you?"

Nerevsky pressed his lips together before responding. "You think my former ... employer ... is happy I am working for the Subsidiary? You think they don't worry that I may have provided sensitive information to those who may not have mother Russia's best interests at heart at all times? You think the SVR, they can't hold a grudge over past grievances ... past mistakes?"

Dick shook his head and spoke slowly and deliberately, in a smooth, soft monotone. "Not at all. I believe the SVR, like the KGB before it, is full of ruthless sons-of-bitches who care about nothing and nobody but themselves and wouldn't give a second thought to endangering women and children if it could help keep some batshit awful thing they did in the past covered up for an extra thirty seconds." He caught Nerevsky's eye and held it. "And that's the God's honest truth."

"I like you better when you lie," replied Nerevsky.

"And I like you better when you're not putting my family in harm's way for reasons I don't know or understand. So, just tell me this, Nerevsky. What's the secret they are trying to make sure doesn't get out? What the fuck happened at Banjawarn Station in 1993?"

Nerevsky sat silent, staring off into the corner of the gymnasium while warm-ups for the next match began. Finally, he turned to Dick.

"Don't you understand? I don't know. I've never known. Don't you remember your mission briefing? That's what you're supposed to tell me."

"Like you wouldn't lie in a mission briefing ... whether for sport or in order to not impact my 'objectivity.' It makes no fucking sense that you don't know. You were *there*. You made up the damn cover story about Aum Shinrikyo testing sarin gas on sheep. You said so yourself.

You can't make up a credible cover story without some clue what the actual facts are. So, I'll ask again. What were you covering up?"

"They didn't tell me. Believe it. Don't believe it. That's of no concern to me. But, that's the truth. You have to understand, this all happened not that long after the fall of the Soviet Union. The KGB was dissolved and the SVR and the GRU were jockeying for position. Everyone was jockeying for position in Russia, including Aum Shinrikyo. The politicians asked me to concoct a cover story, in particular a story which would implicate Aum Shinrikyo. That was relatively easy to do as the sect was in the process of purchasing the gargantuan sheep station nearby. I did what I was told. They seemed satisfied, even if the public still had questions. But they never told me what really happened and when I asked, things began to go quite badly for me."

"What do you mean? How?"

"The details are not important. Just understand there are reasons why, when the Subsidiary was formed after 9-11, I was open to their overtures to head up their Internal Audit function." He let out a long breath. "Nobody ever thinks about anyone else's career path but their own."

"Not good enough," said Dick. "I'm looking at my kid's career path, my wife's goddamn life expectancy. I need more information."

Nerevsky turned away. "I've said too much, much more than I should have already. My troubles in the past are none of your concern. Finding out what happened in Western Australia in 1993 and what may be happening again now *are* your concern. I'll see if there is anything I can do to eliminate or, at least, confuse the Russian opposition you have faced, but I make no promises. You must proceed with haste."

"And, where exactly should I proceed to in haste?" He waved his arm at the court below, where play was about to commence again. "Should I subscribe to *Obscure Sports Daily* and figure out the next bullshit place to meet on your fantasy fan tour and hope it's got some connection to this case? Cause my leads so far have given me nothing but a little electronic woopty-do out woop woop."

Nerevsky sat motionless, as if he hadn't heard Dick at all. The match started. Dick just waited as several points played out, watching Nerevsky's eyes follow the action of the ball or whatever the fuck they called the round thing in this stupid sport. Eventually, his contact spoke.

"The Russians must have been involved in what happened or they wouldn't care so much about covering it up, especially not something which occurred before the fall of the Soviet Union. They excuse many things by saying they occurred in Soviet times, but not this. That means it must be big and it must somehow still be ongoing or have present or future repercussions." He sighed. "I've tried to follow the leads my speculations have conjured up on this for years and come up with nothing. You must follow your thoughts, not mine, if there is any hope the results will differ."

"So that's it? You've got nothing else for me?"

Nerevsky smiled. "I'll send you a subscription to *Obscure Sports Daily* for Christmas. You really should check out Bandy. It's like hockey, but with a ball and an iced field the size of a football pitch with eleven men on each side. Or, maybe Kabaddi, from Bangladesh. It's a tackle version of a combination of the American kids' games of tag and Red Rover, but the person running must hold their breath until they score or are tackled."

Dick left without saying anything else. He was on his own. Sure, he might get more information from Nerevsky at some point. But he wasn't holding his breath, especially not until he scored or was tackled.

Chapter 20

Ace wasn't impressed when she arrived at The Tesla Science Center at Wardenclyffe in Shoreham, New York. The large parking lot next to the dingy, red brick building was nearly empty. And the bright, modern signs touting the exhibits inside and the restorations to come once fundraising was completed struck her as a bit flashy and desperate. Still, the picture of the new statue of Nikola Tesla to come from Serbia, and the plaque indicating the site had been put on the National Register of Historic Places, looked nice—at least fresher than the rest of the place.

She doubted there was anything she could find out here she didn't already know from surfing the internet about Tesla, but you could never tell. That was the whole point of field research. Of course, the whole "mission" was undefined and pointless. But then, her life had been undefined and pointless before she joined the Subsidiary. At least here she was trying to ... to what? ... save the world? No, just doing some drudge work to help her former partner work his way out of a bad spot with someone at work with more sway than he had.

She went inside. For a place that was all about a guy who wanted to light the world with wireless electricity, it was more poorly lit than she expected. It was also clear that plenty of restoration work was still going on inside the structure. She skipped past the photos of kids' entries for the best model of the lab made out of Lego blocks and looked for some substantive signage. After a few moments, an older gentleman with a balding head, a white moustache, and a belly that hung over his belt line like a head of foam trying to escape a glass of cold draft beer, came through a doorway and approached her.

"Walter Riordan," said the man brandishing a yellowed smile and offering a meaty hand to shake. "But you can call me Walt. I'm your guide to all things Tesla here at Wardenclyffe." He looked her up and down, slowing at the usual places, but at least not leering. "What can I tell you that you want to know?"

Well, at least he was direct.

Ace could be direct; in fact, she preferred it. "I'm interested in hearing about Tesla Towers and the various electromagnetic weapons and energy shields Tesla worked on while he was here."

Walt's mouth gaped open. "Really?"

She narrowed her eyes and gave him an icy stare. "Why? Is that a problem?"

"Oh, no ... no ... not at all. It's just that you're not the ... ah ... usual demographic for those interested in supposed death rays and earthquake generators and force shields and all that."

Now it was Ace's turn to say: "Really? What is the demographic for questions about secret weapons?"

"Older, male—" said Walt. He gestured at himself with an open-handed wave with his right hand down the front and side of his body. "Quite frankly, someone who looks a lot like me. Some ex-military, but more often retired guys from skilled blue-collar jobs. Plumbers, electricians, and the like. Factory workers who watch a lot of history shows and documentaries now that they've got too much time on their hands and never learned how to golf."

"You're describing my grandfather exactly," Ace lied. "He doesn't get around so well anymore, so he asked me to stop by and ask a few questions." She tilted her head toward the ceiling for a second. "Too bad they tore down the Tesla Tower so long ago. My grandpa's really interested in them. Guess that's just all ancient history now."

"Certainly, the one that was here is long gone, but there is another one."

"Oh?"

"Down in Milford, Texas. Just built in 2017."

"Whatever for?"

"Supposedly they're doing research on Zenneck Surface Waves."

"What the hell is that?"

Walt smiled condescendingly at her. "Your grandpa will know. It's the scientific mechanism behind wireless transmission of electricity."

"Oh," said Ace. "So, not a weapon, then?"

"Damned if I know." Walt grinned. "Most new inventions, they can have a military component to 'em if you look at 'em hard enough that way."

"And, did people look at Tesla's inventions that way?"

"Well, not Tesla. At least not offensively. Tesla was against war, so the energy devices he was looking into were defensively oriented. He wanted ways to prevent enemy planes from getting close to a city, for instance, by zapping them out of the air. The Japanese supposedly looked into that in their so-called Ku-Go project. Killed a couple rabbits from across a field, but not much else. Didn't work out that they or anyone else could shoot planes down at a distance, but the Brits and others used some of those same ideas as key components in developing radar, which is very effective as a defensive device giving warning of approaching aircraft."

"And the supposed earthquake machine?"

Walt waved a hand dismissively. "There's folks who think the Russians stole the technology. Chit chat on the web about a Tesla scalar howitzer constructed by the Soviets at the Sary Shagan Missile Range in what is now Kazakhstan back in the day ... oh, maybe forty years or so ago. Same kind of story with the remote earthquake generator: the Russians have it and did something with it, but no hard proof."

"Couldn't someone just look at the plans nowadays and tell if they would work? I mean, science has progressed a lot since Tesla's day, hasn't it?"

"Maybe," mused Walt, "but nobody knows for sure what happened to the plans for that device, if they ever existed. The FBI raided his last hotel room, but claim there was nothing of value there. Some cable TV guys got the notion the plans might have been hidden here."

Ace gestured around her. "In this space?"

Walt tilted his head downward. "In tunnels underneath. Tesla supposedly had tunnels underneath Wardenclyffe so his tower could 'grab hold' of the earth to infuse waves of energy. These reality TV sleuths searched for the tunnels with ground penetrating radar and interviewed some old timers who claimed to have explored them years ago, but nothing ever came of it. Just like Geraldo exploring Al Capone's hidden vault."

Ace had no idea what he was talking about, but it didn't seem like it was about Tesla, so she let it slip ... er, slide. "So, were there tunnels? Are there tunnels?"

Walt scratched his chin. "Seems likely there were underground tunnels for wiring or whatnot, but I can't imagine anything still being down there, if anything important ever was."

"Too bad," said Ace. "That would be interesting."

#

A crisp knock, then an underling came into the room.

"Nerevsky's traveled to Perth," he reported, holding out a sheet of paper.

Yuri took the paper and scanned the itinerary. "So smart, yet so dumb. He demonstrates his eagerness with every move. He is cautious enough to send a proxy to do the investigation he has so long dreamed of pursuing, yet he foolishly flies into the country for a personal report."

"So it appears," said his assistant. "What could explain such behavior?"

Yuri swiveled his chair and squinted at the gray light streaming through the cheap Venetian blinds on the office window. He could have a nicer office, but like most of his contemporaries in the SVR, he preferred to divert spare office funds to pay for a better apartment for his mistress. "His power at the Subsidiary is perhaps less than we thought, and his confidence in his own cleverness perhaps greater than it should be. He obviously decided an in-person report was less of a risk than the risk the Subsidiary would intercept any electronic communications. In his paranoia, he fears the risks he best understands—electronic surveillance—and underestimates the risks associated with an adversary which he does not understand at all. As always, we are one step ahead in both instances. Remind me to thank Tsing Tse at the MSS for selling Nerevsky that phone."

"Yes, comrade. Excellent." The minion dipped his head briefly and exited the office.

"Satisfactory," murmured Yuri. "Satisfactory for now."

#

"*Sakra!*" For once, Ace was glad to be an orphan. If she did this kind of thing for a work partner—a *former* partner—what kind of lengths would she go to for family? Maybe Dick had thought this would be a simple expedition. Go to Wardenclyffe and take the tour, chat up the local experts about Tesla's military experiments and equipment and stumble upon some obscure piece of information which would suddenly reveal some insight into the history of a man who had already been studied and revered and belittled and discussed for a century.

Yeah, like that's how investigation works.

Except the big-bellied old man on the tour of the museum at the site of the former laboratory did make an offhand reference to tunnels Tesla had workers dig beneath Wardenclyffe. That deserved a look.

A bit of online research and some poking about at the local library in Shoreham revealed nothing more than speculation and conspiracy theories. But, of course, the historians and speculators who had looked into the possibility of tunnels didn't think like spies. They certainly didn't think about how spies might operate if they needed to do so clandestinely, which, of course, is how any foreign agents interested in Tesla's work back at the time would have had to operate.

Dick had sent her a link to Harry Mason's Bright Skies postings. If he was to be believed, the Russians and Japanese were the most interested parties in any potential experimentation or development of

Tesla's earthquake generator or a force shield capable of dropping planes from the sky and keeping an invader out of territory protected by a shimmering dome. Russian or Japanese spies would have had a keen interest in accessing the Wardenclyffe Tower tunnels during or after the laboratory's operations.

Ace left the library and located the local tax assessor's office. After studying some plat maps for an aerial view of the region, with markings setting forth the real estate parcel numbers for the assortment of residential properties abutting the edge of Wardenclyffe's property (historically broader than the museum's current property), Ace had a long list of property parcels to look into. Hours of tedious cross-checking later gave her what she needed just before the office closed for the day: a nearby property which had been owned by someone with a Russian surname and later sold to a Japanese corporation after World War II.

Which is how she found herself in the dark of night breaking into the basement of a poorly-maintained bungalow in Shoreham, New York. Once she wriggled inside the pitch black cellar, she used both surgically-gloved hands to feel along the cement wall on the side of the room nearest Wardenclyffe. Her nimble hands slid quickly over the smooth, cool surface, until one finger caught the edge of a shallow groove. She repositioned herself and focused her tactile exploration on that groove, confirming a section of bricks in a broad area with a curved top, undoubtedly blocking off a room or exit or tunnel which breached the foundation of the old house.

She imagined Dick would have grabbed a hunk of C-4 from his backpack and blown up the brick wall, continuing into the black maw it revealed even before the dust settled.

Ace was a bit smarter than that.

First things first.

The air was stale, but not musty. The place was probably used, just not that often. She left the site of the wall and, flicking on a mini-flashlight, located the stairs up to the house, ascending with slow, sure movements. After listening at the top of the stairs and testing the door handle, she turned off her light and opened the door and stepped through. All was dark and quiet in the living room. The kitchen was neat in the soft shimmer of a nightlight. A faint smell of pizza lingered in the air.

She snuck down the hall and peered in the doorways on either side. In the first, the screen of a desktop PC glowed along with a nightlight in what looked to be a home office. In the second, an overweight, balding man in a t-shirt and boxer shorts sprawled on his stomach, snoring atop the covers on a double bed, yet another dim nightlight in a wall outlet giving enough light she clicked off her beam. She moved quickly and quietly to the far side of the bed, nearest his face. Reaching into her pocket, she removed what appeared from its label to be a canister of pepper spray, clicked the nozzle counterclockwise, pointed it at the sleeping man and, keeping it at arm's distance, pressed down on the nozzle. A translucent fog emanated from the tip of the nozzle, engulfing the man's nose and mouth just as he inhaled for his next rumbling snort. The cloud of fog stopped expanding as it was sucked into the subject's prodigious, quivering nose.

Ace froze in place, ready to spray again if needed, until two, three, then four breaths passed. The already relaxed features of the man seemed to soften further in the dim light, and his snore became looser before disappearing entirely. Now, he wasn't just asleep, he was out and would remain out for at least eight hours.

She hoped he didn't have an early appointment the next morning.

Once she was certain there was no one else in the house to hear her, she went back downstairs, wrapped a dish towel around a short-handled sledge hammer she found on the tool bench and assaulted the brick wall. It wasn't long before there was a hole big enough for her lithe, wiry body to slip through. There was no reason to make the hole bigger—that would just mean more repair work when she returned.

Once in the tunnel, she took her flashlight in hand and made her way along the straight and narrow confines stretching before her. The tunnel was merely packed earth at first, but after about fifty feet broke through the terminus of a better constructed tunnel. This tunnel was walled in brick, forming an archway about a foot above her head in the center. Metal pipes and cables were affixed about two feet off the floor on both sides before exiting into the ceiling where the walled tunnel ended.

She made good time, counting her paces and running the necessary arithmetic to know she was closing in on where the bulbous-headed, one-hundred-ninety-seven-foot-tall Tesla Tower had originally stood behind the laboratory. Eventually, the tunnel ended short of that location in a pile of fallen bricks and packed and collapsed earth.

No secret stash of papers. No electrical equipment. No corpses of guards or assassins. No schematics of a death ray or an earthquake generator or a force field generator or anything like that. Of course not; things like that only happened in the movies.

But what she had found was enough. Confirmation, at least in her mind, that the Russians and probably the Japanese had been monitoring what was going on at Wardenclyffe decades upon decades before she was born and had gotten access to whatever might have been in the tunnels before or after Tesla died.

Kurva! Maybe Harry Mason had been onto something.

Do prdele! Maybe Dick Thornby was onto something.

Knowing Dick, how long would it be before something big blew up?

She was just turning to trudge back to her exit when a flicker of movement near the bottom of the rubble pile blocking the tunnel caught her eye. She turned back and bent down, bringing the flashlight to bear with her right hand. As the shadows shifted with the change of direction in the source of light, she again caught a glimpse of something white against the blackness in what appeared to be a gap or hole in the loose dirt at the bottom of the debris pile. She reached toward the hole with her left hand as she centered the soft-edged gap in the rocks and dirt with the beam from her flashlight. Just as she got her hand to the edge of the hole, she heard a hiss and the white against black shifted again, this time more rapidly.

What the fuck? Her mind raced, trying to figure out if there were any venomous snakes in New York. She didn't know, but instinctively froze in place, her arm outstretched, her hand halfway in the entrance to something's lair.

Suddenly, something wet splashed against her hand and arm as an overpowering stench assaulted her.

Sakra!

The stink and her instinct drove her away from the source of the scent, her eyes watering, her lungs constricting, as if a tear gas canister had popped off in the enclosed space. What kind of beast was this? There was nothing in the Czech Republic, nothing she knew of in all of Europe, which could spray such a foul, burning liquid to defend its turf.

She ran without real thought, but the path was clear and there were no spurs or intersections to navigate or slow her flight. After a minute or two, she realized there was no sense to her rush. Whatever had attacked her was far behind and not pursuing her. The still shockingly powerful smell assaulting her nose and eyes was from the oily residue on her hand and arm.

Then it came to her. A skunk. It must have been a skunk. The stench it sprayed wasn't what she imagined from the cartoons she'd watched at the orphanage.

She slowed to a fast-paced trudge, retracing her steps to the hole where the tunnel from the suburban basement accessed the subterranean passage. A minute later she was back in the basement and at a utility sink near the washer and dryer, doing her best to scrub the stinky, oily residue off her arm with running water and a squeeze bottle of bargain dishwashing detergent.

She'd originally planned to replace the brick, so as to cover her break-in from immediate discover, but the "tidy up" plan was no longer viable. The entire basement reeked. She needed to get out before the potent chemical weapon of the black and white beast woke the lightly drugged occupant upstairs. The most she could do was hope the sink would dry out before anyone investigated and the tumult of bricks would be mistaken for a natural collapse, perhaps due to the foul-smelling beast trying to get inside the basement.

She left, disgusted by her own smell. She dared not stop until she was back home, cursing up a storm as she brought her malodorous self into her apartment and soaked in a tub filled with suds and a dollop of chlorine bleach.

Sometimes being a good partner stunk. Being a good partner to Dick Thornby stunk like the chemical plant in Kralupy-nad-Vltavou outside of Prague after it exploded.

Kurva!

Chapter 21

Dee's intercom buzzed. She put down the report she'd been reading on the latest tactics of cybercriminals and pressed the reply button. "Who?"

Her assistant replied. "Anatoly Kremarsky."

What could he want? "Remind him the next meeting of the International Oversight Board is the day after tomorrow and I can chat with him then, or beforehand, if need be."

"He said it's not about Board business and that it's urgent."

"Very well. Tell Glenn to step in and listen." Dee took her hand off the reply button and picked up the receiver for the desk-set phone, clicking the flashing button to take the call.

"*Zdravstvujte!*" said Dee by way of greeting with all the faux enthusiasm she could muster.

"*Zdravstvujte!*" came the reply, but with a thick Russian accent and very little enthusiasm. "I'm afraid this contact is not social."

"None of my contacts here are, Anatoly. What seems to be the problem?"

"My government has asked me to lodge a protest with you concerning a current operation."

"I see." Dee slowly let out her breath and arched an eyebrow as Glenn Swynton entered her office and stood by the door. She pressed the button to put the call on speaker. "That sounds quite serious. If you could just give me the designation of the mission you are protesting, I'll call it up on my screen so I have the operational details and most recent reports while we chat."

"There is no mission designation."

"Ahh, you didn't bother to look up the designation before calling," Dee scolded. "Location? Agent? Objective? I can ask one of my people to do a cross-search while you brief me."

"There is no point to these administrative questions," snapped Anatoly. "The mission is not official. It has no designation."

She caught Glenn's eye. He replied with a knowing nod. Nerevsky and Thornby, no doubt. She wasn't, however, about to admit that to Anatoly Kremarsky.

"I don't know whatever you mean, Anatoly. I run a tight shop here. You know that. I'm not off gadding about on personal vendettas and implementing secret agendas."

"That may ... or may not ... be, Dee. But my sources tell me you have someone running amok."

"Running amok?" She replied with mock indignation. "I didn't even realize it was the season for Pon Farr."

"For what?"

Dee smiled. It had been a long, long time since she watched television—especially old re-runs—with any regularity, but there was nothing like a dated pop-culture reference to confuse foreign emissaries.

Glenn nodded knowingly as Dee continued the conversation. "Never mind, Anatoly. A minor witticism for which it appears you have neither the cultural background nor the patience."

"You need to take this seriously, Director Tammany."

"My apologies, Anatoly. I will take this very seriously once you actually tell me what you want. I can't stop, start, or investigate anything until I know what the problem is."

"I think you know what I'm referring to. I'm ... I'm not at liberty to say more."

She felt like tweaking him with Patrick Henry's "Give me liberty or give me death!" quote, but she knew better than to prod a Russian bear too much. "Then I'm not sure what I can do about an alleged mission in an unknown location with an unknown objective."

She paused, but the line remained silent. She decided to throw her counterpart a bone.

"Perhaps I should ask our Internal Audit Division to look into whether someone is conducting unsanctioned activities."

"NO! Er, I mean ... no, I don't think that would be productive ... uh ... until I can get you more definitive information. But rest assured I will. And, if I find out with certainty you or your personnel are running off-the-books operations targeting Russian interests, there will be consequences. Serious consequences."

The line clicked, but Dee made certain to kill the line on her end before saying anything. Once the light went off on the phone, she again arched an eyebrow at Glenn.

"Did you hear that? *Serious* consequences."

Glenn walked over to her desk. "Are there any other kind?"

"They obviously know Nerevsky's up to something, but don't want to admit how they know that or exactly what it is he's up to and why that upsets them."

"Undoubtedly."

"Of course, we also know Nerevsky's up to *something*. But we can't admit that, and I *don't* know exactly what he's up to and why that would upset them."

"Precisely."

"No," said Dee. "Nothing about this situation is precise in any way."

#

"That's pretty vague and speculative," said Dick. Once again, he and Ace were connecting via Shangrilyfe.

"*Zavři hubu!* What the hell do you expect? That with no resources or backup, I'm going to be able to solve in only a couple of days the question of whether there really was something to the conspiracy theories about Tesla having some kind of secret earthquake weapon? And just by visiting a damn museum? You need to temper your expectations with a little reality, big guy."

Dick tried to gather his thoughts into some kind of apology, but Ace didn't wait long enough for him to even get an "I'm sorry" out.

"Look, Dick, my logic about the tunnel being evidence of Russian spying may be speculative, but it is sound. And the Japanese connection when the house was sold firms the pudding even more. The whole situation smells almost as much as—"

"I'll pay to clean your clothes."

"To je pěkná pičovina!"

Dick sighed. "I don't know what that means."

"That means 'That's some nice bullshit!' I stripped off my clothes and dumped them in the trash before I went into my apartment."

Dick suspected she meant that literally.

"You can, however, pay for steam cleaning the upholstery in my fucking car."

"Sure, sure. No problem."

"Look, I can't say there's a smoking gun about the Tesla thing, but there is enough to give some credence to the speculation in Harry Mason's postings saying the Russians and the Japanese may have been experimenting with Tesla devices back then. And, if those experiments created whatever the hell happened in Australia back in the day, it sure seems like there's enough credibility to the existence of the machinery to mean they'd still be pushing the boundaries as to what the device can do today ... and keeping the whole thing a secret."

Dick took a deep breath, then slowly exhaled. "Yeah, that makes sense. That also means the whole great circle theory connecting the Exmouth facility to an outpost in Antarctica to locations in Japan and Russia and Maine bears some looking into, too."

"Probably, but I don't see any way for you to find some cover which would allow you to saunter into the Amundsen-Scott base in the middle of winter in the Southern Hemisphere. And trying a HALO drop so you could try to infiltrate a place like that in the dark and the cold would be the stupidest thing you've ever done. And that's saying a lot."

"Actually, I've been looking at the maps and reading up on the various Antarctic bases. I think the Russian bases at Mirny and Vostok line up just as well and are more likely. Hell, Mirny supposedly does seismological work."

"Doesn't matter what base you pick. This time of year, your dick would break off if you tried to take a leak outside. And before you suggest I wouldn't have that problem, let me remind you I don't have your layer of insulating fat."

"Honey-dipped bacon does have some advantages."

"Look, I can take a road trip to Maine if you want, but I'll need some time to arrange to do so without the powers-that-be knowing I'm up to something."

"Yeah. And I don't want to take advantage ... at least, not yet. Exmouth is nearby—"

"It is?"

"Okay, twelve hundred kilometers away. That's nearby by Australian standards. Let me check out things there, first. If I need you to go to Maine, I'll let you know. In the meantime, get your car detailed and send me the bill."

"Already done. Cost me two hundred dollars. Two nineteen with tax. *Sakra!* You pay a lot of sales tax here."

"It's the land of the free, not the land where everything is free."

"Zavři hubu! To je pěkná pičovina!"

"Yeah. Well, I owe you."

"I know. We just talked about that. Two nineteen. Remember?"

Chapter 22

Dick checked a few more websites, then turned off the laptop and left the hotel room. He found Melanie and Seth having a light meal at a table near the windows at the hotel's Atrium restaurant.

"Relax and enjoy the day. We check out in the morning."

"Home?" asked Melanie. Dick didn't think she was hinting; she just didn't know what came next.

"Nah. You never go home until the ... task ... is finished. Headed up to Exmouth, way up north on the coast."

Melanie took the news in stride. "What's up there?"

"According to the tourist website, it's the gateway to the Ningaloo Reef. Dolphins, turtles, manta rays, a lot of whale sharks, and, this time of year, humpback whales. Great snorkeling and the clearest turquoise water anywhere in the world."

A slight crease appeared on Melanie's forehead. "I thought you said we were staying out of the ocean."

Dick smiled. "Yeah, sure. They have glass-bottom boat tours for those who don't want to get wet."

Seth turned to his mom. "I'm sure the organized snorkel tours are safe and well-managed. It's not like they're going to just leave when the time is up without checking to see if everyone is aboard." Seth shifted his eyes to Dick and gave him a wink. "Not like you'd get abandoned in *open water* or anything."

Dick caught the reference, but didn't wink back. The last thing Melanie needed to know was that the *Open Water* shark movie was based on an actual incident which occurred in Australia. Sometimes it's better for a mother not to know of all the possible dangers of the real world—hell, the entire *raison dêtre* of the Subsidiary was to discern threats to the smooth functioning of the world and eliminate them before the public ever realized they existed.

Melanie apparently missed the subtext altogether. "Somehow I don't think you're headed up to Exmouth for the whale sharks."

Dick had to be careful—talking in a public place was not nearly as safe as most people thought. Parabolic microphones, listening devices, and even lipreaders all were well-used in Dick's line of work. He maintained his cover. "Some pretty interesting UFO sightings up that way." He reached over and took a few french fries off of Melanie's plate. "Some people think they're attracted by the ultra-low frequency antennae and transmission system. It's used to communicate with submarines when they're still deep underwater. Only the long wave lengths of ultra-low frequencies can penetrate deep into the ocean."

"Oh, yeah," said Seth. "I think I saw something about it on TV once. It's this huge pentagram or something. You can see it from space!"

Melanie did not seem to share Seth's excitement. "How far away is this place?"

Dick tilted his head as he ran the numbers through his brain. "About seven hundred fifty miles."

"That's a long drive," replied Melanie.

"Too long," agreed Dick. "Even the tourist board admits it's a two-day haul from here."

Melanie sighed. "I'll pick up a book to read from the gift shop this afternoon."

"Sure, but I've already checked into flights." He lowered his voice. "Lots of lonely stretches of road. Don't want any more car trouble on this vacation. Off-season, so planes aren't very full. We'll pick which flight we want to take at the last minute." It wouldn't hurt making the gun-toting yahoos on their tail scramble to keep up with them and leave their weapons behind if they wanted to keep Dick and his family in sight.

There was just one more thing he needed to do before he left Perth.

#

The suburban house was small by American standards, but well-kept. The flowerbed was bright and weed-free. He glanced at his watch and then over at the driveway leading to the two-car garage. A bright blue compact SUV was parked in front of the double door. No surprise, it wasn't yet sunset, but late enough that the occupants, Mr. and Mrs. Calloway, would likely be home from work or errands, relaxing at the end of their day.

He took a deep breath and walked up the sidewalk to the front door.

This was going to be hard, but he had to do it. He'd promised himself he would as soon as he'd found out he was headed to Perth.

A shiny brass knocker gleamed in the low sunlight. Dick lifted it and rapped once. Then stood in a relaxed, parade rest stance, waiting for someone to answer. It wasn't long before a wiry man in a short-sleeved, plaid, button-down shirt and khakis opened the door part way. He was about Dick's age, more or less.

"I'm sorry, but we don't encourage solicitors," said the man, his manner polite, but firm.

"That's fine, Mr. Calloway," Dick pronounced the name Aussie style, with a long i sound at the end, rather than a long a sound, the way Luke had always done. "I'm Richard Thornby, sir, from Catalyst Crisis Consulting. I ... uh ..." Damn, this was harder than he'd thought it would be. "I ... well, I worked with your son."

The man's head swiveled away from the door. "Katherine. There's a man here who worked with Luke." He turned back to Dick and opened the door wider, then spoke in a quiet, urgent voice. "It's been so long. Have they found the body?"

Jesus. He should have anticipated that question. When a Subsidiary operative dies in a secret underground facility which is rendered impassable due to lingering radiation, it's impossible to recover the body, so a cover story had to be invented. Of course, they'd ask about it. "No, no," said Dick. "I'm just vacationing in town with my family and wanted to drop by and pay my respects."

He'd felt guilty about Luke's death. Both the fact of it and the manner of it. Perhaps it was a mistake to have come by ... a selfish mistake. He never intended to bring back their pain. But he was committed now. He'd do what he'd come to do, what his conscience told him had to be done.

Mr. Calloway ... Mark as he insisted being called ... led him into the living room. A tall thin woman, her blond hair graying around the temples, came in from the kitchen, her eyes already moist. "You worked regularly with Luke?" she asked, then bit her lower lip as she sat on the couch. Her husband joined her, leaving Dick the easy chair across the coffee table from the two of them.

"This is Katherine, my wife," said Mark. "Luke's mother," he added unnecessarily.

Dick dipped his head in greeting as he sat down and answered Katherine's question. "Not regularly, but on one big project ... uh ... near the end."

Katherine folded her hands together, probably, Dick guessed, to keep them from shaking. Mark put his arm around her shoulders. She took a deep breath. "Were you with him at the end?"

Yes. Damn it, Dick had been with him at the end, but he wasn't sure what to say.

"On the boat," Mark added. "Such a surprise. He was always a strong swimmer. Made the swim team at university in Melbourne."

Of course, the Subsidiary had to have a reason why Luke's body had never been recovered. Dick remembered the cover story now. An outing with a few people from work, sailing. Luke had dived into the cold Atlantic Ocean and never surfaced. The working theory of the Coast Guard was the shock of the cold water had caused a massive heart attack, causing him to expel his air and sink into the depths without surfacing.

"I was there," Dick said, staying as close to the truth as he dared. "But I didn't see him die."

"Were you the one piloting the boat?" asked Katherine.

Dick shook his head. "We were both in the same boat, but I sure wasn't the one driving it." Deep down, Dick knew Luke's death wasn't his fault, but that didn't stop the guilt. "I ... I just wanted to tell you something you already know, but needs to be said. Your son was smart and clever and hard-working and, well, just about as good a guy as could be. Certainly, as good as I have ever known. And he helped more people in his job and his life than you realize."

An hour later, Dick was back in the rental car. He drove a few blocks away and pulled over. He parked and let the tears he'd been holding back flow. Twenty minutes later, he headed back to his family and to his mission.

He'd done what he came here to do, for Luke's parents, and for himself.

Chapter 23

Seth was right. The communications array at North West Cape near Exmouth was fucking huge. Although the commercial flight into the Exmouth Aerodrome south of town was a fair distance from the facility north of town, Dick couldn't help but see the sharply geometric hexagonal shape of the tall antennae array at the tip of the peninsula as the plane banked slightly to line up for its landing. The tall antennae of Area A, as it was called, was a mere four miles from the buildings of the main base, which was called the Naval Communication Station, Harold E. Holt, or "NCSHEH" in military jargon. What was harder to see, but Dick knew was there from his perusal of satellite maps courtesy of Google Earth, was a similar hexagonal-shaped facility thirty-some miles south of the taller, flashier array. Known as Area B, it was the receiver which corresponded to the better-known transmission capabilities of the station.

The plane landed, and before long Dick had rented another oversized, dark-colored vehicle and booked them into the finest local accommodations Exmouth had to offer. While Melanie unpacked, Dick fired up the laptop and started pecking at the keyboard.

"Here," said Seth, nudging Dick on the shoulder. "Let me do the data entry. My keyboard skills are faster than yours."

Dick acquiesced, sliding out of the straight-backed desk chair and relinquishing it to Seth while he paced behind.

"What else do we know about the facility at Exmouth?"

Seth's fingers skittered across the keyboard. A Wikipedia page flashed onto the screen. "Started out as a U.S. base in the sixties. Increasing resistance from the locals starting in the seventies through to the nineties, mostly protests about having a U.S.-run base on Australian soil. Slowly transitioned to a jointly-run base, with most U.S. Navy personnel leaving in 1993. The Space Surveillance Telescope was just recently transitioned from White Sands Missile Base in New Mexico to Exmouth."

"That's good. Any self-respecting UFO fanatic would find the Space Surveillance Telescope interesting stuff." He stopped pacing and looked at Seth. "Anything else like that?"

Seth scrolled down the page. "In 2008, two Qantas flights had to make emergency landings after a series of automatic pitch down maneuvers in commercial craft traveling nearby." Seth clicked to a new page. "Twelve people had serious injuries, including fractures, lacerations, and spinal injuries, with another hundred and seven with minor injuries."

Seth clicked again and again, pages flashing by too quickly for Dick to focus on them, much less gain any useful information. "Some people think the signals from the Exmouth transmitter interfered with the automatic guidance system."

"That's good, that's good," muttered Dick as he paced again, but then noticed Melanie's eyebrows raised in alarm. "I mean, that could be useful for our ... my ... purposes."

Seth was still surfing the net. "No big surprise. There have been UFO sightings that people associate with the Exmouth facility."

"That's really useful," said Dick. "Given my cover, that gives me a plausible explanation for being on the grounds of the facility if I'm caught."

"Excuse me?" said Melanie in what Seth always called her mom voice. "Are you saying you're about to break into a secure military installation in a foreign country?"

Dick stopped pacing and stepped over to Melanie, putting what he hoped was a comforting hand on her shoulder. "It is the kind of thing I do in my job, but don't worry. I'm very good at what I do."

"You'll have to be more than good," said Melanie. "Did you notice the countryside when we were landing? It's practically all open ground. There's no place to hide. The guards will see you for sure."

Dick knew she was right, but he didn't want to admit it when he knew he had to go forward anyway. Suddenly, a thought hit him. He smiled and said, "Not if they're looking someplace else."

He turned to his son. "Seth, can you post things on social media without anyone knowing it's you?"

"People do it all the time."

"I didn't ask if it could be done. I asked if you could do it."

"Sure, I guess. It's not that hard."

"Don't guess. Be sure. I don't want superficial anonymity. I want the kind of phantom posting which can stand up to some scrutiny, but still remain anonymous." Another thought popped into his mind and he snapped his fingers. "Even better. If it is looked at hard by someone with reasonable skill, can you make it look like it came from a Russian bot or trolling firm?"

"Yeah. Back when Brian and I were on Reality 2 Be..." Seth's face reddened and his words faltered. Dick guessed it was because while both Seth and Melanie knew Dick was a spy, Seth likely wasn't sure how much his mother knew about his clandestine activities on Reality 2 Be before the fire which had injured him so severely.

Dick came to the rescue. "Your mom knows everything." It was a lie, but he'd deal with Melanie later.

"Okay. That's good ... good to know." Seth took a breath. "So, Brian was pretty into the whole anonymization thing. You know, phantom servers, bouncing the signal around the world. Encryption. That kind of stuff. I can do what you want. Faster, though, if I can get his help."

"Get his help," said Dick.

"He owes you," added Melanie. "You saved his life."

Seth reddened again. "I did my part, but Dad, Dad saved us both."

Dick shook his head. "If not for me, you wouldn't have needed saving." He knew Seth thought that his own clandestine activities on Reality 2 Be had been the sole cause of the fire. Maybe he was right. But Dick had never really believed it. He thought Pao Fen Smythe was the puppet-master for all that had happened. That was why Dick had gone to Jurong Bird Sanctuary in Singapore to settle the score. But Seth didn't know that. Dick would rather live with his own guilt, than live with any condemnation that might come from his family if they knew the truth.

In some ways, Dick was a coward.

Just a coward with a strong sense of duty.

He smiled at Seth. "Here's what I need you and Brian to do."

#

Dick had hoped to act as soon as he got to Exmouth, before anyone could possibly have tailed his family here, but an operation like this required substantial planning. If he'd been alone, he might have just winged it, but his family was in the crosshairs, too. He wanted ... no, he *needed* ... to minimize risk and give them some cover in case everything went wrong. After all, this was a quasi-military operation. There were always SNAFUs. Things always went wrong ... or "arse up" as the Aussies liked to say. Of course, the Brits used "tits up" to mean the same damn thing, which made for some convoluted anatomy.

In the meantime, he'd familiarized himself with the Exmouth installations as best he could, both Area A and Area B. His main focus was on Area B, but Area A got a lot more attention on the internet. The fact that the antennae of Area A were not only arrayed in a star-pattern easy to associate with witchcraft was a draw. And since the center tower was, for a long time, the tallest structure in the Southern Hemisphere, it got more than a few looks. Of course, the close to four hundred kilometers of copper wiring in a huge mat underground beneath the towers pulled in lots of attention from the Tesla fanatics and conspiracy freaks of all sorts. The fact that Harold Holt, the Australian Prime Minister after whom the base was named, disappeared mysteriously in a swimming incident three months after the facility was commissioned, made things even more interesting from a conspiracy theory perspective.

During his research, Dick also learned for the first time that a group of Australian demonstrators had occupied the base briefly in 1974. A few people were arrested and a couple songs were written about it, including *Omega Doodle*. Dick had no doubt it was a dandy. But the historical tidbit did give him an idea of a few more organizations Seth and Brian might add to their surreptitious contact list.

The day after tomorrow was Saturday. That would be when his plan came together. More importantly, Saturday night was the night. The new moon had already come and gone, but it looked to be overcast—as dark as he could hope for under the circumstances. He prayed it would be dark enough and that, if it wasn't, his cover would hold.

#

The nice thing about Brian being on the other side of the world was that once they'd set up their anonymous identities for posting to Facebook, Twitter, Instagram, Tik-Tok, and all of the smaller, but up and coming, social media platforms, at least one of the two of them were awake at all times to keep the flow of misinformation going. For something to go viral on social media, you couldn't just post it and forget it, you needed to keep posting, then sharing, retweeting, liking, tweaking, modifying, commenting, mocking, and generally stirring the pot. You needed constant views and attention. Friendly was fine, but controversial was even better. To accomplish that, they used additional fake accounts to post angry comments about their own stories and pics, hoping to fan the flames and get more attention. And they tailored several different approaches to appeal to different groups: UFO enthusiasts; Tesla fans; conspiracy buffs; Australian nationalists; environmental purists; anarchists; anti-military peaceniks, and the save-the-whales crowd. Time was short; they needed all the bodies and attention they could get.

Chapter 24

The unmistakable thud of a small explosion nearby woke Ace from a deep sleep. Instincts kicking in even before she opened her sleep-filled eyes, she rolled off her bed away from the window, snatching up the Glock 26 she kept under the extra pillow reserved for guests. She pointed the Glock at the open bedroom door as she opened her eyes to ... well ... nothing out of place. The dim early morning light permeating her olive-green curtains revealed nothing but the spartan, if a bit messy, surroundings of her apartment ... of her life.

A wavering of the light outside caught her attention and she used her free hand to vault over the double bed and land softly on the beige shag carpeting next to the window. She positioned herself along the wall and peeked through the crack at an oblique angle without giving her position away by touching the drapes, like pretend spies and amateur actors playing cops always did on American TV.

Ježiši! Her car was engulfed in red and orange flames, oily black smoke roiling into the bright blue sky. Two neighbors already stood in the condo complex's parking lot watching the conflagration. More stood on the pathetically narrow balconies outside the living room of their pathetically small pieces of the American dream. No one seemed excited or particularly concerned about the firebombing; certainly no one seemed out of place.

A distant siren confirmed somebody had already dialed 911.

Ace pulled on a T-shirt and slipped into a pair of sitting-around-the-condo shorts and ambled out to the combo living-room/kitchen, then out the front door and down a flight of stairs to the parking lot.

Mornings not being a high crime time period for suburban New Jersey, a police car with a pair of local peace officers was rolling up, with a large, noisy, fire truck right behind it. An ambulance followed, then pulled over away from the activity, waiting for potential customers, no doubt.

The fire crew was efficient, but there was no hope there would be anything salvageable of her vehicle. As she was watching the firemen work, she noticed a folded piece of white paper on the ground next to the door she'd come out. Before reaching down, she looked around without swiveling her head to see if anyone was watching her. Unfortunately, the local law enforcement yokels had stopped staring about the area with stupid expressions on their faces and zeroed in on her. She just left the paper alone and, instead, made eye contact with the approaching cops. She immediately dubbed the older, more intelligent-looking one "Dutiful" and his younger, more dimwitted-looking companion "Clueless."

"That your vehicle?" asked Dutiful as he tilted his head toward the smoking hunk of metal now hissing out billowy clouds of white steam.

"What's left of it," replied Ace.

Clueless squinted his eyes at her. "Pardon me, but you don't seem that upset." Clueless had a thick Jersey accent, but with clear enunciation.

Ace also noted a tinge of accusation in his voice, but she knew better than to ramp up his testosterone by making a snide remark. Instead, she simply shrugged and waved a hand at her torso. "Woke me up. Haven't had my coffee. I'll get more pissed once I'm awake and dealing with my insurance agent."

"Name?" asked Dutiful as he took out a notepad.

"Acacia Zyreb."

"Employer?"

"Catalyst Crisis Consulting. They're in Philly. It's a consulting firm with offices all over the world. We do work for big companies that ... well ... need advice on how to get bigger, mostly."

"Occupation?"

"Abstracter."

Clueless interrupted. "That mean you paint rectangles and blotches for your company's offices?"

"No. It means I read documents and summarize them for the consultants and analysts, so they can be more efficient in finding the information they need to give advice."

"Any idea why someone would torch your car?" asked Dutiful.

Ace spread open her hands. "It's summertime in America. I assume some local team won or lost a game of some sort last night. People celebrate with violence. Drunk people especially."

"Uh-huh," said Dutiful.

"Any reason why these drunks would target your car?"

Ace made a point of rolling her eyes in an exaggerated fashion. "Who the fuck knows what motivates drunk yahoos to do anything but shovel Cheetos in their mouths, washed down by cheap beer?" She flashed an insincere grin. "Maybe they wanted me to come outside in the cool air without a bra on."

Clueless's stare immediately dropped to tit level. Dutiful proved the experience of his extra years on the job by looking elsewhere. Unfortunately, since his eyes had been dropping to chest height, he covered by quickly looking all the way down to the stoop.

He bent down and picked up the piece of paper. "What's this?"

He opened it so they could all see it. In block letters, it read: "STOP ASKING QUESTIONS OR NEXT TIME TOPSY WON'T BE THE ONE FRIED."

Clueless pulled his gaze away from the note and her tits, looking her straight in the eyes. "Who the hell is Topsy?"

Ace didn't need to act. "I have no idea."

"Sure, sure. Like you don't know," said Clueless.

Dutiful also looked up from the note. "Is Topsy what you call your car?"

Ace started. "People name their cars?"

Clueless gave her a slit-eyed look and straightened his posture, she guessed so he could look more intimidating without actually doing body-builder poses. "A lot of people in America do." He tilted his head and looked her up and down. "I'm noting a slight accent. You from overseas? You come from some place far away?"

She gave Clueless a slit-eyed look back. "What you noticed was a lack of a local accent. You from this town? You ever been some place far away?"

Dutiful intervened. "Just answer the question, please, ma'am."

Ace bristled, but complied. "I'm from the Czech Republic."

"Czechoslovakia?" asked Clueless.

She gave him the stare the nuns used to give her when she said something stupid. "Is Brooklyn the same as New York City?"

"Nah. It's just part of it."

"Bingo. Except, you know, history."

Clueless flushed red, but Dutiful de-escalated the encounter. "I think we have the basics. A detective will contact you for a full report in the next day or two." He pointed at the wet, scorched remains of her car. "You might want to take a few pictures for your insurance company before the tow truck comes to haul the burned-out husk away. It can speed up the process."

"Thank you, officer," Ace said.

Dutiful touched the brim of his hat, then elbowed Clueless, who was steaming as much as her car. Then they both turned and left ... with the note, of course.

#

Yuri Lemarov used all of his patience not to tap his foot while his underling got around to reporting.

"Car torched. Message successfully delivered. No witnesses."

"Sounds adequate. I'm more impressed we found out about her snooping than I am that we can set a car on fire in suburban New Jersey."

"I told you it was worthwhile to keep tabs on Wardenclyffe."

"Indeed, you did," said Yuri. "But I don't recall authorizing any budget for surveillance, and I didn't know we had a source inside the museum."

"Uh, you didn't and we don't," agreed the underling with more enthusiasm than Yuri thought necessary.

"Then, how?"

"Kind of hard to miss the news story," replied the man. He held out his phone, on which there was a story titled: *Skunk Spray Blows Down Basement Wall in Shoreham.*

"Ahh, the internet is a wonderful thing, sometimes."

"After that, it was just basic follow-up. It didn't take much work to figure out a woman who works for Catalyst Crisis Consulting was snooping around town the same day."

"Perfect. Just the kind of interaction that suits our purposes."

#

Once the smoke had cleared and the Centerpoint Condo Complex had gone back to its dreary normal, Ace checked in with Dick via ShangriLyfe.

"A thousand," she said by way of greeting.

"A thousand what?"

"That two nineteen you owe me is now a thousand—actually one thousand two-hundred and nineteen."

"Jesus! Your car detailing place is stealing you blind. I hope for that price they got the skunk smell out completely."

"Doesn't smell like skunk at all anymore. Now it smells like firebombed metal and plastic, with a side of gasoline."

"What?"

Ace explained the morning's events. Dick remained quiet throughout, until she got to the part about what the note said.

"Do you call your car Topsy?"

"*Ježiši!* Do people here really name their cars? It's just a hunk of metal; it's not your identity."

"For some people, it is. Or, you know, it's a term of endearment for someone ... or something ... you spend a lot of time with."

"Ahh. That explains it. I had heard guys in America liked to name their penises ... probably for the same reason."

"Yeah ... uh ... no ... uh ... I wouldn't know," Dick stammered.

"Don't worry, big guy," Ace replied. "I know you didn't name your penis." She paused for a beat. "Obviously, it named you, *Dick*."

"Ha, ha. Hilarious," snarled Dick. "Can we get back to the note?"

"I don't know a Topsy," replied Ace. "Certainly don't know one which has anything to do with Tesla or this case ... whatever it is."

Dick snapped his fingers. "But I do. Topsy is the elephant that Thomas Edison electrocuted."

"Thomas Edison electrocuted an elephant?"

"He did. He was trying to prove alternating current was dangerous during the current wars with Tesla. You know AC versus DC."

"I do, but you probably shouldn't talk that way if your wife might come into the room."

Dick sighed. "I have to teach you the most basic idioms, yet that one you know."

"Didn't you get the memo? The youth of the world are inordinately fascinated with sex, drugs, and rock 'n roll." Ace's fingers skittered over her keyboard. "Actually, it seems like you're the one who doesn't know the real facts about AC/DC. According to Wikipedia, that slur on Edison is a myth. Topsy's electrocution occurred ten years after the current wars and Edison wasn't even there."

"Doesn't matter. Whoever torched your car and left the note obviously wanted to reference Tesla in an obscure way so you'd get the point without anyone else being the wiser."

"Okay, but how would they know I was helping you?" Ace furrowed her brow in thought before answering her own question. "You think there's a spy at the Subsidiary?"

Dick laughed. "There's nothing but spies at the Subsidiary, but this doesn't sound like Nerevsky or Swynton or Tammany. This smacks of the Russians. They must be keeping a *very* close eye on Wardenclyffe."

"But why?" asked Ace. "There's nothing there."

"Not that we know of. Maybe that's the point."

"I could check out the tower in Texas."

"Nah," said Dick. "Manpower is limited and I've decided I'd rather have you check out the facility in Cutler, Maine, after all."

"Makes sense," said Ace, her voice dripping with sarcasm. "Have the Eastern European infiltrate a base in the United States and the American 'Hero of Lake Michigan' sneak into a base on foreign soil."

"Yeah, well, I'm already here. Besides, I don't need you to infiltrate Cutler, just monitor its transmissions from someplace safe, but nearby."

"Can do, but there's no reason to go nearby. The whole point of super low frequency transmissions is that they go a long way and permeate into the ocean deeper than the higher frequencies."

"Then set up at home ... or at the office for all I care. Just get what you can on the transmissions from Cutler."

"Can do, but you know they're all super-encrypted, don't you?"

"Don't give a good goddamn about what they say. Just let me know number and duration."

"Sure thing. That's all women care about, right?"

"Fuck you," replied Dick.

"So, I'm guessing Melanie isn't listening in at the moment. Want to know what I'm wearing?"

"No," said Dick. "But I'm guessing it's not khakis, like Jake from State Farm."

The connection terminated.

What the fuck? Sometimes Americans made no sense at all to Ace.

Chapter 25

Dick had to admit he was impressed with what Seth and Brian had cobbled together in short order. The crowds gathered in the open terrain near the Yardie Creek Road entrance to the Exmouth facility weren't huge, to be sure, but there were a lot of people for a dusty, backwater location in a dusty, backwater country. The diversity of activists was even more impressive. UFO and alien enthusiasts circulated, some accusing the base personnel of covering up evidence of, or even contact with, flying saucers, faster than light technology, and ominous Grays. The new arrival of the Space Surveillance Telescope was a lightning rod for those who already suspected the giant antennae array was communicating with a "mother ship" hiding behind the moon (or even inside the "artificially created and hollow" moon, which ominously rings like a bell when struck by meteors). Anti-military and local nationalists decried the use of the base by a warmongering foreign power (the United States) to communicate with submarines carrying nuclear weapons. The GreensWord types joined forces with the Peaceniks for Whales to decry the impact of the low-frequency signals emanating from the base on cetaceans around the world. Portions of the local tourist industry most integrated with viewings of the majestic and docile whale sharks joined in, even though whale sharks are actually fish, not mammals.

According to Seth, a second crowd at least twice the size, mostly skewed toward the oceanic environmental types, was also gathered on the other side of the base nearest the ocean at the main entrance right off Bundegi Beach.

A few professional anarchists even roamed through the crowd risking heat stroke in their black jeans, black hoodies, and black motorcycle helmets, as they clutched their black umbrellas and burner cell phones looking for whatever chaos they might take advantage of. Dick wasn't happy they'd joined the protesters, but demonstrations were like college parties. Once you invited a bunch of people, you had no control over how many friends of friends of friends got the invite and showed up ... and who might crash the bash even though they weren't wanted. Dick handed one of them a placard reading "Dismantle Tesla's Death Ray Towers" to brandish, knowing the rowdy youth had no fucking clue what it meant and didn't really give a shit about what he was protesting anyway.

Dick also spied a television news crew from Perth circulating through the crowd, taking video and interviewing the most vocal and outrageously dressed protesters. Many of those in attendance had their cell phones—including phones on selfie-sticks Dick thought had long ago gone out of fashion—up and panning the crowd. Some were no doubt just recording their own fun, but most, according to Seth, were streaming the protest over Facebook or some blog or site or podcast Dick didn't understand anything about. People—not just these people, but people all over the world—seemed to have way too much time on their hands. At least, in this instance, the Subsidiary could make some use out of the modern generation's penchant for navel-gazing and 24/7 protesting.

Dick grabbed up a homemade placard reading "Storm Exmouth, Australia's Area 51!" and made sure to be seen thrusting it up and down while adding his voice to the chants and shouting of the crowd. It went against his nature as a spy to engage in activity he knew was being recorded, certainly by both protest participants and plants the base's security forces had undoubtedly sent to the demonstrations to gather intelligence. But he wanted to add to both the size of the crowd and the enthusiasm and provocative nature of their protests. That's why Seth and Melanie were also attending the protests. This unruly tumult was a key piece of his tactical plan and his cover story if caught later tonight.

He circulated through the crowd, encouraging everyone he interacted with, whatever flavor of craziness they lapped up, with loud exhortations to stay the course and party all night. He even mentioned the location of piles of scrub and driftwood Melanie and Seth had helped him gather the previous day for use in bonfires after dark. Then, he leaned in with *sotto voce* exhortations to storm the main base at Area A from both southwest and east in the wee hours of the night when the "fascist war-mongering foreign imperialists and their indoctrinated military lackey stormtroopers" were least likely to be alert and able to resist an uprising and takeover of the "murderous, alien facility." If the reaction was at all favorable, he'd add a knowing wink and say, after looking conspiratorially over each of his shoulders, "they can't stop us all and they're too afraid of publicity to actually shoot anyone."

He repeated the process over at Bundegi Beach, where Melanie was stationed with a group of Mothers Against Atrocities and Monstrosities, rousing the rabble in her own, quiet, homespun way. By late afternoon, Dick left the demonstrators to their own devices for a few hours and went back to their hotel in Exmouth.

Once there, he checked in with Ace via Shangrilyfe. She was in a mood, but not a chatty one.

"*Ježiši!* I've barely gotten set up! There's not enough data for even the most basic pattern recognition software to make sense of anything. All I know is there are a lot more broadcasts than I would have expected."

"You had expectations?"

"These facilities are for official communications for submarines under deep cover. They're not providing WiFi for lonely sailors scrolling through Match dot com. Yeah, I didn't think there would be much traffic."

"Huh," said Dick.

"Well said," replied Ace.

"I'll have to ponder on that. Talk to you tomorrow, when I know more, if there's more to know."

He signed off and hit the bed to catch a few hours of sleep, putting up the "Do Not Disturb" placard on the outside door handle. He wanted to make sure he was fully awake and alert for his planned evening expedition.

Normally, Dick had no problem falling to sleep for a few hours before even the most dangerous missions, but this time he tossed and turned on the uncomfortable hotel mattress for almost a half hour before forcing himself into a fitful slumber. Of course, on all of his previous missions, whether in the Army Rangers, the Chicago Police Department, or the Subsidiary, he actually had some useful intelligence and knew exactly what he was doing and why. Here he really had no fucking clue what was going on, who he was really up against, and what needed to be done to save the world or at least accomplish his mission.

It wasn't just that, though. Usually Dick had only himself to worry about, and he had a hefty dose of confidence he could handle himself in almost any situation. The few instances in his past he'd had the most difficulty with had involved others. Fellow agents like Ace, fellow Subsidiary employees like Luke, and innocent civilians who he'd avoided turning into civilian casualties, but who had not escaped run-ins with him unscathed. But this time, Seth and Melanie were literally out there on the front line, marching around with signs, antagonizing people with bullets and canisters of tear gas and heavy wooden batons.

Sometimes his job sucked. This was definitely one of those times.

Sometimes the people you worked with ... or more especially *for* ... were evil assholes who didn't deserve the power they had. Pyotr Nerevsky was definitely one of those evil assholes.

Whatever happened, Dick made a vow Nerevsky would pay for what Dick's family had to go through on this godforsaken road trip out woop woop and back again.

#

"Report," demanded Yuri. "What is Thornby up to now?"

The underling dropped a small sheaf of papers onto Yuri's functional desk. "He is in Exmouth, participating in a demonstration outside of the facility for low frequency transmissions to submarines and—"

"No doubt a diversion of some sort."

"Yes, comrade."

"We can't let him infiltrate the facility."

"Er ... of course. But what is there for him to find?"

Yuri glared at the aide. "That is none of your concern. Your job is simply to do as I tell you."

"Yes, comrade."

"Take him tonight."

The aide gave Yuri a curt head bob. "Of course. As you command."

"Take care of the other one, too."

"Another abduction?"

"No. His part in this performance is complete. Time for him to take his bows."

#

Nothing much scared Pyotr Nerevsky. You didn't last long in the KGB, the SVR, or the Subsidiary if you were a coward. And, of course, a significant piece of his work in the Internal Audit Division was making sure the headstrong and sometimes reckless agents didn't do things which went too far—too stupid, too expensive, too destructive, or too high profile. And to do that job, he had to cultivate a cold, calculating, and, quite frankly, violent reputation in order to be sufficiently intimidating to do his job.

Still, he wasn't an idiot. He didn't take foolish risks. He knew his move to the Subsidiary was viewed with considerable suspicion and apprehension by the ruling powers back in Mother Russia. If they even suspected what he was up to by proxy through Dick Thornby, they would be even less pleased. Consequently, he avoided travel to Russia. The state intelligence operations were much too pervasive to give him comfort that he would remain incognito there. On the other hand, things were much more relaxed in Kazakhstan—or, at least, much more disorganized and inefficient.

So, while Pyotr wouldn't think of going to Russia to take in a game of bandy, stopping by Almaty in the former Soviet republic for a little spectator sport was, by his assessment, not a problem. The Russians certainly had some close ties to the country—including a launch site for the Russian space program and, of particular interest to Pyotr, the Sary Shagan Missile Range. The Russians had supposedly tested a Tesla scalar interferometer energized by Moray generators at the range years ago, but now it was abandoned.

Kazakhstan had an independent streak, too, though. It sent engineers to assist the United States in Iraq, participated in UN peacekeeping missions in Libya and Haiti, and had a number of joint economic projects with China. Most notably, it provided humanitarian aid to the Ukraine during its struggles with "Russian freedom fighters."

Most importantly to Pyotr, though, Kazakhstan had a surprisingly strong commitment to traditional winter sports for a hot, predominately Muslim county. It had even put a bid in for the 2022 Winter Olympics. When it lost out to Beijing, Pyotr lost any hope bandy would become an official Olympic sport. Still, the Asian Bandy Federation was headquartered in Almaty, and this was his best chance of catching some good games outside of Russia in the near term.

As usual, he arrived at the field well before the game, interested in watching the pre-game warm-up and assessing the ice conditions. The crowd was pretty thin, but Pyotr headed into the thick of it at center ice, near enough to hear the banter from the players as they practiced and prepared. Sometimes you could pick up information during warm-ups which could prove useful when betting on a game. Pyotr always bet on the games he watched, not because of a compulsive need for money, but because it always made things more exciting when you had something to win or lose. And, if you're going to bet, you need to gather enough information to bet smart. So, he worked his way through the throng of people to get closer to the action.

That was the final mistake in the series of miscalculations which had led him from a dusty field in Western Australia almost thirty years ago to a frigid conference room in the bowels of Catalyst Crisis Consulting's Philadelphia headquarters for the Subsidiary, then to Perth and on to Almady.

He felt the stabbing jab in his lower back—sudden, sharp, and swift. He might have dismissed it as a muscle cramp were it not for the radiating warmth spreading from that point within his body and the sensation of warm, trickling liquid on his skin emanating downward from that same location.

He wasn't stupid. He knew the methods Russia liked to employ for their wet work. He knew he was already dead. Cesium, poison, or maybe something more esoteric these days. It didn't matter. He would die and quickly. There was only one thing he could do and that was to identify his attacker. He whirled around, searching for someone moving with steady, deliberate speed away from him. Most likely with an umbrella or a cane—something the assailant could use to hide a blade or a needle from casual search. He caught sight of a dark, shadowy figure headed for the nearest exit, but Pyotr's eyesight was already fogging. Dark crept in around the edges. He shivered from cold, though he was not really that close to the ice.

He'd always known he would die this way, but he had hoped he would end his idealistic quest, that he would know what actually happened near Banjawarn Station in Western Australia before he died. He should have known better. Spy agencies are where ideals go to die—where everything and everybody is shaded in gray and the ledgers of life and death are all calculated with cold, practical precision. His life had been cold and gray. His office at the Subsidiary had been the same. Now his death would be cold and gray, too.

With his final, labored breath, he hung on to only one spark. Dick Thornby was on the case and that foul-mouthed, pyromaniacal grunt was as obstinate as they came. He'd been sent on a mission and he would do whatever it took to get the job done.

#

Dick rolled out of the bed in the dark and dressed without turning on the light. He'd made a point of showing his face earlier in the day, but now it was night, when all the real action happened. Everything from this point forward would be shrouded in secrecy. What he was doing now wasn't a peaceful protest, it was clandestine covert action against a sovereign power—actually two, both of which were members of the Subsidiary's International Oversight board. On top of that, there were other forces at work with unknown operatives, unknown agendas, unknown capabilities, and unknown allies, whether terrestrial or alien. Dick could get captured and thrown into a hole so deep and so dark he would never see the light of day again, no matter how long or hard he screamed.

Yep, just another day at the office.

Chapter 26

Dick didn't take the rental car. Cars meant lights and traffic cameras and easy surveillance and tracking. No, the rest of the mission would be on foot. And, he wanted to only bring things a protester would carry when infiltrating a base to find evidence of a UFO cover up. These days, that meant a cell phone with the camera app open, a plastic bottle of water, and a small cloth protest banner. He grabbed the kangaroo tourist bag and dropped the items in with his tube of sun-block, then rolled it up and tucked it into the back of his jeans. Having it along made it look like he'd come straight from one of the groups protesting all day in the sun. So did having his aviator-style Subsidiary-issued sunglasses—and they were more than useful day or night.

He, of course, had never retrieved the gun he'd dropped and covered over along the shoulder of the wide gravel roadway of Fimiston Super Pit, but that didn't bother him. Guns were a big bugaboo in Australia—there's no way a tourist would be packing.

Fortunately, this wasn't Patton force-marching troops to Bastogne during the Battle of the Bulge. It was a quick stroll around the outskirts of the Exmouth Golf Club to the beach. Dick wore the shade of dark clothing favored by the anarchists he'd encountered earlier in the day, but without the ridiculous and stifling hoodie, so it was relatively easy to stick to the shadows and avoid two sets of teens obviously too young to have their own apartment or car, but old enough to want to chance creating their own clueless kids.

In no time, he was on an irregular path to the beach. Once there, he headed north as the waves lapped and surged rhythmically onto the pebble-studded sand. He donned his aviator sunglasses and switched them to night vision mode. No sense twisting an ankle in the dark.

It didn't take long for Dick to reach Area B. He would have gotten more steps in on his workout routine if he'd actually been on vacation and played eighteen holes at the Exmouth Golf Club, rather than pretending to be on vacation and skirting it to access a foreign military facility. He reached the point where the perimeter of Area B was closest to the ocean and passed it, continuing along the beach. That was probably the spot most watched, if indeed anyone was watching anything along the perimeter of Area B during the wee hours tonight. With any luck, the thin security force for the Holt base was concentrated on Area A, watching the bonfires and protesters gathered on either side of the base for any sign the noisy frolickers actually intended to follow through on their boasts of storming and occupying the place.

With a little bit of luck, some yahoos emboldened by too many pints of local brew would charge the fence and attract every bit of attention the beleaguered guards had to give.

Not much farther along the beach, Dick spotted the gulley he'd spied on the satellite photos of the base kindly supplied by Google Earth to the denizens of the World Wide Web. Though North West Cape—the peninsula which jutted out into the Ningaloo Reef and on which both Exmouth and the ponderously named Naval Communication Station Harold E. Holt sat—was all arid and caked sand, the shallow wash provided drainage from Area B to the ocean when storms raged through. He crouched and made his way up the small incline from the beach to the perimeter fence.

Just as he'd hoped, the gulley had washed away some of the dirt under the chain-link, providing dirty, but relatively easy, access inside the perimeter fence without cutting or scaling it. Dick used his gloved hands to scoop out enough additional loose sand and small stones to allow even his stocky girth to wriggle through until he was on the inside, officially committing a felony and breaking the national security laws of Australia and maybe the United States.

He stayed flat on the ground for at least a minute to make sure his intrusion was so far undetected, then stood in a low crouch and crept toward the center of Area B, still using the wide, shallow drainage gully for whatever minimal concealment it provided. Scrubby bushes were especially prevalent along the gully close to the outer perimeter of the facility. That helped, but Dick knew from the aerial photos the vegetation thinned more and more as one moved further from the perimeter fence. The central area, housing the only sizeable buildings in Area B, had an entirely cleared area in a roughly two-hundred-meter radius around the complex. There would be no hiding there, other than darkness and inattention.

He moved as quick as he dared, praying most or all of Area B's regular security personnel had been re-assigned to watch the protesters congregating around—and threatening to breach—Area A. Or, if not, hopefully the remaining guards had monitors tuned to both Areas and the higher level of flashy activity there would catch the eye rather than a subtle flutter of black-on-black skulking about Area B.

He checked the luminous dial on his watch. Some poor third world woman probably was fighting cancer because she licked her brush tip when applying the luminous paint, but it was a damn convenient thing to have during black ops. Nine minutes.

In less than ten minutes, Seth and Melanie would lead their respective throngs of ragtag protesters in rousing renditions of protest songs from the last occupation of the base. Seth would belt out *We Don't Want No Yankee Bases* with the group at the Yardie Creek Road entrance to Area A *a cappella*. Melanie would orchestrate *Omega Doodle* with the accompaniment of a dozen plastic kazoos from the partying protesters near the beach. Short of rigging explosions, it was the best Dick could do to maximize distractions at Area A at the moment he wanted to breach the building in Area B.

Dick reached the edge of the open area, took off his aviator sunglasses and tucked them into his front pocket. With light from the buildings, they were a hindrance now. He waited a few moments to let his eyes adjust to the ambient light. Then he took a few deep breaths and sprinted across the open ground at full speed toward the secondary fence surrounding the main building. He leapt up, half-somersaulting, and using his gloved hands and flexed arms to push up and off one of the metal posts while in the air, like a ninety-pound prepubescent Russian gymnast. He guessed the fence was electrified, but he hadn't the time to check and as long as he wasn't grounded when he touched it, even if not gloved, he should be safe. These guys might be using secret Tesla technology to threaten the world, but they didn't know squat about the best way to protect a building from a sophisticated, determined intruder.

He landed on his feet, letting his knees collapse, as he dove forward into a roll to absorb the momentum from his run and jump. He came up into a crouch below the level of the building windows and waited for a few beats to see if his approach had raised any alarm.

All was quiet. All seemed safe.

He didn't really know what he was looking for, so there was no obvious plan for how and where to infiltrate the building. His best guess was that if someone really was doing something secret and bizarre here (other than sending and receiving highly encoded military messages to nuclear-armed submarines on deep station patrols), they were most likely doing it someplace underground, where fewer people went and nobody could look in from outside. Accordingly, when he turned to the side and raised up to look in the corner of the nearest window, his first priority was to find the nearest stairwell.

No luck from his first vantage point, so he crept along the outer wall of the building a little more toward the center of the facility and checked again. Nothing. On his third attempt, he finally found what he was looking for. Next up, he needed to find an emergency fire exit near the stairwell. He'd surreptitiously accessed enough buildings in the course of his career that popping an emergency exit without tripping the simple circuit-breaker alarm system was not a problem, even in the dark in a country where people drove on the wrong side of the road and liked to watch kangaroos box instead of people.

He found a door and got to work.

Maybe circumventing the alarm took more of his attention than he thought, because he didn't see the two black-clothed thugs who ambushed him from either side as he was working the door until it was almost too late.

As they converged, he ducked and put his left hand flat on the concrete pad near the door, giving him a contact point that allowed him to lash out with both legs at once. Unfortunately, he only made grazing contact with his right leg on one assailant and nothing but air with his left. He attempted to spin counterclockwise with his legs still extended in hopes of clipping the two thugs behind their knees, but they avoided his legs by jumping atop him in his awkward, crouched position. He was forced to move his contact hand to avoid a sprain ... or worse ... from the sudden additional weight.

He fell to the hard cement and attempted to roll away from the building, where he had more room to maneuver and possibly escape his opponents, but it was too late. He was trapped, with one arm folded beneath him and his legs flailing ineffectively. One arm against two opponents was a losing proposition, even if he could really see what was going on. But his viewpoint was from a partially blocked position and the shadows from the building and spilling lights made a mish-mash of glaring angles of light and dark.

Still, he tried to fight back more effectively—there was no point to being stealthy and quiet once you were found out by the guards of a military facility. But he never got a real chance to either use his professional-grade street-fighting skills or his ersatz amateur UFO-ologist and protester protestations about use of force. Instead, Dick felt a sting in his neck and the shadows enveloping him somehow managed to fade to an even deeper black.

Between Dick's stocky build and his healthy adrenal response to fight or flight situations, whatever they'd dosed him with was on the ragged edge of insufficiency. The black filling his vision lifted for short moments of ... not really lucidity, but more like foggy, trippy, translucency. He heard a *boom* and felt himself being half-carried, half-dragged, his feet forming furrows in soft, then wet sand. Later, he half-woke to a bobbing motion with the smell of moist salt permeating the dusty, stuffy confines of the bag over his head.

What the fuck? He was being taken out to sea. Those hadn't been guards from the facility. Someone else was taking him god-knows-where.

Not good. Not good at all.

As he faded into oblivion once more, he comforted himself with one thought. At least Melanie and Seth weren't with him when he was taken. At least his wife and his son were safe, singing protest songs around a campfire with the salt of the earth. Gullible, groovy peaceniks and idealists, but well-intentioned people.

#

Seth didn't actually know the words to *We Don't Want No Yankee Bases*, but he followed along as best he could, though he always dropped out at the word "Yankee" out of respect for his country—the country his dad fought in the Army to serve and the country which, despite all of its faults, still remained a bastion of freedom and ingenuity and success. He stared into the bonfire, wishing not only that this distraction meant his dad would succeed on his mission, but that the world could be an even better place.

He glanced around the bonfire at the earnest, smiling faces. Certainly, many people wanted to make a better world, just like he did. Of course, he knew from his experience with Chinese dissidents on Reality 2 Be and what he knew of his dad's work with the Subsidiary, there were a lot of different paths to that same purpose.

He shook himself out of his reverie to turn and scan the crowd away from the bonfire, just to make sure nobody was doing anything stupid. Back when his activism in the *Free Tibet!* Movement had been revealed, his dad, a former cop after all, had given him one rule to keep in mind whenever involved in a protest march. *Pay attention to and police your fellow protesters, because if you allow criminal elements to take over your protest and commit felonies, not only will you undercut whatever your message was supposed to be, but some scared or poorly trained or injured guard will use deadly force to protect himself or his fellow officers.* Keepng tabs on a diverse, spread-out crowd was harder to do than Seth liked. He couldn't just keep an eye out for people brandishing rocks and Molotov cocktails. These days frozen water bottles were the weapon of choice for rioters. Still, he had to try. As someone who sought a better world, Seth wanted to propose solutions, not cause more problems.

Unfortunately, staring at the bonfire had screwed up his night vision and all he could see in the distance was blackness punctuated by the blinking red lights of the antennae and the harsh security lights of the central compound of Area A. He closed his eyes to speed their adjustment to the dark and counted silently to thirty as yet another protest song started. Finally, he opened his eyes and caught a flicker of shadowy movement to the north and slightly east of his position, where the westernmost antenna jutted out of the flat desert high into the night sky. A couple individuals wearing black clothing and black motorcycle helmets were scrambling over the perimeter fencing. As they moved into the shadow of dim light nearest the tower, he saw them place something at its base, then run to the fence and scramble over, drop down, and run away at full tilt.

A moment later, a bright white flash burst at the base of the towering antenna and a lonely *boom* thundered across the vast emptiness of Exmouth peninsula.

The protest song fell off raggedly into stunned silence.

Then there was the unmistakable creak of twisting metal as the westernmost tower of the NCSHEH faltered and sagged as its base disintegrated. A sudden *snap* and the *twing* of a failed cable sailed across the air as the antenna leaned to one side, then gained momentum and fell to the earth with a wrenching, groaning, rumble.

An alarm started blaring at the central complex.

Fucking anarchists. They ruin everything.

Seth didn't wait for the men with automatic weapons who were no doubt pouring out of the central complex of the station to arrive.

"Run!" he shouted. "Everybody leave now! Move!"

The problem with protesting at a remote location on a narrow peninsula in an undeveloped part of the country was there was only one road out. If they didn't make it to Murat Road and south, at least into the town of Exmouth, the whole lot of them would be taken into custody and imprisoned for the acts of the anarchist fringe, who were already roaring past the group on their motorcycles.

If the security guards were smart, they weren't headed to the site of the explosion or even to the intersection where he and the other protesters were singing their songs, they were headed to block off Murat Road at this very moment.

What a total cluster.

As he jumped into a car with another protester, he hoped his mom was okay and was on her way back to town, too.

As for his dad ... well, he had the distraction he needed.

#

The first thing Melanie thought when she heard the explosion was that Dick was in trouble. Deep, deep trouble. But even as she whirled toward the sound of the boom, she realized she was turning northwest and Dick was to the south, southwest, far from the site of the explosion.

Her next thought, even more horrifying, was that there was an explosion where Seth was monitoring the gaggle of other protesters. But then she saw the light on the westernmost antenna wink out as it fell and she realized the explosion must have taken place there, away from the intersection where the main protest group was encamped.

She grabbed her cell phone to call Seth, to tell him to run, to get back to town, but she realized he was smart enough to figure that out for himself and the only thing that might slow him down was calling her to tell her to do the same. She stifled her maternal instincts and let her nascent espionage instincts come to the fore.

Time to get the hell out of Dodge ... or, at least, Bundegi Beach. She accepted the hurried invitation of another demonstrator and waded out to a small speedboat just off the beach. Boats were slower than a car on open road, but a lot more difficult to roadblock. Soon, she was staring through the salt spray as the boat skittered south, toward Area B, where Dick was supposedly in the midst of his infiltration.

A sudden lurch of the speeding boat almost propelled her overboard, but she grabbed the gunwale in time, hanging on white-knuckled as her face dipped downward, hovering over the foamy water streaming past with the boat at top speed. She arched her back to regain her balance, then turned to look at the pilot, who was extending a raised middle finger at a larger boat, retreating into the darkness.

"What was that?" she asked as she wiped salt spray from her face.

"Bloody wankers! Partiers cruising full-on without running lights. Who the bloody hell does that?"

Melanie looked to the west. The lights of Exmouth twinkled to the southwest. They were just abreast of Area B. She looked astern, but could no longer make out the speeding boat which had made them swerve. All she could see was the white froth of its wake, dissolving from foam into a glassy black sheen on the dark water.

She silently prayed with all the fervor she could muster that the culprits who had already disappeared from view were idiotic partiers ... bloody wankers ... and not something or someone much, much worse.

Chapter 27

Later still, much later by his estimation, Dick crawled from the depths of unconsciousness toward reality.

Reality sucked.

He didn't know where he was or even when it was, but the humidity was higher here and he felt the purring vibration of a powerful, but finely tuned motor. Then his neck was pricked a second time. Once again, a curtain of blackness fell over his vision, but this time in the blackness a blue-ringed octopus cavorted with giant Portuguese Man-o'-War jellyfish, stinging him again and again and again.

The next time he awoke, dappled flashes of bright sunshine flitted over the outside of the black bag amid the sound of buzzing insects, intermittent muttered curses, and animal sounds, including a Kookaburra. He knew it from his experience as a birdwatcher to be a Blue-Winged Kookaburra, not the Laughing Kookaburra used in so many old Tarzan and similar movies as a substitute for monkey howls. Dick could tell the difference between jungle sounds and tropical rainforest sounds, and this was the latter.

There was no rainforest near Exmouth, just sand and scrub and whale sharks surfing the turquoise ocean. And the Blue-Winged Kookaburra's range didn't extend that far south of the northern coastal shores of Australia, especially not in the western part of the country.

He was somewhere north and east of Exmouth, given the sounds.

But exactly where the hell was he?

More importantly, why was he being taken far away from Exmouth ... and his family?

#

Thank God Seth was already at the hotel and packing up the car by the time Melanie arrived. She grabbed him in the parking lot and hugged him to herself before he could make the typical teen protest against public displays of maternal affection. But her elation was short-lived.

"Is your father here?" she asked. Even she could hear the near panic in her tone. She took a deep breath—she had to hold it together for Seth.

"No, he's not. And he said not to wait if this kind of thing happened. He said to leave and not wait."

Melanie managed a tight smile. "I think his words were: 'If things go south, go south—as soon and as fast as you can. I'll meet you back in Perth. Maintain cover.'"

Seth nodded as he headed back to the room. "Just one more suitcase and we're loaded." He tossed her his room key. "Check us out."

She caught the key. "It's awfully early. The sun isn't even up."

Seth stood at the open hotel room door for a moment, then shrugged. "If anyone asks, we're getting an early start on the day. Tourists do that all the time."

In less than ten minutes, they were headed south, out of town. Perth was more than twelve hours away, but Melanie wasn't planning on making any stops along the way. Seth explained what had happened at the westernmost antenna, but after exchanging information about their respective escapes, they fell into silence. About an hour later, Seth fell asleep in the passenger seat and she let him sleep for as long as he wanted. Despite being up all night, she didn't need him to help keep her awake as she drove. Her mind was a whirl of thoughts, fears, and emotions.

Was Dick all right?

Where was he?

When would he meet them?

What should they do to maintain cover in the meantime?

When Seth finally awoke, he didn't ask what time it was or where they were or when he could stop for a bio break. He had only one question.

"If someone asks us about Dad, what do we say?"

"I thought about that while you were asleep. We stay as close to the truth as we can, but we maintain his cover."

"But, how do we—"

"We tell them we came here to vacation while your father checked out UFO sightings and he simply went out by himself into the dark with the hope of completing his quest, with plans to meet up with us again back in Perth."

Seth bit his lip, then looked into the distance. "But what if some time goes by and Dad doesn't meet us in Perth?"

Melanie didn't hesitate. She'd thought this through. "We tell them the truth. We don't know where your father is. For all we know, he was abducted by aliens."

Seth wrinkled his nose. "Aliens?"

"Definitely," said Melanie. "All of the locals we've met have been much too nice to have abducted your father. So, it must have been foreigners ... aliens."

#

Dick heard low, muffled voices, probably from outside or maybe another room nearby. He couldn't make out the words, but he was pretty sure they weren't speaking English. Not locals, then. He chuckled to himself. He'd hit the UFO buff vacation trifecta: seeing weird lights in the sky at Rendlesham Forest; stumbling upon a strange artifact uncovered by winds in the remote desert near Banjawarn Station; and being abducted by aliens in the wee hours of the night. If Nerevsky ... or Dee Tammany ... fired his ass after this bizarre, botched caper, at least he could self-publish a UFO conspiracy book. Hell, he might be able to get a show on the History Channel. There were stupider shows on television, he told himself. He could be a reality television success. And, he'd been in worse binds than this, he told himself. He could still eke out a mission success.

He heard a chair scrape across the floor in the other room and the door to the room he was in opened. "Ve haf a few questions," said a gruff voice, the accent unmistakably Russian. "You vill provide answers. Da?"

Of course, he'd have to survive a round or six of torture before he could eke out that mission success.

#

Actually, the torture turned out not to be so bad.

Of course, torture is one of those things ... like holiday fruitcake or infomercials ... which is always painful. A perfect world wouldn't include any such things. But the guy with the Boris Badenov accent didn't really ask him any questions; he just tuned him up a bit. Unusual, but not unheard of. The bizarre thing was the guy seemed to have a fetish for tidiness, cleaning the bloody spot on Dick's face where the skin had stretched too tight when hit and had split open. He even put the bloody paper towel into a ZipLoc bag, rather than set it down on the nearby table.

It took all kinds. Even brutal psychopaths could have their fetishes and fears. Maybe the guy was germophobic. Dick's best guess was that this guy was just the warm-up for the main act. Not really here to do the main interrogation, but just to let him know that his captors meant business, that he could really be hurt by someone willing and able to inflict pain if answers weren't forthcoming once the real interrogation began.

And, by the time the initial pummeling was over, Dick was pretty sure as to what his game plan was going to be during the main session.

He was going to talk.

Oh, he wasn't going to tell them about Glenn and Dee and operational details about the Subsidiary or its agents, but it was clear these goons—ape-like relatives of the Russians who had chased his family into the Super Pit—already knew he was looking into some connection between UFOs and Tesla and he was doing it at the behest of Pyotr Nerevsky. At this point, Nerevsky had already put his family in danger for no good reason. He had no loyalty to the Head of Internal Audit; they could fry the son-of-a-bitch for all he cared.

Of course, that plan went out the window of the windowless hole he was being kept in. They'd taken the bag off his head while they were tuning him up. Not a good sign, since it meant he could I.D. everyone in the room if needed, so they weren't planning on letting him leave. One silver lining to the dark cloud that was his life was that after beating him up, they untied his ropes and let him roam free in his squalid hell-hole. Sure, that meant they probably intended to keep him for a long time and didn't really need the stench associated with letting him soil himself again and again, but it also meant he could scope out the location to plan an escape. The smattering of sunlight creeping in from the cracks around the door, the only relief from the solid cement block construction, didn't really help much on that score.

Fortunately, they'd searched him and let him keep his empty water bottle, sunscreen—suggesting he might use it to supplement his diet—and his protest sign. They'd also left him an old coffee can in which he could relieve himself, even though with the trickle of water they gave him and the amount he was sweating off in this hole, there wasn't much liquid in his body left to pee. They'd destroyed his phone, of course. Unfortunately, they'd also taken ... or somewhere along the route he'd lost ... his best resource, his Subsidiary issue aviator glasses. Not only couldn't he use the Subsidiary's tech marvel to signal for help, he couldn't even use the night vision mode to scour the place for potential tools to help him escape. He'd have to make do with what he had.

That wasn't much. There were few places to look and fewer things to find. Some miscellaneous trash—foil from cooking something from over an open fire, trashed remains from a broken flashlight, a plastic cup, and a few nudie magazines. Still, he cataloged the surroundings, both animate and inanimate, and steeled himself for what was to come.

Then, he waited. Typical spy work.

Chapter 28

At first Seth did his best to keep up the cover story and to help his mom do the same. They walked along the riverfront, had lunch at trendy cafés and dinner at high-end restaurants—touristy things to mask the fact they were marking time until his dad, an international spy, could make his way back to Perth after infiltrating a highly classified military installation.

For the first few days, there was also plenty of coverage of the "terrorist incident" in Exmouth in the local press, including both the daily *The West Australian* newspaper and the local television stations. Reporters had, of course, also covered the protest he and Brian had created out of thin ... hot ... air, so there were plenty of shots, both still and video, of crowd members brandishing signs and shouting slogans. Not having dressed as a druid or an alien or a *Crocodile Dundee* wannabe, none of the pictures featured Seth or his mom, but he still found several with one or another of them somewhere in the background. Given that they'd registered at the Exmouth hotel under their real names and had beat a hasty retreat after things went bad, he guessed any competent police force or national security apparatus would know exactly who they were and where they were now.

By the third day, Seth simply stayed in the hotel room watching television and playing games on his laptop while his mom alternatingly paced and stared out the window. In their own separate ways, they were both waiting for the same thing, for the knock at the door which would bring the authorities into their lives. Their return flight wasn't until the middle of the next week, and there wasn't any other plan for what to do except wait for his dad to return and tell them what to do.

Still, Seth looked up the number for Catalyst Crisis Consulting's nearest office, in Sydney, only four thousand kilometers—about twenty-five hundred not-so-comforting miles—away. He, of course, knew the number of his dad's office in Philly by heart, but Philly was a long, long way away, so he memorized the Sydney number, too. Just in case.

Days passed, each one longer than the one before.

Finally, there was a knock at the door. His mom merely started in shock, then stared at the door as if it were a wild beast come to devour her. Seth strode past her, yelling a faux cheery "Coming!" as he approached the door, hoping perhaps to forestall a battering ram followed by a flash-bang and a swarm of shock troops or whatever Australia's equivalent of SWAT was, as the powers-that-be came for them.

When he opened the door, though, he did a double-take. There was a somewhat familiar man wearing what looked like an ultra-expensive three-piece suit.

The man made no movement toward the door, but simply held out a well-manicured hand. "Glenn Swynton, Catalyst Crisis Consulting. May I come in?"

His mom looked almost as shocked as Seth felt, but she recovered more quickly. "Yes. Yes, Mr. Swynton. I ... well, I believe we've met."

"We have," said Swynton, as he took Seth's hand, gave it a firm shake, then dropped it. Seth took a step back and Swynton glided into the room, moving to his mom with both grace and urgency. He took her hand, too, but instead of shaking it, he held it and placed his other hand alongside it, the way politicians always do when they're trying to appear comforting. "I believe it was at the family holiday gathering three years past."

Up until now, Seth had never thought about the fact that Catalyst Crisis Consulting held holiday parties and hosted clients at corporate boxes at football and baseball games just like any other big consulting firm. From the look of astonishment on his mom's face, he figured she'd never thought of it, either, and was just now realizing that everybody she'd ever met from his dad's workplace was really a spy.

"Yes. Yes, I think you're right," his mom said, then waved Swynton toward the sofa to sit.

Seth watched as the man did just that, with a practiced micro-tug of each pant leg so the fabric didn't stretch over his knees as they bent. Then his mom sat and looked up at Seth expectantly. Seth hurried over and settled on the other end of the couch.

Swynton closed his eyes for a second, then pursed his lips together before speaking. "I've come with news about your husband ..." He turned his gaze to Seth. "... your father."

Seth had been little when his dad was an Army Ranger and still somewhat young when his dad was a Chicago cop. But he knew what all families of those who put their life on the line feared, the knock on the door by someone too formal, too high-ranked to be there for a social call, the knock that was inevitably and irretrievably followed by the words "I regret to inform you ..."

Seth's stomach dropped as all the color drained out of his mother's face.

"I regret to inform you that your loved one is missing and presumed dead."

His mom's face flashed an instant of relief at the first part of the statement, then fell quickly to anguish. She closed her eyes and he could see her struggling to control her emotions.

"Missing? Just missing?"

"Yes," said Swynton, "but presumed dead."

Contrasting emotions continued to flicker over his mom's face and flutter through his own mind.

"But just presumed?"

Swynton took a deep breath. "I don't want to extinguish any spark of hope, but I do not want to kindle that faint spark, either. We do not make presumptions lightly in ... ah ... our consulting business. We base our assessment on facts and evidence. In Richard's case, we grew concerned when he suddenly disappeared. Our concern grew as time passed without any communication from him or any sighting of him by our electronic and human surveillance sources. Then, a week went by with no contact. In addition, it was disturbing his disappearance coincided with a sizeable explosion, particularly because forensic analysis shows such explosion to have been the result of the use of Nobel 808."

"I'm sorry," said his mom. "I don't know what that is."

"It's an unusual type of plastic explosive."

"So?" interrupted Seth.

Swynton let out a deep breath. "Your father was given a tube of Nobel 808 when he arrived in country."

"Still," said Seth, "that hardly seems—"

"I hadn't finished," said Swynton, cutting him off, dashing his hopes. "A tech found some blood on one of the supports for the destroyed antenna at Exmouth. The DNA analysis has come back and it is a positive match for ... well, for Richard Thornby."

There were other words, but Seth never heard them. A white haze of static buzzed in his mind. It made no sense. Dad wasn't at the tower; he'd said the whole point of the demonstrations near Area A was so he could access Area B. Could he have set the explosives earlier, perhaps, to provide a more pressing distraction for the security forces?

But when Seth's vision and his mind finally cleared enough to ask more questions, he saw Swynton, now sitting next to his mother, holding her as she cried, her tears streaming down her face onto the fabric on the shoulder of the man's suit, and he knew this was not the time for questions or false hope. It was time for him to step up and take over providing the comfort his mother needed.

A half hour later, Swynton left with a promise of whatever assistance they needed, both in departing Australia and in dealing with matters back home in Philadelphia. It occurred to Seth that Swynton must have done this kind of thing before, that this kind of notification, and the compassion and support that came with it, was part of the job of someone who worked as some kind of manager or director or whatever at a spy agency. Swynton had enough practice to know how to do a terrible, terrible job well. That said more about the dangers of being a spy than anything else Seth could think of.

And yet, when he wasn't thinking about missing his dad or comforting his mom, Seth was thinking that he wanted to pick up the torch his dad had dropped when things went bad at Exmouth. Seth decided right there and then. He wanted to work at Catalyst Crisis Consulting. He wanted to be an agent for the Subsidiary. He wanted to be a spy.

Just like dad.

#

More than a week passed in dull monotony. Unrelenting heat. Buzzing insects. Some half-hearted punching by the practice squad. Instead of wasting his energy and risking internal injuries with displays of bravado, Dick did his best to avoid provoking his captors. He also pretended to be weaker and groggier than he truly was to both subtly encourage them to let down their guard, and perhaps entice them to treat him better lest he die in their care. He was also performing a second balancing act. While healing and resting up to be ready for an escape attempt, he had to make sure not to wait too long. The lack of food and water would eventually weaken him too much to make any escape impractical.

One day was the same as the next. Eventually there was the sound of a speedboat approaching, then voices and a bit of commotion outside the narrow confines of his world. Finally, the door squealed open and a short, slightly stout man with graying hair and a sallow complexion scarred by childhood acne walked into the place like he was in charge.

He apparently was, because the thug who had tuned Dick up ambled into a kind of parade rest stance and looked at the floor. Personally, Dick didn't see what was so intimidating about the bureaucrat who'd arrived. He didn't even carry, at least nothing but a folded newspaper. Dick recognized it as *The Western Australian*, the largest circulation daily—well, six days a week—newspaper published in Perth. Dick focused on the paper. The headline read: *Explosion at Exmouth* above a large picture of the mangled remains of one of Area A's large antennae. Smaller pictures beneath showed wide shots of the protests Dick had recruited Seth and Brian to orchestrate.

Shit. Things had gone bad at Exmouth. Very, very bad.

"Oh," said the bureaucrat, "I see you've noticed the headline. But, of course, I doubt that is any surprise to you, Mr. Thornby, given your ... fondness ... for explosions."

Shit. Shit. Shit. Dick didn't need to talk when the torture started. This guy knew way too much already.

"Lots of speculation in the article about violent protesters, professional provocateurs—Would that be you, perhaps?—and international terrorists. Yackety-yack. What passes for news and analysis these days. Wrong on the facts and clueless about the actual reasons behind what's going on right under their noses."

Dick stayed silent. The more this mook talked, the more likely he'd pick up some useful information.

"So, here's what's going to happen. I'm going to ask you some questions. Maybe a few; maybe many. You're going to answer, at least most of them. After all, you actually might not know the answers to a few. As familiar as I am with Pyotr Nerevsky's *modus operandi*, I know he keeps his operatives in the dark about many, many things, and I don't want to blame you for his training, with which I am intimately familiar."

"And what do I get out of this? A fast death rather than a slow death? Less motivating than you might think."

"Nothing so ... ephemeral. No, should you be less cooperative than I think you should be, Otik here will use you as a sparring partner, but with no gloves and no punching back. He didn't make the Russian Olympic team, but he does know how to break ribs with alacrity. Very painful from what I hear."

"He might make the next team. He's been practicing at least once a day since I got here."

The bureaucrat chuckled. "That wasn't practicing. That was warming up. If he'd been practicing, you'd be wincing every time you took a breath and there'd be a hollow whistle when you spoke."

"Yeah. But then you take the chance I fall unconscious ... or die ... and you get no information at all."

"A keen observation. After all, I didn't come all the way to Yilgalong Creek to watch you die. Direct violence can be unpredictable, which is why I prefer other motivational methods." The man glanced down at the folded newspaper he was still holding. "The demonstrations and explosions in Exmouth caused quite a stir. Both the police and Australia's national security apparatus are involved in finding those responsible, and emotions are running high."

"I suppose they are."

"All that puts your wife and your son at considerable risk."

Dick grit his teeth, but said nothing.

"No doubt," continued the bureaucrat, "you provided them with instructions on where to go and what to do if things went wrong, but you had no real idea how wrong they would go, how much pressure there would be to find them."

"Assuming you're right," growled Dick, "I don't think your incompetent local goons could do much of a job finding and protecting them."

His interrogator pursed his lips and grinned. "You have a point. But, you see, we don't have to find them. Been there, done that, as you Americans are so fond of saying. And I wouldn't really say we're protecting them." He waggled his head. "No. More accurately, you're protecting them ... at least so far ... from us. From me. That's the real story. Otik is just here for ... training."

Fuck! This asshole from Nerevsky's past might be lying, but Dick couldn't assume that. Dick wasn't a traitor. He wasn't a turncoat and he wasn't a wimp. But he was a husband and a father, one who loved his family. It was a good thing he'd already decided to talk ... at least about some things ... because he dared not stay silent with their lives in the balance.

"Message delivered. Ask your questions."

The bureaucrat snapped his fingers and a couple of guards brought in a wooden chair for him to sit on.

"Did Pyotr Nerevsky task you with investigating the Banjawarn Bang to find out what really happened back in 1993?"

"Duh," replied Dick. "You already know that."

"Do you believe the Aum Shinrikyo detonated a nuclear weapon there?"

Dick snorted. "I don't even think the remnants of Aum Shinrikyo believe that."

"And what do you think happened there?"

"Hard to say. My inclination is to say some sort of natural phenomenon, but then, if that was the case, types like you wouldn't care. So, something more sinister, more bizarre. Some of the UFO buffs seem to think that an alien spaceship landed and the world made first contact with the Grays or lizard men from Mars or some shit like that."

"That's a bit far-fetched, don't you think?"

Dick shrugged. "Too much in character for my cover, maybe."

"Any other theories?"

"You've seen the chatter amongst the conspiracy crowd on the internet, no doubt. From all I understand, you Russians are all over the internet."

"Hmm-hmm. And how did you end up in Exmouth? What's the connection?"

"Not quite clear," replied Dick. "Your goons nabbed me before I could finish my facility tour. Some potential connection with energy weapons."

The man's lips puckered for a moment before he spoke. "What types of energy weapons?"

"You're still asking me questions I know you know the answers to," Dick replied. "The type connected with old Tesla research. Death rays, energy shields, earthquake generators."

"Why would you say I know that?"

"Because I owe somebody a thousand bucks for a new car."

"Sounds like a bargain. Who would that be?"

Dick shook his head. "Off limits. Not going there. Either you already know and this banter is just filler you're using to build *rapport* or you don't know and I sure as hell am not going to tell you."

The bureaucrat inclined his head toward Otik and the thug stepped forward and jabbed Dick once in the upper ribcage. It hurt like a son-of-a-bitch, but Dick didn't feel anything pop or crack.

The bureaucrat inspected his nails. "You're right, of course, but non-compliance does have a cost."

Otik stepped back and Dick's interrogator continued. "What's the connection between Exmouth and Banjawarn Station?"

Dick took a breath and winced, but only for show. Let Otik's handler think his pet thug had over-performed. "Don't you guys read the conspiracy sites on the internet? I heard you like that kind of shit."

"Which sites in particular are you referring to?"

"Harry Mason's stuff, mostly. 'Bright Skies,' he called it. You know, earthquake generators, great circle routes, Russian bases in Antarctica, Exmouth, Cutler, Arecibo, electro-magnetic weather control. Yada, yada, yada."

"Ahh. Some fine reading there, although Arecibo's last purported attempt to control the weather seems to have gone rather spectacularly awry." Again, his inquisitor puckered his lips during a brief pause. "But let's get down to serious business. What do you know about Exmouth that I couldn't find on the World Wide Web?"

Dick hesitated before responding, taking a breath and providing another faux wince to buy time for thought. The true answer was he didn't know jack, but he didn't think this guy was going to buy that. He decided to bluff with the only bit of information he had which, based on what Ace had told him about Cutler, Maine, might be true, but without revealing his source.

"I know," he said, "there are a whole lot more ultra-low frequency transmissions from Exmouth than make any possible sense if all it is doing is communicating with submarines in deepwater stations."

The bureaucrat started, but quickly tried to pass it off as a laugh. "Really? And who do you think Exmouth is in constant communication with?"

How the fuck did he know? Aside from submarine communications and the occasional self-destruct order to certain drone models, Dick had no clue what ULF communications might be used for. For all Dick knew, the constant stream of transmissions was nothing but meaningless filler, sent so that anyone monitoring the unbreakable code wouldn't know when real communications were actually occurring—kind of the flipside of terrorist groups getting quiet just before an operation. But he wasn't about to say that, just in case it might be true. Dick was just making shit up at this point, doing his best to keep the questions coming in the hopes of learning something from them, just in case he ever got out of this place. He played to his cover. "UFOs? Black Triangle Motherships? Aliens?"

"Aliens."

"They brought that Space Surveillance Telescope in recently. Maybe it helps direct the signal."

"Exmouth's been operational a long time," said the bureaucrat. "The Space Surveillance Telescope is a quite recent addition."

"Fine," said Dick. "Maybe the lizard men from outer space are busily infiltrating society and keep in contact with their leadership through ultra-low frequency communications."

"Is that so?"

Dick had thought his wild speculation would draw a chuckle from his captor, but the bureaucrat's eyes did not twinkle in amusement. They were dead cold.

"It's a theory."

"And, what? There are thousands of 'lizard people' as you call them roaming around the planet undetected?"

What the fuck did this guy want? A plotline for a SyFy movie? "Not at all," answered Dick. "They take human form. They take over the bodies of human hosts."

"And what happens to the minds of those humans?"

"I don't know," said Dick. "They scream in terror, trying to get out?"

The bureaucrat smiled. "Not really. I'm told it's pretty boring, unless, of course, there's something that happened before the assimilation that was truly terrifying."

What the fuck?

"Did you ever consider that when someone does something illogical and say their 'lizard brain' made them do it, they might be telling the truth?"

"Eat shit and die," said Dick.

That made the man laugh out loud. "We're done here." The bureaucrat got up from his chair and turned to leave. He looked down at his hand, still holding the folded newspaper as if he'd forgotten he had it. "The lizard people part was a nice touch. But, of course, alien life could be no larger than a bacterium, a parasite which attaches to the brain and is capable of receiving ULF transmissions. Less visually exciting for cinematic purposes, but still quite effective at controlling the thoughts and deeds of the host body."

Dick rolled his eyes. "*To je pěkná píčovina!*"

His interrogator's eyes narrowed. "I don't know what that means."

"No, you don't," replied Dick. "But, then, I don't know what you might understand because I don't really know who I'm talking to, do I?" This entire interrogation was bullshit and Dick was getting tired of it. "Who am I talking to? Russian SVR? GRU? Or are you just a meat puppet for some parasite that just needs a good dose of penicillin to clear out?"

"Someday you'll know. The world will know, but not yet. Which reminds me—" He tapped the newspaper. "Interesting top story, but that isn't really why I brought you the paper. Headlines can be so sensational, but it's the human-interest stories which really inspire the average reader to keep subscribing. Entertainment gossip, helping homeless kittens, and the local police and emergency blotter. Have you checked your horoscope lately?"

He dropped the paper on the ground and turned to Otik. "No more workouts. His body needs to heal before he is ... suitable ... for what comes next." With that, he left the cement block prison with Otik and the rest of the guards. Apparently, the interrogation was over.

What in the world ... or out of the world ... was going on?

Chapter 29

Dick didn't really believe alien lizard men or alien space bacteria existed and he was going to be used to host one. Russians loved to lie. They loved to fuck with people. They probably took *Men in Black* and *The Andromeda Strain* way too seriously. But he did believe the Russians might use him to host a whole ... well ... host of unsavory things. Tracking or surveillance chips, lethal contagious diseases, debilitating jungle parasites, or who knows what.

Time had come for Dick to make his move.

His ace in the hole in terms of escape was the tube of sunscreen—actually Nobel 808 plastic explosive—and the detonating fuse handles of the kangaroo shopping bag still in his possession. Unfortunately, the fuse required a flame to light it and Otik hadn't offered him any cigarettes and matches so he could bask in the afterglow after their last one-on-one session. He'd simply taken away the chair. An electrical outlet might have helped, but the cement block building was not wired for electricity, and he hadn't even heard the cough of a generator the whole time he'd been at this humid, sweltering camp from hell.

He found a piece of glass from the broken flashlight and spent a few minutes seeing if he could somehow use it to concentrate the sunlight filtering in through one of the cracks in the door, but the slivers of light were thin and at a poor angle to be useful for much of anything. Besides, the small piece of glass was almost flat—not the best for focusing light, even if held at an oblique angle. Instead, he used the small piece of glass as a miniature platform to hold bits of lint recovered from his pockets off of the floor in the sunlight, so as to dry out the meager tinder he had should he discover a way to produce a flame.

Then he went back over his tiny aggregation of supplies once more and sat on the floor to think. Even though he didn't relish rushing through parts unknown in the dark, it was probably best to wait until the middle of the night when most of the guards would be asleep, drunk, or slow to respond.

He picked up the newspaper both to pass the time and to see what the bureaucrat's reference to his horoscope might mean, if he wasn't just pulling his leg like he'd been with the whole alien lizard men nonsense.

That's when he saw it. Not his horoscope, but on the same page along with the weather forecast, the tide chart and the phases of the moon, and the police blotter: *Two Dead in Auto Crash* read the headline. He almost passed it by, but then a name caught his eye ... his name, but not him.

Emergency crews recovered the bodies of two American tourists, Melanie Thornby and her son, Seth Thornby, from the twisted wreckage of a rental automobile which apparently went off the road along the Northwest Coastal Highway several kilometers south of Manilya. Responders speculate the driver may have fallen asleep during the long drive from points northwest en route to Perth. A third person, Mr. Richard Thornby, husband and father, respectively, to the deceased, was believed to be traveling with them, but his body was not found in the wreckage. It is unclear at this time whether he may have been thrown from the crash or was traveling to Perth separately.

Dick was a calm person. You had to be in his line of work. But he felt his blood pressure rising as he read the article. It continued to rise after he'd flung the paper down. His head throbbed and he could feel the blood vessels in his neck throbbing.

That fucking bureaucrat. He'd known this. He'd not only known this, but Dick had no doubt, no doubt whatsoever, that he'd done this.

He had to die.

Dick couldn't wait for the cover of darkness. He needed to escape now, before the man who killed his family left this godforsaken camp, apparently along the Yilgalong Creek, to Moscow or Vladivostok or the United fucking Nations to spin his lies and kill other innocents. Nerevsky, he had to die, too. But that was for later, when his vengeance would be cold. Right now, his vengeance was white fucking hot. He had to find a way to trigger the Nobel 808 in his sunscreen tube before his head exploded a thousand-fold from sheer anger.

He took a deep, cleansing breath, then let it out through his mouth. He counted to ten, then twenty, then a hundred and forty-fucking-seven before the ragged stars around the edges of his vision stopped pulsing in time with his carotid artery.

He wasn't McGyver, but he had gotten survival training back in the Rangers. He focused all his training, all his anger, to the task at hand. And this time, while sorting through the remains of the trashed flashlight, his mind seized upon the single Double-A battery which powered the pocket device. Of course, he didn't know if it had any charge left, but if it did ...

He bolted toward the corner of his prison where he'd found a bit of aluminum foil from a fire-cooked food item. He flattened out an inch-wide piece about the length from the tip of his little finger to the tip of his thumb when he did the traditional Hawaiian shaka sign. No, he didn't want to hang loose, but he did want to try to create a useable electric circuit.

He kept the third of the flattened aluminum foil on either end as is, but painstakingly tore away the foil from the middle third so it left only about a sixteenth of an inch of foil on one edge. He set that aside for a moment. He pulled the cord fuse off of one of the tourist bag's handles and took out the tube of Nobel 808, squeezing out a line of it along the corner of the back wall and righthand wall of the shelter, along with a few cross-hatches along the mortar crevices of the cement blocks it crossed, then emptied what was left of the tube in a glob about halfway up the corner stripe. He pushed the cap of the tube upside down into the explosive and used the small plastic hook in the recess of the top to attach the fuse. He then dropped the open tube back into the now one-handled tourist bag, along with his long-empty plastic water bottle, the nudie magazines, and, after quietly ripping off a strip from the bottom of the last page, the newspaper his tormentor had brought along.

He retrieved the sunshine-dried lint from near the door and placed it in the dirty plastic cup he'd found, set it aside for the moment and recovered his can of piss and watery shit from the other back corner of the room. He dumped the foul liquid out in a disgusting, thin sheet inside the door so anyone rushing through would lose their footing and, after they fell, hopefully their lunch.

He recovered his plastic cup and shredded up the strip of newspaper he pulled from the back page, arranging it in a nest shape around the dry lint. He grabbed up his one-handled bag and his aluminum strip, along with the Double A battery, and huddled in the back corner where the fuse and the Nobel 808 stood ready. He creased the aluminum lightly in the middle, so the wide edges were pulled somewhat closer to one another and the thin filament formed an angular V shape. Holding the tourist bag awkwardly so he could use the opposite walls of it as insulators to keep from grounding whatever meager charge the battery might produce, he edged the point of the V close to the lint in his plastic cup and placed the hopefully charged battery between the two wide ends of the aluminum foil.

The battery still carried a charge because the thin filament connecting the two ends of the battery quickly glowed with heat. He touched it to the lint and shredded paper until they browned then briefly flamed. He dropped his foil device and quickly pushed more shredded paper toward the almost imperceptible fire he'd created. The flame sprung up, and he held the now burning paper fire in the plastic cup toward the end of the fuse hanging from the detonator tube cap he'd shoved into the jellified plastic explosive. The fuse lit and Dick scuttled to the left wall of the shelter, near the front of the hut. He squatted down to provide as little profile to the shock wave as possible and threw his arms up to cover his head and chest, as best he could, using his thumbs to press down on his ears in hopes of saving his eardrums from the sound of the coming blast.

B-B-BOOOOOOOOOOMMMMMM!

The blast wave slammed Dick against the left wall, knocking him from his crouch into a sprawl, and his ears rang. The Nobel 808 did exactly what the inventor of the Peace Prize had intended explosives to do when he was out making his fortune. The cement blocks in the back, right corner of the room were either pulverized or hurled into the rainforest outside.

Dick didn't bolt for the sudden hole in the door. Instead, he got to his feet and stood against the front wall, behind where the door would open when guards rushed inside.

Even through the ringing in his ears, he quickly heard the snap of the lock, then the door pushed open. Otik rushed in, followed quickly by a regular guard with an AR-15, their hands waving away the cement dust hanging in the air from the explosion. The guard slipped on the wet, shit-strewn floor and collided with Otik, sending both of them down in a tangled, disgusting heap, the AR-15 clattering to the floor.

Dick stepped from behind the door and snatched up the assault rifle, which he noted had been converted to full auto (illegal in the U.S. and way beyond illegal in Australia), and fired two rounds at close range. Blood and brains and flecks of bone joined the piss and shit on the floor. Dick took a quick look out the open door to see the rest of the guards grabbing guns and heading his way. Avoiding the mess on the floor, Dick sprinted to the hole blasted in the back of the structure, snatching up the kangaroo tourist bag by the remaining handle as he did so.

Once outside, he blustered straightaway into the undergrowth of the rainforest, praying he hadn't been taken far enough east to have to worry about the invisible nettles of the gympie-gympie plant and its painful neurotoxins. He doubted he'd been taken as far as Queensland, but he wouldn't put it past these fucks to plant the stuff outside of their hidden rainforest prison. It didn't matter. Speed was critical right now—he'd chance whatever pain might come.

He crashed forward at full speed, making no effort to mask his movement, then, when he came to a small creek with a relatively clear access, turned and sprinted upstream thirty yards or so before turning back into the rainforest, headed back toward the camp. This time, however, he moved stealthily along a track parallel to his lumbering escape route, found a stout tree, and pulled himself up twenty feet into the canopy. Here he could see the camp not far away and the clear path he'd made in the underbrush blundering away from his prison. True to their mediocre training, the remaining five guards appeared at the gaping hole in the cement block and discovered the path. Within seconds, they headed for it, forming a single file as they did.

As was his training when facing more than a trio of opponents, his mind automatically assigned names to his targets to ease his combat processing. Lined up as they were, circling past his vantage, they became planets: Mercury; Venus; Mars; Jupiter; and Saturn. He skipped over Earth—his job was to save his own planet, not shoot it.

Once they were on the path, Dick raised his purloined weapon, aiming to pick them off from his elevated vantage point. The plan was to move from back to front, so as to not alert those in the front of the line of death as to exactly what was going on.

Pop. Saturn dropped with barely a rustle.

One down, four to go. Just like he'd learned from Gary Cooper in *Sergeant York.*

Pop. "Ahhh!" Jupiter thudded to the ground noisily.

Damn! Why couldn't the bad guys all go down quietly?

"What the fuck?" muttered Mars, the next guy in line. He twisted away as Dick was lining up the shot. A broad leaf blocked sight of the target's head. Dick held for a beat, waiting for his sightline to clear.

"Sniper!" yelled Mars as he turned back to the rest of the team. "Light it—"

Pop. Dick sentenced him before he could finish his sentence. Three down, but the two still up weren't going to be so easy. Both Venus and Mercury started firing on full auto into the vegetation that surrounded them, shredding leaves, bushes, saplings, vines, and any semblance of a controlled response. Flecks of green, yellow, and brown ballooned into the air at speed, then floated down, first in front, but quickly on all sides of the beleaguered and bewildered bad guys, who snicked in fresh magazines as fast as they could empty them.

Dick would have been in trouble if he'd been hiding at ground level. Dumb luck has saved many a bad situation. But the stupid sons-of-bitches had no clue he was above them.

Pop. "Aiiiieeeee!" As Venus went down, he maintained a death grip on his weapon, his finger clenching the trigger of the AR-15. A thundering line of fire arced up and left into the trees. Dick jerked back, trying to gain what little cover he could while the bullets tore through vegetation as the path of destruction headed for his perch. There was nothing he could do but wait for the end ... or at least for the wound which would curse him to die slowly where his body would never be found.

Thankfully, the magazine ran out before the arc of devastation reached Dick's private perch or his private parts.

Mercury, the lone survivor, finished his magazine and reached to grab another, but found none. He turned, Dick supposed to loot Venus or, more likely, Jupiter for fresh ammo, but instead hauled off, running full speed back toward the camp.

Cowardice wouldn't save him from Dick.

Pop. Pop. Pop. Crash, rustle, thud.

What could he say? Mercury had been running, with partial concealment.

Dick waited for a few moments to make sure the planets were all down and that the bureaucrat—who Dick's combat mind suddenly and fittingly named Uranus—wasn't coming to see how capturing the escaped prisoner was going.

No one else appeared. He listened, but it was hard to tell whether his ears were still ringing from the explosion or there were just so many insects buzzing he couldn't really hear well.

After a couple minutes, though, he heard the chuffing fart of an outboard motor. Uranus was getting away!

Dick dropped from his perch and double-timed it back to the camp and past the hut. He saw a dock along the edge of a lazy river surrounded by green rainforest. He dashed out on the wooden structure and saw a boat speeding downstream, the short, pudgy bureaucratic asshole he now knew as Uranus at the wheel.

Dick dropped to one knee, steadied the barrel of the AR-15 on one of the wooden supports for the dock and took aim. He didn't have a scope, but the channel was relatively straight here. He didn't need to lead his target.

Pop.

Aim. Exhale.

Pop.

Aim. Exhale.

Pop.

Aim. Exhale. Wait.

Pop.

The figure on the boat slumped over the wheel, slamming into the throttle. The boat engine screamed as the boat sped up, fleeing like the devil at a slight angle toward the far side of the main channel, while the Yilgalong River took a leisurely curve the other direction as it widened. A few moments later, the boat slammed at speed into a log near the far shore, flipping it and its limp contents into the maze of trees and vines and plants along the shore.

The screaming engine whined into an even higher crescendo, then sputtered and stopped.

The planets were aligned. The bad guys were all dead and he was free. Not easy to accomplish, but somehow still too easy for his comfort.

Still, he was lost in space, alone in the fucking never never, beyond more black stumps than he could count. He didn't know where he was, in which direction civilization or rescue might be, or how long he'd have to survive before seeing another human being, not that he would be particularly good company at the moment. But, still, getting somewhere with a phone or a radio or a fucking ultra-low frequency transmitter was what needed to be done right now. And Dick always did what needed to be done.

Sometimes it really sucked to be a spy, even when you were good at your job.

Chapter 30

The speedboat—the only boat about as far as Dick could see—was totally wrecked and the only radio Dick found in the camp had been smashed when something fell on it, presumably during the Nobel 808 blast. He had no choice but to walk to freedom. He didn't relish the journey, not only because he didn't know where he was, where he should be going, or how to get there, but because it all seemed so pointless now. The mission was a bust, a mishmash of theories and maybes and who the fuck cares. His family was gone, whether killed by accident or intent. The bad guys he knew of were all dead.

What did he have to live for? Work? The people at work used and manipulated him, most especially Nerevsky.

Nerevsky.

Nerevsky was a reason to live. More accurately, killing Nerevsky was a reason to live, at least long enough to perform that one last task. For himself, for his family, for the whole damn world.

He gathered up his tourist bag, filled his water bottle, grabbed a bag of crisps and the half six-pack of Emu beers he found poking about the camp, and snatched up a nine-millimeter automatic pistol and two spare magazines. From the lack of supplies he found, he could only conclude the bad guys had never unloaded things from the boat or there was a cache hidden someplace he couldn't quickly find. He didn't want to tarry too long; he didn't know if a supply boat or reinforcements were on the way or would be sent if regular contact was lost. There was probably more to forage, but he didn't want to carry too much on what might be a long walk.

Given the abundant foliage, he didn't think he'd die of thirst.

He headed downstream along the bank of the wide, slow-moving water of the creek. Almost everyone in Australia lived near the coast, so his odds were better downstream. You could also see—and be seen—better at distance over open water, if he got to the shore. And, should the terrain become drier and hotter as he walked, ocean breezes would be good. Being able to dip in the ocean to cool off was also a potential lifesaver.

It didn't take long for him to reach the coast. Of course, the coast at the mouth of the creek was a tangle of water and brush and marshy bog, no doubt infested with snakes and salt-water crocs, but there was no choice but to continue toward civilization. On the assumption he was still in Australia—he doubted Yilgalong Creek was an Indonesian name—he concluded he was somewhere along the northwestern coast of the island continent. So, when he hit the coast, he turned left, in the direction the setting sun confirmed was westerly. From his recollection of the maps of Australia he'd seen, there was nothing sizeable for thousands of miles along the coast to the east. He hoped by heading west, he was headed back toward someplace where he might find help.

He didn't want to stop in an untenable place for sleep once dark fell, so he found a spot with a lonely tree on a relatively flat, dry patch of beach sand as the sun began to kiss the fiery horizon and prepared to settle in for the night. There was a small island, maybe a kilometer offshore, but it was rocky and showed no signs of habitation, so it meant nothing to him. He sipped some water, then carried the beer cans down to the ocean and settled them in a rocky crevice in a nearby tidal pool to cool. He sat in the soft sand to ease his weary muscles and pass some time resting before having a cool beer as a foamy nightcap. He'd climb up the stout tree and sleep in the crook of a branch to keep clear of critters later, when he was ready to sleep.

Somehow, though, this walkabout felt too relaxed, too comfortable for a hike for survival. He pulled the newspaper out of his bag and turned to the back page, figuring to use the last light to remind himself of what had happened, to stoke his rage for the travails he knew would be ahead.

He started at the top of the page and quickly scanned down, past the boxes for the weather and the tide reports and found the story about his family. He read it three times before starting to fold the paper to put it back into his bag. That's when his eyes lit upon the tide report, right next to a small graphic about the phase of the moon.

That wasn't right. That couldn't be right.

He flipped over the newspaper and confirmed the date on the front page, then flipped it again and found the same date in smaller print running along the top of the back page. Then he stared at the graphic again and the small print indicating the time of high and low tides, moonrise and moonset, sunrise and sunset. True, the moon wasn't up in the sky yet and he wasn't sure exactly what day it now was—he'd been unconscious part of the time—but he did know what day he attempted to infiltrate Area B and what date the paper purported to be from—a few days after the Exmouth debacle. But the moon phase was all wrong. Every Army Ranger who goes on a nighttime raid knows when the moon will rise and how much light is it likely to shed on his operation. He closed his eyes and felt the texture of the paper, all the time thinking back to how it felt reading the paper between slices of honey-soaked bacon at the hotel back in Perth.

Too smooth. Too expensive. The newspaper he had in his hands was a fake. No doubt the bureaucrat had brought it with himself from Mother Russia, straight from the forgery department of the SVR. The forgers at the Subsidiary faked things all the time. Why should the capabilities of the SVR be any different?

How much of what he read in the newspaper was true? How much was a lie? The forgers could have lifted stories and pages—maybe even most of the layout—for the faked paper from the internet. But something about how things fit together for the back-page layout, where they wanted to place a fake story about Dick's family had led them to replace the moon and tide chart with something from another date, one weeks out of sync with reality.

Uranus, the bureaucrat who talked to him, had for some reason wanted to torture him, to break him, with something besides physical torture. To get what? Not more about Dick's mission—he knew plenty about that already and Dick hadn't been shy about telling him what he knew. No, either he wanted what he knew Dick wouldn't give—operational details about the Subsidiary and its agents—or he was just a sick bastard who liked to make people suffer.

No. There was one other choice. The Russian didn't want to get information from Dick; he wanted to give information to Dick, without seeming to do so, then fire him up enough to make him attempt some kind of escape.

Before Dick knew it, darkness surrounded him and stars sparkled in a blanket of wonder across the sky, crowding into a blur to form the Milky Way. It was a miracle to behold, but it was completely outdone by the true miracle of Dick's day. His family was alive. He had a reason to go on. Not just to survive this trudge out woop woop through the sucking shores beyond the black stump, but to live a full and happy life once more.

He closed his eyes for a moment and let his anger flow into the warm sand beneath him as the cool salt air from the shore flowed into his nostrils and into his lungs, as if replenishing his soul. He basked in the feeling for a few minutes, then decided it was time to really celebrate. He opened his eyes and walked back toward the water, where he'd left the beers to cool. The starlight did little to light his path, but when he searched the darkness for the glint of the edge of the tidal pool, he saw something else, something wonderful.

A pinpoint of light bobbing up and down on the gentle swells of the ocean. A boat. This was no *Fata Morgana*. He saw a boat. Always hard to judge distance over water. Harder still to do so in the black of night. But then he remembered the rocky island he'd seen offshore before the sun set. The boat had to be in the channel between the shore and the island. He was a quarter, maybe half, a mile from rescue.

He took a few steps forward and his toes hit a cool, wet rock. He reached down into the tidal pool, fumbled in the water for a moment and pulled out a cold beer. He shot-gunned it for energy, then angled off onto the sandier part of the beach and strode into the ocean and began swimming toward the small boat sheltering in the lee of the rocky island for the night.

He swam for freedom. Sure, there could be salt-water crocs, man-eating sharks, stinging jellyfish, and deadly blue octopusses, but he'd chance it. At least they didn't have AR-15s. Besides, he didn't fucking care about the risks.

Now that he knew he had one, he swam for his life.

#

Less than a day later, Dick was finally able to call Melanie and tell her where he was, just like he'd promised her he'd always do. After a long pause, both Melanie and Dick blurted out the same thing at the same time: "I thought you were dead."

It was a long call, full of laughter and tears and explanations, but by the end of it, not only had Dick and Melanie assured each other they were alive and well, Dick knew for certain for the first time in a long, long time that their marriage was, too.

Melanie would forgive him for being dead, eventually.

Epilogue

"Nice to see you alive," said Dee by way of greeting as Dick walked into her office.

Glenn Swynton was already there, relaxing comfortably in one of Dee's client chairs in yet another crisply-pressed bespoke suit, the silver cuff-links on his French cuffs setting off the silver and charcoal swirls in his double Windsor knotted silk tie. Dick didn't care enough about fashion to know how many suits Glenn had in his rotation, but he couldn't remember ever seeing him wear the same tie twice. Glenn was to ties as Imelda Marcos was to shoes. The unbidden thought made Dick glance at Glenn's shoes. Polished to a sheen, of course, with the sole of the one visible because of Glenn's crossed legs pristine and unscuffed. Jesus, the Subsidiary must pay the guy a lot. Of course, given that the Director of Operations was always at the office, Dick supposed the fellow didn't have much to spend money on besides his attire.

Ace was there, too, dressed in a sapphire cocktail dress which showed a lot of leg and even more skin in other places where Dick was smart enough not to let his gaze linger.

"Nice to be alive," Dick finally thought to reply. "Would have preferred it if you hadn't told my family I was dead."

Glenn flushed red and opened his mouth to speak, but no words came out. Dee looked oddly pleased at his discomfort, as if she'd been waiting a long time to see it happen. Finally, Glenn replied, his tone bordering on defensive. "I did say 'presumed dead.' The DNA on the blood found at the explosion site was damning."

"Obviously they planted blood spatter they got from me afterwards, when I was in captivity. Whether at the site or at the lab, doesn't really matter."

"Yes," said Glenn, "but they obviously didn't know about the Nobel 808 or they wouldn't have let you keep it, so why did that match up?"

"Could be coincidence," murmured Ace.

"More likely," said Dick, "they knew I'd gotten some when I arrived in country, but didn't know I had it with me disguised as sunscreen. Maybe through a leak in Nerevsky's channels or maybe because they just know the local spooks still use the old-fashioned stuff."

Dee waved her hand in dismissal. "I don't care why we *thought* you were dead, so much as what it means."

"You don't get why I'm alive?"

"Don't be obtuse," Glenn interjected, his voice as smooth as the fabric of his tie. "You're a trained agent of the Subsidiary. Of course, you're alive. That's your job. That's what you're supposed to do—once the mission is accomplished, naturally."

"And you always do what needs to be done," added Ace.

"Yes, yes," said Dee, "but I don't get the point of the entire operation: what was going on in Western Australia in 1993; what Nerevsky was ordered to cover up; why he sent you on this mission; what's going on there now; why they captured you, but didn't kill you; and what it means in terms of Russia's current weapon capabilities." She stared out her window for a moment. "My job—the Subsidiary's job—is to know these things. I'm not naive enough to think the member nations of our international oversight board don't hide things from us. That's what countries do. Trust is not the dominant trait of successful nation-states, especially superpowers. But I do expect there to be some basic, or at least superficial, rationality in their course of conduct over the decades."

"I had a long flight to think about that and good WiFi access onboard for a good part of it," said Dick. "I can't say anything for certain, but I do have a few ideas. Ideas which are logical enough to me that I'm not going to lie awake trying to suss it all out in more detail."

"Do tell," said Glenn.

Dick closed his eyes for a moment to gather his thoughts. "Where do you want me to start?"

"I thought you knew how to do a debriefing, big guy," said Ace. "Don't you ever do anything by the book? Start at the beginning. What happened in 1993?"

Dick shrugged. "Don't know. Don't care. Probably doesn't matter."

Ace shook her head. "That's helpful."

Dick closed his eyes again, this time so no one would see them roll. "Look, my best guess is the historical incident was probably a meteor skimming the atmosphere of the planet. You've got a bright trail of light and a big boom, but no impact crater of any kind, so nothing ... or, at least, nothing sizeable or with any oomph behind it ... hit the ground. That kind of thing happens. Take the Tunguska incident."

"Ahh," said Glenn.

"Okay," said Dee.

"*Jdi do prdele!*" spat Ace. "What's that?"

"There was a big explosion in Siberia in 1908. I mean, really big. Nuclear weapon big, but, you know, *not*, because it's 1908 and there are no nuclear weapons. Knocked down almost a hundred million trees over close to a thousand square miles of forest."

"Actually," interjected Glenn. "I think your figures are at the high side of the actual ranges calculated."

Dee shot her Director of Operations a sharp look. "Don't interrupt and don't argue with Agent Thornby about the size of explosions. We all know his expertise in that arena."

"Whatever," said Dick. "The Russians had something similar occur in February of 2013 above Chelyabinsk. Some meteors, they don't hit the earth, but they don't exactly miss, either. They hit the atmosphere and heat up and explode from the friction. The one in Siberia in 1908 was maybe three to five miles up. Put out close to thirty megatons of energy, with the burst triggering a ground shock—like an airburst of a nuclear weapon—which would have measured maybe a five point zero on the Richter scale. Chelyabinsk was supposedly four point two."

Dick rubbed his chin. "The Banjawarn Bang was maybe three point six or three point nine on the Richter scale and not so much damage—

not that there are many sizeable trees out woop woop … er, in the Outback … to knock over. Still, the explosion there was probably smaller."

"But that doesn't explain the red dome glow afterwards, does it?" asked Ace.

"It probably does. Back in the late fifties, the U.S. conducted some nuclear tests in the upper atmosphere. Operation Hardtack, they called it. The blasts all created the same kind of ionization associated with aurora effects, though more in the reddish range. At a distance, the red glow expanded in a sphere which lingered for a good long while and was witnessed by those at a distance at ground level as a reddish dome or hemisphere on the horizon."

Dee swiveled her chair to stare out the window again. "That's a good explanation of the 1993 event, but it doesn't explain why the Russians would order Nerevsky to come up with a cover story about Banjawarn rather than just explain what they thought really happened."

"Doesn't it? Look, even though the Russians probably had the best leg up on what really happened in Western Australia back in 1993, because they know more about the Tunguska incident than pretty much anybody, they weren't expecting it. And, initial reports were that it might have been a nuclear test. One which, by pure happenstance, occurred near a big piece of property where Aum Shinrikyo had been testing for uranium not long before. We may not know a lot about what Aum Shinrikyo may have been up to back then, but I do think the evidence is pretty good that the Russians were involved with the Japanese cult. Maybe they worried that Aum Shinrikyo members had actually gotten hold of a nuclear device—maybe that they'd bought or stolen an old Soviet weapon. Or maybe the Russians really were working with or without the Japs on some wackadoodle Tesla energy weapon design. If so, that would have been need to know and Nerevsky might not have needed to know."

Glenn frowned. "That's a lot of speculation."

Dick sniffed. "Sure, it is. I don't *know* any of this for rock solid certain. You asked what I think happened. I answered. I do what I'm told. You know what? So does Nerevsky. He goes and provides a cover story about why Aum Shinrikyo is out woop woop. A story that makes them look bad, but doesn't really explain a damn thing. And that's the end of it as far as his involvement is concerned."

"But not as far as the Russians are concerned," said Glenn. "Right?"

"Look, maybe Tesla is the genius everyone said he was. Maybe he created an electromagnetic earthquake device, a force field shield, a death ray, wireless transmission of electricity, and Colonel Sanders' secret recipe of eleven herbs and spices for fried chicken, for all I know. The Russians would dearly love to have all of those things. So would the Japanese, by the way, especially since they're not allowed to have a standing army and rice is pretty bland. But what's the next best thing to all of that?"

The room was silent for a few moments before Ace spoke up. "An international franchise program for Kentucky Fried Chicken?"

"Bingo," said Dick. "That and making the world think you just might have an electromagnetic earthquake device, a force field shield, and a death ray—it's hard to fake wireless transmission of electricity with wires hanging all over the place. The Russians, they remember all of the lessons of World War II, and one of the most memorable lessons was that of Operation Fortitude, most especially that the First United States Army Group under the command of George S. Patton was going to spearhead the Allies landing in Europe at Pas de Calais."

"Instead of Normandy?" asked Ace. Dick suspected the young Czech spy was the only one in the room not familiar with the incident, a nice piece of wartime counter-intelligence.

"Exactly. Except there was no First United States Army Group. FUSAG was a figment of the imagination, a ghost army created on paper with a communication trail designed to make the Germans think it was real. After all, it was commanded by one of the Allies' best four-star Generals."

Dee interrupted. "The Russians played a similar game during the cold war. They included huge ICBMs in their military parades that were much later revealed to be fakes."

Dick began to pace as he warmed up to his explanation. "Of course, they did. And, why not? The United States spent massively to keep ahead of the Soviets in nuclear weapons, never knowing how far ahead they already were. The same principle applies here. Whether or not you have an earthquake-generating weapon, it's good for your adversaries to think you have one. Perhaps it will give them pause if they think you can lay waste to their cities without the need to deliver nuclear weaponry via plane or ballistic missile. At the very least, it may make them waste large portions of their research and development funds trying to catch up. It's simple misdirection. Hell, not long ago the United States Navy publicly filed patents about using extremely high electromagnetic energy fluxes for anti-gravitational devices or some bullshit like that."

"Even though," mused Dee, "the Navy is permitted to file patents confidentially?"

"Exactly," said Dick. "But they file in the open so the world knows the United States wants to close the Death Ray gap."

"True, as far as it goes, Dr. Strangelove," said Glenn. "But, how does what the Russians were doing here correspond to that? This is obtuse, indirect, even confusing in comparison."

After all of the clues and conspiracy theories concerning Denver International Airport and what was really going on there, Dick couldn't fathom how it could be they didn't understand. "The Russians, they understand disinformation at an instinctual level. You don't think they just started manipulating Western elections via the internet from a standing start, do you? Sometimes I think they just fuck with things to find out what fucking with those things will do. Then they apply the lessons they've learned. I also think that over the years they've figured out you can get a lot of leverage out of electronic disinformation if you sprinkle a few actual events in reality to make the fiction look credible."

"I'm not sure what that means," said Dee.

Dick looked at his boss. "You do stuff in the real world which tends to confirm your electronic disinformation, so it all fits together in some whacko worldview way when you spin your conspiracy theories. In this case, post Banjawarn Bang you do a few tangible things to further spread confusion, like spy on groups trying to further Tesla's research or send agents to Western Australia to poke around every so often, just to keep your presence in the area alive. Maybe the mooks you send really spy on the submarine communications or radar defense installations while they are there, but they're not as clandestine as you'd really want them to be. Is that because you *tell* the agents to do a half-assed job? No. That brings too many people into the subterfuge. But maybe you send your newest or clumsiest agents, knowing they'll be noticed, maybe by other intelligence outfits, but certainly by the locals."

"Pretty convoluted," said Ace. "And I've been looking some more on the internet about the Tesla stuff and there's plenty posted, including that the Soviet Union built a scalar interferometer device that would do all the stuff that supposedly happened at Banjawarn Station. Seems too detailed not to have some basis in truth. If the Russians are so omnipresent on the World Wide Web, how's the stuff that gives too much away stay alive?"

Dick chuckled. "I may not be super tech savvy, but one thing I did pick up from my kid is that nobody controls the internet. Once something's posted and shared it is damn near impossible to get rid of it. Besides, if you really want to make sure that something true isn't given the time of day, what better way to do it than leak the information to conspiracy buffs? They may broadcast the hell out of the information, but they taint it with their—"

"Craziness?" volunteered Ace.

"—single-minded fervor," continued Dick.

Glenn spoke up again. "You could be right. Our intelligence on the Russian's disinformation efforts on social media is consistent with your theories. It's not so much that they back one candidate over another—though God knows countries have been doing that surreptitiously for all of modern history—but that they provide an echo chamber for extremist viewpoints and outlandish conspiracy theories. Their effort is geared not only at distracting the world from more substantive geo-political events, but at getting people to distrust one another and almost all sources of information. That creates conflict and confrontation, undermining the fabric of free societies. I don't know of an internet conspiracy theory the Russians don't have their bots share and retweet at every opportunity."

"And Harry Mason?" asked Ace. "You think he was a Russian plant?"

Dick snorted. "Not at all. Most likely a true believer and not because he was gullible or stupid, but because he was misled. Like Glenn said, most of the misdirection that occurs, especially on the internet, isn't because someone is making shit up, it's because they are repeating and echoing whatever other people make up or misunderstand or misstate over and over and over again."

He took a deep breath and let it out. "Sadly enough, there's no need to ask people to lie. People lie all the time. They tell interviewers what they think they want to hear. Sometimes because they get paid for the interview, sometimes because they just want the notoriety or attention, sometimes because they are pathological liars, and sometimes because they are batshit crazy. People even remember things that never actually happened; it's called the Mandela Effect. And don't forget, something actually did happen in Western Australia. Aum Shinrikyo really was running around doing cultish things. There was really an earthquake in Kobe, Japan. There are actual military installations in Cutler, Maine, and Exmouth, Australia. And people—non-crazy people and trained observers—do see UFOs all the time. Harry just tried to connect the dots ... or maybe the great circle routes."

"Perhaps," said Glenn, "but what about the more recent sighting of lights in the area?"

"Looked into that," said Dick. "All of the indications from the Desert Fireball Network are that it was an ordinary meteorite, just flashier than most. Being it was considerably farther west than Kalgoorlie, they got some brief images of it. It's only real importance in this narrative is that it spooked Nerevsky into ramping up his historical quest."

"And now?" asked Dee. "What about all the stuff that happened to you? Who was behind that? What's really going on at Exmouth and out ... woop woop? How'd the Russians even know you were trying to infiltrate Area B?"

"Same old thing, just modernized. The Russians are obviously interested in the area. I, for one, don't think it's coincidental that the concrete block shelter where I was held is due south of where the Brits tested atomic weapons in the fifties off Australia's Montebello Islands. Of course, nothing we know of is happening there now. But whatever the Russians do or don't have or whatever they are keeping an eye on, they do know Nerevsky desperately wants to know what is going on. Confusion suits their purposes, so they string him along."

Dick scratched his chin. "Confusion and mistrust always suit their purposes. Whether or not they knew I had any connection to Nerevsky at first, by corollary, they string me along. They send agents to tail me and my family, to chase me, to shoot *at and around* me without actually ever hitting me or anyone in my family, to shout dire warnings at me, and to capture me and feed me exactly the type of bullshit they *think* because of my UFO background or my connection with Pyotr Nerevsky that I'll believe. They probably didn't plan on me killing everybody at the camp—certainly not the bureaucrat in charge—but they may have expected, even planned for me to eventually escape so as to spread their lies. Letting me keep most of the shit I was carrying when nabbed was a curious decision otherwise."

Dick fluttered his hand to preemptively dismiss any discussion about whether he was meant to escape. "As for how they knew where I was to nab me, well, they obviously monitor Exmouth pretty closely, whether it's a secret Tesla weapon station or not. The social media regarding the protest couldn't possibly have escaped their attention. Being spies, they probably figured it was a diversion—which it was—and monitored my movements."

Glenn arched an eyebrow. "And the incident at the old, collapsed Tesla Tower the wind uncovered near Banjawarn? That's the one that makes my fingers tingle."

"Was it old? Did it collapse? Did the wind uncover it? Or was it put there to be found, if not by me, by some local mending water pumps or prospecting for ore along the ridge line?"

Ace slitted her eyes as she looked at Dick. "That doesn't explain the lights in the sky, the lightning, the zaps to the tower when you were hiding in it. You sounded pretty convincing when you were telling me about it."

"Massed drone displays like at the last Olympics and Superbowl? Actual dry lightning? A faked tower constructed to discharge electricity collected by a solar array or battery back-up if some silent alarm or invisible tripwire is triggered? Hell, the Russkies could have had an agent on the ridgeline with a plasma rifle for all I know. Prototypes supposedly exist. Unless the powers-that-be want to mount an expedition to dig up the place and see what is actually there and how old it is, I doubt we'll ever know."

Glenn huffed. "As a close observer of the 'powers-that-be' at the Subsidiary, I doubt there would be any interest at all."

Dick's upper lip curled. "Make sure Nerevsky gets that memo." He felt his brow involuntarily furrow. "On second thought. Let me deliver the message in person. I think there may be some postage due."

Dee spoke up. "That won't be necessary. Nerevsky won't ... be getting any memos from anyone ever again." Her brow furrowed. "The Russian representative called to thank me for taking Nerevsky out, so I assume they were actually the ones who did. I think they were more pissed about our recruitment of him than I ever realized. Maybe this was just their excuse for eliminating him while misdirecting us at the same time."

Dick didn't realize he'd clenched his fists until he felt the hands relaxing. "Good. He needed to be taken out, no matter who did it. Better than good. Fucking great." He inclined his head toward Ace. "I owe Acacia a thousand bucks for the deductible on her car. Actually, twelve hundred nineteen, when you include the cleaning. Take it out of Nerevsky's last paycheck."

"Done," said Glenn.

"As is this meeting," quipped Dee.

Dick didn't dawdle in the offices of Catalyst Crisis Consulting after the meeting ended. He headed for the garage and was soon on the highway, headed for home, his mind turning introspective during the monotonous drive.

Unlike his mission on the Canary Islands, nobody back at the Subsidiary would think of this recent cluster as world saving. But they would be wrong. Back at Yilgalong Creek, Dick thought the world had ended, that he had lost his family. And they, in turn, thought they had lost him. But in the end, they'd found each other again. Their world and his world, they'd both been saved. Now he had to make their world together the best it could possibly be.

Dick's family—his wife and his son—needed his time and attention after all they'd gone through both in the throes of the mission and in relation to the false reports of Dick's death.

They needed his love. And Dick always did what needed to be done. That's what a husband and a father does, even when he's a spy.

The End

AFTERWORD / ACKNOWLEDGEMENTS

Like my other Dick Thornby Thrillers, *Net Impact* and *Wet Work*, this book is based on real things rabidly discussed on the internet. That's a handy thing because this entire book was written during the Covid 19 pandemic, so all of my research had to occur online. I couldn't go to any of these places or even to a physical library. Accordingly, every decription of a place, verhicle, weapon, or fact is either based on my personal recollection or on something I read or found online. Those online sources are too numerous to track or mention, but there are some major ones which stand out. Not just standard research tools like Google, Google Earth, and Wikipedia, but also websites about water cribs, boats, airlines, sports and sport teams, hotels, restaurants, weather, tourist information, animals, history, and even swear words in foreign languages. I also reviewed extensive online resources on meteors, UFO sightings, Nikola Tesla, massive pit mining operations, government installations, and weapons, both real and alleged. In each case, I did my best to use information given without appropriating it as my own.

This is also the case with the lengthy Bright Skies report by Harry Mason. If the plot of this book intrigued you, you should definitely check out Bright Skies for yourself. My references to it here are but a brief overview of the voluminous detail contained therein and are intended only to summarize and critique portions thereof and not to catalog or appropriate it, and certainly not to in any way disparage it or Harry Mason. Statements about it herein are simply statements of fictional characters in a fictional version of our world. The same goes for references to Nikola Tesla's purported inventions, Aum Shinrikyo, and what goes on at Exmouth and other government installations. Read up on any or all of those things as much as you like, but please don't take this book or anything in it, including various conspiracy theories, too seriously. This thriller was written to entertain in a way which touches on reality, without necessarily conforming to it.

A number of people helped me with advice, information, comments, blurbs, reviews, or suggestions on the book, the cover, and other aspects of its publication, and offered much encouragement and support. Thank you all. Special thanks to Christine Redford, Jean Rabe, Alyssa Bingle, Wes Nicholson, Steve Wales, Lori Swan, Mary Konczyk, Juan Villar Padron, Raymond Benson, Mel Odom, Steven Paul Leiva, Randall Masteller, everyone who read and reviewed *Net Impact* and/or *Wet Work,* and especially my wife, Linda, without whom my life before, during, and after the pandemic, would be pretty empty.

Thanks to all who supported the *Flash Drive* Kickstarter campaign. Listing all of you would have delayed publication, so I'm not doing that here, but please know that each and every one of you have my personal, heartfelt gratitude.

To find out more about my writing, please go to my website at www.donaldjbingle.com. Subscribe to my newsletter or follow me on Facebook, Twitter, and Goodreads @donaldjbingle to get my latest announcements. And, please, if you like this or any of my books, take a moment to drop a review on Amazon, Barnes & Noble, Kobo, Goodreads, BookBub, or your favorite blog. Also, suggest your local library carry this and/or my other books. Independent authors need all the help from readers we can get.

Want a free taste of my other work? Flip a few more pages to read the first chapter of *Forced Conversion,* my first novel. Here's what Hugo and Nebula award-winner Robert J. Sawyer had to say about it: "Visceral, bloody -- and one hell of a page turner! Bingle tackles the philosophical issues surrounding uploaded consciousness in a fresh, exciting way. This is the debut of a major novelist -- don't miss it."

Thanks for your support.

Aloha.

Donald J. Bingle
Writer on Demand ™
St. Charles, Illinois

ABOUT THE AUTHOR

Best known as the world's top-ranked player of classic role-playing games for the last fifteen years of the last century, Donald J. Bingle is an oft-published author in the thriller, science fiction, fantasy, horror, steampunk, romance, and comedy genres, with seven published novels (Forced Conversion, GREENSWORD, Net Impact, Frame Shop, The Love-Haight Case Files, Wet Work, and Flash Drive) and more than sixty shorter stories, many in DAW themed anthologies and tie-in anthologies, including stories in Scary Stuff, On Time, Strange Days, On Loss, Mystery!, Robots!, Dragons!, Sidekicks!, Speakeasies and Spiritualists, Time-Traveled Tales, The Crimson Pact, Steampunk'd, Imaginary Friends, Fellowship Fantastic, Zombie Raccoons and Killer Bunnies, Time Twisters, Front Lines, Slipstreams, Gamer Fantastic, Transformers Legends, Search for Magic (Dragonlance), If I Were An Evil Overlord, Blue Kingdoms: Mages & Magic, Civil War Fantastic, Future Americas, All Hell Breaking Loose, The Dimension Next Door, Sol's Children, Historical Hauntings, and Fantasy Gone Wrong. A number of his stories have been collected in his Writer on Demand™ Series, including Tales of Gamers and Gaming, Tales of Humorous Horror, Tales Out of Time, Grim, Fair e-Tales, Tales of an Altered Past Powered by Romance, Horror, and Steam, Not-So-Heroic Fantasy, and Shadow Realities.

Donald J. Bingle is a member of the International Thriller Writers, Horror Writers Association, International Association of Media Tie-In Writers, and Origins Game Fair Library. More on Don and his writing can be found at www.donaldjbingle.com.

"Visceral, bloody—and one hell of a page turner!"
-Robert J. Sawyer, Hugo Award-winning author of **Hominids**

FORCED
CONVERSION

DONALD J. BINGLE

Check out this sample of Donald J. Bingle's

FORCED CONVERSION

Chapter 1

Derek hated firefights with religious zealots. They never gave up. Even when they faced certain death, they thought that meant they had won, that their reward in heaven was close at hand and even more glorious if they took you with them.

The scene looked peaceful enough: a shallow mountain creek cutting its way through the soil and detritus of a broad valley floor. A scattering of aging Ponderosa pines whispered and swayed lazily in the breeze above, while the buffalo grass baked and dried in the naked glare of the sun.

But the sun and the trees lied when they whispered peace. Violence stalked this place. The bear and mountain lion tracks crisscrossing a bar of silt nearby bore silent witness to the danger. The pleasant gurgle of the creek's bright, flowing water tried, but could not mask the truth of the mountain wilds. Kill-or-be-killed was nature's way.

And today . . . today there would be violence here of a type never shown in the nature vids.

There were at least three mals on the far side of the creek. His enemy was hiding in the more plentiful pines and bushy undergrowth on the north side of the valley. Derek couldn't see them, hadn't seen them even during the coordinated burst of automatic weapon fire that forced him to dive for the dirt several minutes ago, but he knew that they were there. They were spread out along the outside of a U-shaped bend in the coldwater creek. That way they would have a clear shot at anyone fool enough to charge down the loose gravel bank, cross the shin-high water, and attempt to scramble up the opposite side.

Derek wasn't a fool and he certainly wasn't gung-ho enough about this mission, any mission, to charge forward on his own. Instead, he hunkered down behind one of the bigger Ponderosa pines. He gulped for air, breathing in the sweet smell of the sticky sap oozing from where a bullet had scored the trunk only moments before. The sugary scent mixed with the salty tang of his own sweat and the whiff of powder still in the air from his untargeted return fire. His mouth tasted of mud, tinged with metal.

He glanced furtively about for hostiles, then sat with his back to the trunk as he checked his ammunition and waited impatiently for the rest of the squad to move up. They'd heard the gunfire. There was no reason to risk moving back to report.

Still, he counted the seconds and yearned for a radio to call for help.

He'd learned many things in the course of his training: military maneuvers, survival techniques, PsyOps methods. Things he otherwise never would have thought about back home; things Katy would never know or understand; things he would never tell her when he saw her again after his service was complete. But he had never learned why the squad couldn't use a damn radio to communicate on patrol, not even a radio with an encrypted signal. Their vehicle had laser communications gear, but out in the field they used hand motions. So he sat, frozen in place, imagining a hand motion he would love to give whoever had banned the radios, and waited for reinforcement.

He heard the squad before he saw them, which didn't say much for their training, or, more accurately, their leadership. A. K., the hulking squad commander, crashed forward, barely bothering to crouch as he moved quickly through the buffalo grass. Sandoval, slightly pudgy and sweating profusely, trailed diagonally on A. K.'s right, just ahead of Pancek, who moved in the calm, deliberate manner of a professional soldier. Manning, short and wiry, moved quickly and furtively in a mirror position to A. K.'s left, along with Digger, who was older, taller, and considerably more laconic in his movements and his attitude.

Back and center, their resident techno-geek, Wires, crept forward awkwardly with his conversion equipment.

Derek swung his rifle around the side of the trunk and let off a burst into the trees across the creek, both to give the squad some cover and to make sure they knew exactly where he was. The squad would know the sound of his rifle; the ConFoe suppressor rifles made a deep, dull bark—the result of the rubber bullets. The mals used a variety of weaponry—everything from ancient Kalashnikovs to collapsible Uzi submachine pistols, but they all had the sharp yelp and bite of real ammunition made of brass and lead and designed to tear a ragged hole out of your sinew when they hit.

The mal religious fanatics didn't have to play by the rules regarding lethal force. Only the ConFoes were supposed to do that. It's what almost made it an even fight, despite the superior numbers, training, equipment, and transportation of the ConFoes. The Conversion Forces were tasked to locate, capture, orient, persuade, and convert the malcontents, forcibly if necessary. The ConFoes could only use lethal force in defense; the mals used it all the time.

A. K. halted the group's advance in a brief hollow behind a small deadfall. "Bareback," he growled. Pancek, Manning, Sandoval, and Digger simultaneously popped out their ammo magazines and snicked in fresh ones from their belts with smooth, practiced motions. Wires merely continued his slow, burdened effort to catch up; he didn't even carry a gun.

Derek knew that A. K. had no need to switch; he never used rubber, despite the regulations.

Derek made no move to switch magazines either, but for a different reason. "There's no need for that, A. K.," he hissed back to his squad-mates. "We outnumber 'em."

"To hell with that. Damn mals need to learn to run back to their hidey-holes when A. K. comes to town," the squad leader boasted, louder than he needed to. He obviously didn't care if the mals heard.

"There's only three . . ." Derek argued back.

A. K. fixed him with a steely gaze, the muscles tensing in his jaw. "You only saw three." He looked up toward the shade of the more densely packed trees across the creek. The sunlight dappling through the swaying pine branches was the only thing that moved within his gaze. "They only showed you three." His tanned face crinkled slightly as he took in a long deep breath, then loosed a practiced stream of spittle through his teeth. "I smell one behind every tree."

He motioned, first to Sandoval, then to Manning. The signs were quick and precise and ended with a curt nod. Sandoval moved back and downstream, Manning back and upstream. They would cross the creek a hundred yards on either side of their advancing leader and attempt to flank the enemy. Derek had less than three minutes to get with the program before all hell broke loose.

Swearing below his breath, he ejected the partially expended magazine of rubber bullets and replaced it with the real thing. He stuck a couple extra magazines into the waistband of his camouflage pants for ready access and counted the grenades hanging off his belt: three stunners on his right, two incendiaries on his left.

Unfortunately, the mals decided not to wait to be flanked. They opened up on Derek with apocalyptic abandon before he could even turn back around toward them and get his bearings. Bursts of automatic fire tore up the ground in arcs to his left and his right, zeroing in on him as steady fire from the front pounded into the soft wood of the Ponderosa pine, chewing through it, sending wood and splinters flying into his neck.

He knew better than to have remained stationary this long after having been spotted by an enemy, especially with his back to them. Now they had fully triangulated their fire on his position. It was only a matter of seconds . . . .

With a bellow, A. K. vaulted over the deadfall and charged forward to the left of Derek's untenable position. In A. K.'s left paw, a gleaming silver machine pistol spat out a stream of fire and death at the position of the left-most attacker. In his right, an automatic heavy rifle did the same. A. K.'s taut muscles absorbed the recoil of each shot and his shoulders strained to keep the weapons level despite their thundering rate of fire. Even with the dual targeting and his quick movement forward, A. K.'s aim remained remarkably true, pummeling both positions without respite.

More splinters exploded from Derek's tree as A. K. drew even and passed his position, still firing to both sides, his arms outstretched, his chest full and wide toward the center mal, who had been punishing the side of Derek's cover facing the creek.

Pancek and Digger flung themselves wide to either side, each firing in short bursts at the mal nearest them as they gained speed in an effort to rush and jump the creek.

Derek's tree stopped vibrating as the center shooter began to veer his fire toward the charging A. K. It was up to Derek to save the belligerent asshole. He reached down with his right hand to his left side and loosed a grenade, flicking the pin out with his thumb as he had been drilled in boot. He drew his arm back, then flung his arm upward as he twisted around the right side of the tree to fastball the weapon into the thicket directly across the creek.

As the explosion rocked the previously peaceful valley, Derek threw himself toward a large pine to his right, trusting the dust and chaos of the explosion to cover his movement and staying low to avoid the steady stream of lead that A. K. continued to spew in both directions. The tree he chose was half-undercut by the eroding bank of the creek and leaned out at a forty-five degree angle across the water. If he could clamber atop it and sprint across, he could drop down on the other side before he was re-targeted and capture their center opponent.

Derek attempted to shoulder his weapon to leave his hands free and planted his left foot hard to push up onto the angled pine. As he did, the earth gave way beneath him and his leg dropped into a void until his crotch shockingly halted the fall by colliding with a wide tree root. His rifle slipped off his right shoulder as he spun and jerked painfully downward to his left. Blackness and flashes of light flooded Derek's vision as his plan disintegrated with the eroding earth. He scraped his face on the tree trunk as he fell, wrenching his lower back and twisting his right knee in the process.

Derek gritted his teeth to avoid crying out and struggled to remain conscious. The bank had undercut the old pine more than he had realized and his leg had punched through a layer of dirt between two gnarled roots. His left leg now dangled helplessly below the angled tree without purchase. His gun was out of reach, in the open to his right. Shots rang out on three sides of him, but the tree blocked his view of the firefight raging about him. Mud spattered against his exposed leg as slugs slammed into the bank. The automatic fire approached him from the left in a stream so thick that he knew his leg would be chewed off when the dum-dum bullets cut through his flesh, leaving his blood to course down into the pristine water of the creek.

He tried to marshal his thoughts and figure out what to do, but the only thing that could permeate the haze of pain was that this was surely an asinine way to die. Even more so, because only mals died at all anymore.

That was the beauty of conversion.

Where was that damn slowpoke, Wires, when you really needed him?

*****

Icy slivers of water sliced into Derek's face and splashed across his shoulders and chest. He opened his eyes into utter blackness. His body ached, the pain throbbing outward from his privates and his lower back to his legs, chest, shoulders, arms, and face and somehow out further into infinity, his agony reaching out further than his appendages. His head throbbed in time with the spasms of his back. His tongue was swollen and thick, his lips cracked and crusted with mud and sweat. He tasted blood and grit and bile with the sharp metallic aftertaste that always accompanied a burst of adrenaline.

This wasn't what they promised in the conversion brochures. This isn't what they told people, well mals, during orientation.

Either they'd lied or he had died. Maybe the religious freaks were right about an afterlife, just wrong about what it contained.

He drifted back into blackness.

*****

Stinging cold assaulted Derek's face again. This time, when he opened his eyes, the flickering of a small flame broke the blackness. It snapped off as foul smoke and ash assaulted his nostrils. A circular red, white, and gray glow appeared from behind the smoke where the flame had been a moment before.

"If he closes his eyes, splash 'im again, Manning," grumbled the leering visage of A. K. behind his cigar. "He'll either wake up or drown. Either way suits me."

Shapes and shadows came into focus among the trees that blocked and scattered the dim moonlight. Another flame, this a campfire off to his left, crackled and snapped as the pitch of the pine branches boiled and burned.

"I tol' you," said Sandoval's voice somewhere behind Derek. "I tol' you, Wires, that you was wastin' your time setting up the machinery. No way 'ee needs to be converted yet. Poor bastard has to finish 'ees service in the ConFoes, just like the rest of us."

Derek saw Wires, to his far right, unpacking and assembling the scanner in a small clearing. Even in the dark, the techno-geek's hands moved deftly, with quick certainty, snapping components together, toggling nuts onto well-oiled bolts, and plugging connections in with alacrity. He looked over to Sandoval without pausing at all in his tasks. His voice was soft and emotionless, "Just the same, I will continue. He looks terrible and you know this process takes some time. I'd prefer to be ready in case my services are needed."

Digger squatted next to the crackling campfire, squinting into the flames and breathing in the pungent, piney smoke without coughing as he warmed his leathery hands. "If it's all the same," he drawled, "I'll wait and see. Friggin' bedrock's too close to the surface hereabouts. No use diggin' a hole, less'n you need it."

"I'd try to live if I were you," chuckled Manning, fingering another canteen full of cold water. "Wires ain't ready yet, Digger doesn't want to be bothered to bury you, and A. K. ain't even got around to chewing you out over your lame-ass assault technique."

It came to Derek that he had neither been converted nor had he died. Instead, his life in the squad and his tour of duty in the Conversion Forces continued. Perhaps it was the pain, or even the drugs that Manning had undoubtedly given him in an unsuccessful effort to dull his searing agony into an all-consuming full-body ache, but Derek felt no joy in discovering he was alive. No joy at all.

"What, what about the mals?" he croaked out raggedly, his words slurred and slow, his throat cracking with the effort.

Manning chuckled again. "Two wasted. Me on the one side—A. K. drove him headlong straight into me. It was bee-yoo-ti-ful! Pancek got the one on the other side."

"Hey, man, I keeled him too," interjected Sandoval. "Why do you think he run so slow? Shot him in the ol' rumpola. Come next spring," he continued, gesturing expansively at the clearing about him, "his ass will be grass!"

A. K. stopped sucking on his cigar and smiled thuggishly. "Pegged the bastard in the middle, too, but he got away. Wires was screaming for help so loud I had to come back and take care of you just to shut 'im up." He blew a putrid smoke ring into the thin, clear alpine air. "We'll follow the blood-trail to verify the kill come morning." He stuck the stogie back into his mouth and inhaled deeply. Like most smokers these days, he always fired up the strongest, most loathsome, extra-nicotine laced chubbies he could get his hands on and sucked the smoke deep into his lungs, holding it there as long as possible before exhaling. After all, fouling your lungs really didn't matter anymore.

Which was a good thing, Derek thought, as he pulled the asbestos coated emergency blanket up to his chin to stave off the cold 'til dawn.

*****

Derek still felt like crap in the morning, but Manning's drugs had taken hold enough to make him ambulatory. Just barely. He wouldn't want to jog uphill with a full pack or take on a mal in hand-to-hand, but he could move as fast as Wires could with all his equipment. That meant the squad was back in business.

Getting going wasn't easy, though. Not only was Derek stiff and sore, but his hands were so numb from the drugs he had been given that he actually had to look to see if his fingers were gripping the zipper of his fly when he unzipped to take a morning piss. Even with the powerful drugs, he still winced in pain, then gritted his teeth as he fumbled gingerly at his crotch. His privates were swollen and discolored in ways never intended and not at all amorous. There was blood in his urine and pissing hurt like a son-of-a-bitch.

It was a good thing his equipment was no longer needed for procreation. Like others of the unconverted, he used his recreationally from time to time, but it would be weeks before that would be enjoyable again. Derek zipped up and headed back toward the camp.

Pancek, quiet and reserved as always, greeted Derek on his return with only a brief nod. Pancek's dark brow was furrowed like he had a headache and he had bags under his gray eyes; no doubt he had been on perimeter guard duty most of the night. But Pancek didn't complain. He simply shouldered his pack and kicked dirt into the smoldering remains of the campfire. Then he walked calmly to the stream, stooping to fill his canteen. Finally, he stood, patiently waiting for the others to be ready to move out, as he screwed the cap back on the ConFoe-issued container.

A. K. came back into the campsite after reconnoitering ahead. "Bleeding like a stuck pig . . ." he sneered, gesturing to a clear trail through the buffalo grass.

"I don't think their religion allows them to bleed like pigs," smirked Manning.

"I don't think peegs are a problem for thees religion, Manning," replied Sandoval as he hefted his pack and slung his rifle.

"Pigs, cows, chickens . . . all these religious types are wacko. The government offers them heaven . . . whatever heaven they choose, but they're too stupid to take it," complained Manning, "which is why, ladies, we have to sleep on the friggin' ground and haul our sorry asses up a friggin' mountain."

"Manning, my friend," said Digger as he put a friendly arm around his small, wiry squad-mate. "Perhaps they do not know that heaven awaits them. It is our job to bring them the truth, to orient them to the possibilities, to let them choose, to give them an opportunity to convert. Not missionaries, but on a mission for their good and ours."

Most of the squad winced visibly at Digger's sarcastic recitation of text from their Conversion Forces training manual.

"I don't haul this equipment around for nothing, you know," noted Wires quietly. He had finished disassembling the conversion scanner with one hand as he had eaten his breakfast with the other.

". . . And, if they reject our generous offer of eternal life, then we'll just hafta' blow their asses to kingdom come," retorted Manning, patting his automatic rifle like a faithful dog.

"In which case, I get to do my job," finished Digger as they headed out, trying to keep pace with the ever-aggressive A. K.

Derek held his tongue during the exchange and wondered for the thousandth time what a misguided sense of duty and a slick recruiting vid had gotten him into. Back in his real life, before the Conversion Forces, he had been told he was a good-looking guy: average height, brown hair, with an athletic build from playing sports and a broad, white smile. And, back then, he had a bright future ahead of him in one of the new worlds, just like everyone else.

Now look at him. Dirty, banged up, and bruised, with greasy, unkempt hair that looked almost black, three day's worth of stubble, and a hobbled, bent-over gait that reminded him of his grandfather. And he couldn't remember the last time he had smiled.

Worse yet, he couldn't imagine the next time he would smile.

He had a violent, miserable, and dangerous job. And the future, at least the immediate future, didn't look all that promising. In fact, it looked like hell.

* * * * *

He hated firefights with religious zealots. The gangs and the loners could be vicious opponents, too, but at least those mals mostly fought in a straightforward, military way. They would battle to protect turf or supplies or to cover while their wounded were evacuated to safety. Occasionally, they would simply run away in retreat. Sometimes, the gangs and the loners would even peaceably surrender.

But the zealots never surrendered. They feared conversion more than anyone else, more than anything else. They not only fought for their lives, they fought for their eternal souls.

Books by Donald J. Bingle

Dick Thornby Thrillers by Donald J. Bingle:

Net Impact, Dick Thornby Thriller #1

Wet Work, Dick Thornby Thriller #2

Flash Drive, Dick Thornby Thriller #3

Other Books by Donald J. Bingle:

Forced Conversion

GREENSWORD: A Tale of Extreme Global Warming

Frame Shop: Critiquing Another Writer Can Be Murder

The Love-Haight Case Files (with Jean Rabe)

Stories and Story Collections by Donald J. Bingle

Writer on Demand™ Vol. 1, Tales of Gamers and Gaming

Writer on Demand™ Vol. 2, Tales of Humorous Horror

Writer on Demand™ Vol. 3, Tales Out of Time

Writer on Demand™ Vol. 4, Grim, Fair e-Tales

Writer on Demand™ Vol. 5, Tales of an Altered Past Powered by Romance, Horror, and Steam

Writer on Demand™ Vol. 6, Not-So-Heroic Fantasy

Writer on Demand™ Vol. 7, Shadow Realities

Crimson Life/Crimson Death

Season's Critiquings

Merry Mark-Up

Holiday Workshopping

Santa Clauses and Phrases

Gentlemanly Horrors of Mine Alone

Running Free: A Tale Inspired by Patsy Ann

Father's Day Deluxe 3-Pack

Also from 54°40' Orphyte, Inc.

Familiar Spirits Edited by Donald J. Bingle

Ratfish by Buck Hanno

Surrounded by Love: A Story of Orphans and Family by Marjorie L. Bingle

Semi-Finalist in 2015
Soon-to-be-Famous
Illinois Author Competition

From its lurid, over-the-top prologue to its quirky addendum, *Frame Shop* mixes violence, humor, and occasional writing advice in a format that will keep mystery lovers, aspiring authors, NaNoWriMo participants, and established writers turning the pages.

Harold J. Ackerman thinks his latest cat mystery proves he is the best writer in the Pleasant Meadows Writers' Guild and Critiquing Society, not that the motley assortment of poets, poseurs, and wannabe writers in the PMWGCS provides much competition. But then Gantry Ellis, the NYT best-selling author of the Danger McAdams mystery thrillers, joins the group and wows everyone. Still, Harold hopes to leverage his connection to the famous author into a big break, but soon his efforts lead to murder ... and then more murder.

Visit donaldjbingle.com for more information.

THE LOVE-HAIGHT CASE FILES
BY
JEAN RABE AND DONALD J. BINGLE

Winner of Three Silver Falchions at Killer Nashville

Love-Haight is a comedy, locked within a mystery, hidden in a horror story... Wonderfully clever, stylish, and ghoulish. Delightfully twisted fun!
William C. Dietz, New York Times bestselling author

A seamless blend of horror, romance, and legal intrigue that makes for an urban fantasy-laced cocktail of literary delights sure to thrill readers of all stripes.
Matt Forbeck, New York Times bestselling author

Part fantasy noir, part supernatural legal thriller, Love-Haight sparkles with wit and originality.
Troy Denning, New York Times bestselling author

You have to enjoy a book where they kill the lawyer and he still defends his undead clients.
Jody Lynn Nye, New York Times bestselling author

Visit donaldjbingle.com for more information.

www.ingramcontent.com/pod-product-compliance
Lightning Source LLC
LaVergne TN
LVHW050615100826
845148LV00011B/1602